FIRE SEASON

The Morrigan's Children - Book 1

T E Marts

Names, characters, and incidents are either the products of the author's imagination or used in a fictitious manner. Any resemblance to actual events or actual persons, living or dead, is purely coincidental.

For those who wish for a better world

while stuck in this one.

1

Smoke formed a black cloak that billowed and stretched from horizon to horizon. Orange and red light splashed across the dark shroud as flames danced across the forest below. The mountain stood above it all, the highest in the range of hills that rolled from North to South--a line of hills reaching the sky, now clouded in darkness.

Far above the smoke-wrapped mountain, stars sparkled and glinted in an otherwise clear sky. The full moon gleamed brightly on the grey, attempting to beam the hope of its presence to the land below, but nowhere did it find a gap in the soot-laden haze.

Below the shroud, a small tornado of flame twisted through the eddies of smoke. It swirled as heat rose from the fires, lifting and shifting the smoke. A hole formed in the dark billowing blanket, and a thin beam of moonlight speared through to bathe a small patch of the mountain below.

A figure ran through the beam of moonlight, its feet trampling the pristine snow on the mountain's glacier-covered peak. The trail of footprints behind it led to a small stone hut amid melting ice.

The figure bolted down the glacier, arms and legs pumping urgently. Its breath came in sharp, uneven gasps, each step a frantic attempt to distance itself from the hut--or perhaps to reach the fires below. It barely hesitated as it plunged off the snow-covered edge of the glacier, the icy ground giving way to uneven terrain beneath its frantic stride. Its feet kicked up the gravel and scree of the no man's land between the glacier and the tree line. Intent on its destination, the figure didn't slow as it dodged around an outcrop of rock and into thick brush. The thorn-laden branches tore at the figure's clothing, slowing it momentarily. But the figure was resolute, tearing through the foliage as it reached the tree line. It barreled into the thick forest of pine. It turned and looked back. Panic burst over its bearded face as it turned to continue down the mountain, the urgency of its flight palpable.

The forest erupted in chaos. Branches snapped and shattered as something massive pushed through the treeline; its sheer weight and power sent vibrations through the ground. The crack of splintering wood was replaced by a bone-chilling roar reverberating through the mountainside. The sound echoed across the peak as if the mountain roared in anger. Panic surged through the figure. The roar carried the promise of death itself.

Without hesitation, the figure sprinted toward the fires below, the destructive flames offering a far more merciful fate than the horror that pursued him. His heart threatened to burst from his chest. Heat and smoke stung his lungs, but the fear pounding in his chest drowned out every sensation except the primal urge to flee. Heart racing, he leaped over rocks and roots, every step bringing the creature's thunderous approach closer. Yet the black smoke and crackling flames ahead felt like salvation compared to the monstrous force tearing through the woods behind. To avoid dodging trees, he moved to the ridge line. His calves screamed as he raced up the slope. The far side of the ridge was free of trees, but the rock and ash-covered slope was too steep to risk heading down.

He followed a jagged crest, a ridge etched into existence millennia ago when shifting tectonic plates collided with a force that reshaped the earth, forming starfish-like protrusions radiating outward from the central peak of the mountain. It's volcanic rock now softened by a thin layer of snow that gleamed under the pale moonlight.

As his boots crunched over the icy terrain, the mountain's backbone stretched before him in sharp relief, its ridges cutting against the horizon like the spine of a dormant giant. His gaze swept the expanse, following the winding descent until something caught his eye--a glint, almost out of place. On a distant crest, half-concealed by a thinning line of frost-covered trees, the angular roof of a structure broke the natural symmetry.

The ski lodge.

He froze momentarily, his breath fogging in the cold air as he realized where he was. He knew this place--the ridge, the slope, and the faint sound of rushing water far below. His eyes scanned the horizon, gazing out from beneath a black strip of asphalt that cut through the tree-covered landscape. It was the campground parking lot. Relief surged through him. He had regained his bearings and a flicker of hope, a feeling that washed over him like a wave, filling him with renewed determination.

He adjusted his path, heading directly toward the parking lot.

Maybe I can lose it at the river, he thought. *Can it track my scent through the water?* The idea spurred him on. His steps grew quicker and more deliberate. Each step sent up snow and loose rock as he pushed his body harder.

Behind him, the creature continued to follow, its relentless pursuit like a shadow given substance. The sound of its heavy steps crashed through the stillness of the mountainside. He didn't dare look back-- he didn't need to. The snapping of branches and the thud of displaced rocks told him it was closing the distance. The realization filled him with a deep, gut-wrenching dread.

Its presence was a constant, oppressive weight pressing against him, driving him faster down the slope. His breath came in sharp, ragged gasps as his legs burned with exertion, but he couldn't afford to stop--not for a second.

Each moment felt stretched, the sound of pursuit growing louder, sharper. It wasn't just following--it was hunting. And it wouldn't stop.

2

The most beautiful sunset Jack Season had ever seen filled the sky above the Fallen J Ranch. Orange and yellow blended with red across the low-hanging clouds. The colors merged and flowed together as the light creating them flickered. A low mist hovered a dozen feet off the ground, giving the scene a dreamlike quality. It was one of the most beautiful skies Jack had ever seen.

The sight was deceiving. It was 9 PM in the Pacific Northwest, and the light, low-lying clouds and hanging mist were from the dozens of wildfires burning to the South and West.

Like a monolith, the mountain rose above the long line of the Cascades, a reminder of nature's power and the timelessness of stone. Jack would sit on his back porch most mornings and watch the eagles soar around the slopes. Today, the mountain was obscured by plumes of smoke that stretched for miles.

A shame we had to burn a couple of million acres to get such a beautiful sight, Jack thought.

Earlier in the day, he had watched as cargo planes dumped fire suppressants on the southern edges of the National Wilderness. The bright red dust floated in the air, forming a mist that shone like blood in the setting sun behind it. Since then, the flames had only grown.

Jack felt a deep sense of helplessness as he watched the flames grow. Despite the efforts of technology, the National Guard, and thousands of professional firefighters, the wildfires continued to spread. The feeling of being unable to protect his home and livelihood was overwhelming, a stark reminder of the destructive power of nature.

Like many in the past decades, this year's wildfires ran out of control. Weeks without rain in record-breaking heat had prepared the mountain slopes to burn with an abandon no one in living memory could remember. From the Smith River far to the South to the mountain's slopes, half of three states smoked as hundreds of conflagrations burned up and down the entire Cascade Range.

Thousands of people had been mobilized to fight the blaze. Dozens of area fire stations, smoke jumpers, and the National Guard had been brought in to fight the fires. The wildfires seemed to be winning. The nearby town of Wimac had been warned to be ready to move as the inferno swept down the slopes. The authorities were prepared to lose the eastern valley. Homes west of Jack's ranch were given evacuation orders yesterday. He expected to be evacuated next, if not tonight, sometime in the morning. The impact on the local community was devastating, with many families facing the loss of their homes and livelihoods.

He sipped coffee from a steel mug and watched the distant flames flicker against the low smoke covering the horizon.

"I'm starting to think buying the ranch was a bad move," Jack said.

Beside him, his dog, a four-year-old Newfie, raised its head. Jack inched his pinky off the armrest and scratched the dog behind one floppy, furry ear.

"What do you think, Otter? Should we have stayed in LA?" he said. Beside him, Otter whined, a low rumble of worry at his human's tone.

Jack sighed heavily. He had poured every last penny into the Fallen J, his last hope for a fresh start. If the fire reached this far, he would be left with nothing but a charred patch of land, a stark reminder of his shattered dreams.

"Buy a patch of land out in the middle of nowhere," Jack said, sarcasm dripping from his voice. "What a great idea." Jack sighed, "What the hell was I thinking?" Otter whined and set his head back down on his forepaws. Jack's pinky crooked several more times before settling back with his other fingers. A low woof sounded from the dog.

"Yeah, I like it here too," Jack said.

With no river access and the spring nearly a half mile from the house, the property was more of a hermitage than a tourist Mecca. That had seemed perfect to Jack, a couple of hundred acres of land well off the beaten path, no hustle and bustle, just flat-out country living, back to nature and all that hippy shit seemed like just the life he needed back in LA.

He bought the property, moved up, drilled a well, and invested in converting the old bunkhouse into a six-suite set of apartments. He began renting them out to hunters and hikers who wanted to take advantage of the proximity to the National Wilderness and nearby private hunting preserves.

The last of his savings had gone into finishing the bunkhouse, a gamble that seemed to have paid off. By February, he was fully booked until October. The wildfires had led to a wave of cancellations that threatened his financial stability and the future of his business.

He looked past the bunkhouse to the old hay barn that stood ramshackle and unpainted at the base of the far ridge. Its boards hung on the walls as if desperate to get away. He planned to tear it down next spring or maybe convert it to another bunkhouse, but now the approaching conflagration would destroy it along with the rest of the ranch.

Everything he had built over the last year, on this beautiful ranch that had become his dream, was about to go up in flames. *It's not just a property,* he thought; *it was a new start, a future space I want to exist in.* The thought of losing this idyllic place, where he had invested so much of himself, was almost unbearable.

His wife, he thought, *would tell me to stop complaining.*

It had been four years since the accident, and her voice still echoed through his mind. Her voice would admonish him, point out his flaws, and remind him of life's unpredictability. *Jack, it's the nature of dreams,* she would say. *You win some, you lose some. Life is transient, and its unpredictability is what makes it worth living.*

Jack looked around at the property. Everything he could see, from the ridge behind him to the river edge at the base of the valley far below, was his. He had spent the last year building it up to the point he could make it into a viable business, and he had. The bookings proved it, but the fire would push him back to square one, and he did not have the finances or the energy to build back from nothing. Once again, his life had been changed by circumstances over which he had no control.

Jack sighed, stood, and moved inside.

3

Onyx ran. He passed through trees lit only by the flames that devoured them. Here, deep within the trees, the smoke lay low. It filled the space below the forest canopy. It obscured the trail ahead. He could see less than a dozen yards in front of him. The firelight revealed only the swirling eddies of smoke as they rolled across the forest floor. They curled around trees in ghostly wisps before rising into the heated air to obscure the forest canopy in dense plumes as ash rained down like snow around him. The mountain was on fire, and the flames were spreading. Dry from seasons of drought, the trees were ripe for any spark to set them ablaze, and blaze they did.

His chest heaved. Each breath he took was a struggle against the thick, acrid smoke. It filled his lungs and burned his throat. It's searing pain matched the intensity of the flames behind him. Heavy with exhaustion, his legs carried him up the slope, out of the low valley full of choking air. Every step he took was a battle against the fatigue that threatened to overwhelm him. His muscles ached, his head throbbed, and his vision swam with the combination of smoke and tears.

He ran along a ridgeline on a thin trail worn smooth by hikers. The tall and imposing trees, their once lush green leaves now turned to fiery reds and oranges by the months of drought, stood like soldiers on both sides. Their dry branches creaked in the soft breeze that wafted across the mountaintop. The worst fires were behind him, but flames still loomed ahead, lighting up the rugged terrain. The ground beneath his feet was a mix of loose gravel and compacted earth, and the air was thick with the acrid scent of smoke.

It was behind him. He could feel it getting closer. He had to do something to get away, get it off his scent. He was far enough away for his brother to have gotten to safety. He could lose the beast now. He could circle and get back to their camp at the peak. His brother's safety was his sole focus, and his unwavering commitment was a testament to his love and determination.

The tree next to him erupted in flame. It became a burning candle among the water-starved foliage. Tongues of fire crawled up the trunk and into the branches above. They grasped and raced along the dry timber. They jumped from the first tree to the ones beside it. Soon, a whole section of the grove he ran through burned like hot coals in a forge.

He moved over the ridge and down toward a dry ravine that ran east toward the only part of the mountain not currently on fire. His feet slipped on the carpet of centuries-old volcanic ash below him. He went down hard. Pain shot through his hips. He didn't stop moving. He couldn't stop moving. He had to get this thing as far away from his brother as he could. He slid down the slope a dozen yards, then rolled down into the valley below. He managed to spring to his feet as he neared the bottom. He kept running, each step a testament to his endurance and determination.

They had failed. His brother and his cousins might all be dead--two weeks on the mountain and no sign of their goal. There was no sign that it even existed. The beast, a monstrous creature with razor-sharp claws and teeth, surprised them as they searched. It had mauled his brother, and the creator only knew the fate of his cousins. The creature, a relentless and deadly force, cornered them. With his injuries, his brother couldn't move, couldn't run. So, Onyx ran for him.

He attacked the beast. When it was focused on Onyx, he ran.

Onyx thanked the creator that it followed. It still followed. He thought he had lost it at one point, and he worried that they were too close to his brother's hiding spot, but it still followed. The creature appeared in front of him. He changed direction, sprinting off the trail and into the trees while a dozen trees began to blaze behind him.

He ran along the dry riverbed. The once-wet channel was now a dusty path. He heard the crunch of dry leaves behind him as the creature followed.

He raced through a dip in his path, dodged several small boulders in the center of the once-flowing stream, and turned into a larger creek bed where the stream joined. Water splashed beneath his feet. Behind him, the beast roared as it reached the water's edge.

Soon, Onyx was ankle-deep in flowing water. Trees to the side rustled and shook as the creature pursued him. He kept running, determined to lead the beast as far away from his people as he could manage, even if that meant his death. They had followed him here, believed in his plan, and trusted him to see them through it. They had been wrong. He had been mistaken. Their faith in him had been misplaced, and now they had fallen. The weight of his responsibility in their fall, the burden of his failure, pressed heavily on him as he ran.

Onyx stopped. Calf deep in water, he fought to stay upright. The now rushing stream was trying its hardest to knock him down. The smoke that hung so low in the thick wood above stood just above the trees here. Onyx took several deep breaths. Ahead was a bend in the stream.   As he approached it, the trickle and tinkle of flowing water filled his ears, growing louder. Soon, the sound of rushing water was so loud he couldn't hear his pursuer. Onyx turned. He scanned the tree line. He saw no sign of the beast. He looked back at the way he'd come. The mountain rose high above, wreathed in fire and smoke. The air above the stream here was clear.

There was a roar behind him. Onyx turned to see the beast straddling the stream. It charged toward him. He ran. The water was getting deeper and slowing him down. He moved toward the bank, where another stream joined the one he was on. The bank was too steep to climb, so he continued downstream. He reached shallower water. Now able to make longer strides, he sped up, but the creature behind him kept pace. He could feel its breath on his neck and hear its claws scrape against the riverbed's rocks.

Onyx reached the bend. He followed the stream around it. The land in front of him disappeared as the water cascaded over the side of a cliff. He had reached a waterfall. The beast behind him wasn't slowed. It continued after him. Pain tore through Onyx as the beast's claws raked across his back. Onyx, desperate to escape, leaped from the waterfall. His arms pinwheeled about as he launched himself out into the open air.

He fell without a sound.

4

Jack picked up the remote from the couch and flipped on the news. Governor Reed was on screen requesting help from the Federal Emergency Management Agency to house the thousands of people forced to flee their homes. A moment later, a map of Oregon filled the screen. The fire areas, highlighted in red, covered most of the state to the southwest. Everything between the mountains and Interstate 5 seemed to be on fire.

Jack blinked as Hood River and Wasco County were added to the evacuation orders flashing across the bottom of the screen.

The state preparedness levels seemed juvenile to Jack. The state used three levels for its evacuation schedule: Ready, Set, and GO, like a foot race. Ready meant prepare to leave soon, Set meant be ready to go within minutes, and Go meant GO Now; Jack guessed it helped to convey the importance of evacuating to even cynical residents.

Jack stared at the map on the screen, looking for his section of Wasco County. The area running along the county line with the river was still green, meaning he was still in the Ready stage; he should pack what he wanted to run with and be ready to go. No problem; Jack had spent most of the morning loading his truck with camping gear and those few things he did not want to lose. All he had to do when the order came was hit the road. He planned to head northeast for a couple of hours toward Boardman to a campground he knew of on the Columbia River. He could camp out there until the fire was under control.

Jack looked around the room to double-check that there was nothing he wanted to take. The books and furniture had come with the house, so there were not many personal items he had missed. Childhood and family photos had been digitized and uploaded to the cloud years ago. Family heirlooms and keepsakes had all gone to his sister for safekeeping when he left for college.

Jack sighed. His only real connections were to a dog, a pickup truck, and a failing ranch. His connection with other human beings had always been fleeting. Friends had all revolved around his wife and his work. When those were lost, so was his social circle. By the time he decided to leave LA, there wasn't anyone around to talk him out of it. He made the leap, and now here he was, about to lose everything to the wildfires. He wasn't sure if he was up to building his life back this time.

Jack moved into the tiny kitchen and rinsed his steel mug. He placed it on the counter next to the small coffee pot and wiped down the counter. He thought about the coffee tin momentarily but decided he would need it in the morning. Beside him, Otter whined and set his chin on the countertop. Jack reached down to pat Otter's head. He pulled a dog food can from the cabinet next to the stove. He yanked the pull tab on the can and dumped the contents onto a paper plate, followed by a generous cup of kibble from a small bag under the counter. He set the plate on the ground and watched as the massive dog scarfed down the food.

Jack returned to the living room, where the national news anchor told the nation about the wildfires. A giant graphic next to her head, wreathed in flame, declared Oregon Burns. Images began to replace the graphic as videos of firefighters battling the fires cycled with photos of burnt-out homes and flame-ravaged towns. The story ended with pictures of low-hanging smoke and red-veined skies over the city of Portland, the fires southeast of the city visible in the distance.

A large chest of drawers in the bedroom took up most of one wall. Jack had considered packing it up along with several of the older pieces of furniture, but he couldn't get his head around saving furniture. Objects were just that. If he and Otter got out, preferably in the truck, he would be okay. If losing everything after the accident had taught him anything, it was that things could be replaced.

Jack moved into the tiny walk-in closet. Sensing his entrance, the light turned on, illuminating Jack's wardrobe. A half dozen dress shirts, four suits, and a dozen ties hung forgotten; everything else had been moved to the truck. Jack had not worn a dress shirt, let alone a suit, since leaving LA; his business suit on the Ranch was a t-shirt and blue jeans, maybe a plaid shirt or leather jacket after September. He had packed two suits in the truck earlier in case the unthinkable happened, and he lost the ranch. Taking any more would crowd out stuff he did need to take. Suits could be replaced.

Jack turned to the back wall, where shelves full of trophies flanked a wall display that featured more than two dozen edged weapons. A dozen swords, a half dozen axes, and several long knives hung from stylized hooks on the wall. The weapons were once his pride and joy, collected over the years from fantasy catalogs and private swordsmiths. While some men trained in martial arts, such as Karate or Taekwondo, Jack preferred Historic European martial arts, including the Sword, the Axe, and the Spear. His obsession drove him to push himself to learn more.

He had learned to fence in high school, graduated with a scholarship after placing in several tournaments, and made it to the US finals twice and then to the Olympics. The Saber, Foil, and Epee were extensions of his soul, but it was the heavier weapons he'd learned to master during college that became his addiction.

When he felt he needed more than organized fencing offered, he joined re-enactors and Renaissance enthusiasts to continue learning new weapon styles. His push to learn eventually impacted his official training, and after several missed practices and a series of losses in tournaments, he was cut from the team. That cut his scholarship, and he was forced to drop out.

Jack initially displayed the weapons and trophies in the living room. After several remarks from guests, he decided to move them to a more secluded location where prying questions could be discouraged.   Here, no one would judge him for his past. That was another life. He had spent years learning skills he would never need to use at the expense of a degree that would have helped him make a living. Now, instead of being a wizard of Wall Street, Jack struggled to find an odd consulting gig to supplement the repairs and maintenance on the ranch.

His gaze strayed around the closet. He took in the weapon rack, the clothing racks, and the shelves. In one dark corner, he saw the old cedar chest.

Hope chest, his wife's voice reminded him.

A gift from his parents to their new daughter-in-law. Jack realized that the contents of this closet were the only things to survive the accident: just Jack, Otter, and the trophies. He considered the hope chest but couldn't convince himself to open it.

They are just things, he thought. *Most things can be replaced,* his wife's voice whispered; *the ties we make are all that really matter.*

Jack decided there was nothing else he needed to take. He was ready to go as soon as he needed to.

5

Onyx woke with a shiver. He was wet and cold; his body was partially submerged, half in and half out of the water, on a small sandy beach.

He coughed as he sat up. Water filled his mouth and throat. He leaned forward and spit onto the sand. A gush of water spewed from his mouth as his lungs and stomach rejected the water that had been forced into them. His nostrils and the back of his throat burned. They felt like they did when he swam in the creek by his farm and got water up his nose, a burning sting that filled his nostrils and the back of his throat.

Onyx sat on a small crescent beach carved from the forest at a bend in the river. Little more than a small patch of sand tucked between two large boulders, the beach seemed to be the only way up the river's steep banks. Onyx looked around. The river made a graceful arc here, surrounded by towering pines. Trees corralled the flowing water like a lioness standing watch over her pride. The water was not the raging torrent he had fought above the waterfall; instead, it was a gentle flow that reminded him of that creek back home.

Onyx cleared his throat and took a deep breath. The burning at the back of his throat eased. The air here was cooler than that above the waterfall. The acrid scent of the burning forest was faint, overwhelmed by the natural smells of pine, wood, and wet earth.

Across the river, the bank rose steeply, a wall of dense undergrowth and moss-covered rocks that seemed impenetrable. Downriver, the water continued its journey. It swirled around rocks and splashed against the far banks as sunlight weakened by the smoke-laden sky filtered through the high branches.

The sun reflected off the river's surface in bright flashes of silver.

Sunlight, he thought.

He sprang to his feet, river water slushed down his legs. Sand dug into his palms as his heart sped in his chest. Panic rose like a wild tide. He imagined the worst happening to his brother. He turned to move back upriver. In the distance, the snow on the mountain peak glittered in the feeble morning sunlight that broke through the billowing smoke above. He was a long way from the peak.

"No," Onyx said. His thoughts spiraled out of control, each one more catastrophic than the last. Soon, he was consumed by an overwhelming sense of failure.

He breathed slowly as he tried desperately to regain control of himself.

Onyx stepped out of the river. The sloped ground sent his head reeling. He tried to keep his balance. Pain seared through his back and shoulders. He struggled to stay upright. He reached up to touch one shoulder and brought back a hand covered in blood. The creature had done more damage than he thought. He twisted his head around to see how bad it was. It was no use; all he could see was the blood that now ran down his chest and arms. He couldn't feel anything except the early morning chill.

The cold of the river must be numbing my pain, he thought.

Onyx's first instinct, raw and visceral, was to run toward the peak. His brother was up there injured and in danger. He wanted to sprint through the trees, headlong up the mountain, and find him before it was too late. He forced himself to take a breath. The cool morning air did little to calm the storm in his mind. Rushing in mindlessly could make things worse — he knew that. If he went charging off without a plan, he risked getting lost, leaving them both stranded and defenseless. What if by the time he reached his brother, it was too late because he hadn't thought things through? A wrong turn into a dead-end valley could cost him hours. He had to be smart about this.

Something inside him tugged at his thoughts; a small voice urged him in the other direction. It pulled him away from the peak toward something--something that would help save his brother, he hoped.

He moved up the nearest slope, away from the river, hoping to see anything that might help him from the higher elevation. He searched the woods for any sign of movement as he went, any clue that would make his choice more straightforward, but the forest gave him nothing. Just silence. He weighed his options again, mind flipping between logic and instinct. Seeking help would provide him with backup, more eyes to keep watch, more hands to help fight, but it would take time. Precious time that his brother might not have.

Onyx considered where he was. The map in his head told him the river angled southeast. He was on the mountain's eastern side, his people were far to the west, and no one he could ask for help was nearby, but that strange feeling was pulling him south.

On foot, he wouldn't get back in time to do any good for Ellis. He had lost hours already. The river had swept him farther away than he wanted to be.

What are my choices, though, he thought. *My feet are all I have.*

In the distance, he heard the whine of an engine. Onyx reached the top of the slope to find a paved road that twisted through the valley below. A semi-truck followed a twisted asphalt path to the east, moving away from the mountain. From his vantage point, he could see over the far ridge and down into a series of shallow valleys that stretched westward.   In the distance, a lonely group of buildings nestled against the slopes of a ridge. It wasn't precisely toward the peak, but it wasn't away from it either.

He looked toward the snowcapped peak.   He clenched his fists.
The pulse of urgency thrummed through his veins. He had to
suppress it.

I should run toward the peak, he thought.

Onyx glanced back at the group of buildings. If he could find a ride
back to the peak there, he could return to his brother far sooner than
if he just ran.

What if there isn't time, he thought, *what if the creature made it back to his
brother first?* Could he live with himself then? Every moment he
wasted trying to find help would be a moment closer to disaster, but
a long run up the mountain would take far longer.

What would Ellis do, he thought.

Onyx was the impulsive one.   He didn't hesitate; he acted. Ellis,
though, was the planner. He looks for the best choice and chooses
the one that will be the most effective, ensuring it gets the job done
right the first time. Onyx just followed his instincts and tied up loose
ends later. His instincts always told him to be bold, decisive, and to
act quickly. Right now, though, those instincts were steering him
toward those buildings.

Onyx's breath quickened. His thoughts spun with the blur of
possibilities. He felt his duty demanded that he run at once toward
those in danger. He thought he had to act in the most decisive

manner available to him, but in the end, it wasn't about what he felt. It was about what solved the problem.

What is the problem? Onyx thought. I am stuck miles further away than expected, and I can't run fast enough to get to Ellis before the creature returns.

How do I fix it? He looked toward the road below and the group of buildings beyond. *Run. Either way, I run.*

His jaw set with resolve, Onyx turned toward the distant buildings. If it was the wrong choice, so be it--but he couldn't just stand here and do nothing. His brother needed him now. He made his decision. Without another thought, he turned toward the distant valley and ran.

6

Jack was jolted awake by the blaring fire alarm. He scrambled out of bed. His feet landed inches from Otter's head. The dog peacefully snoozed on the floor. The acrid scent of smoke filled the air. Jack's composure was unwavering. Without panicking, he slipped on his shoes and grabbed a light T-shirt off his dresser. He pulled it on as he searched for the source of the smoke. Jack checked the bathroom and the closet and then moved to the living room. Smoke hung just over his head. It billowed through the open windows next to the back door. A haze of smoke floated across the back porch, through the windows, and into his living room like a fog rolling off some Scottish moor.

"Shit," Jack said. He reached up and pulled the windows closed, then pulled one of the armchairs to the spot where the smoke alarm was screaming. Jack pressed the alarm reset several times, but the siren continued to roar. He ripped the alarm from its mount and yanked the connectors from the wiring. He tossed the alarm onto the couch and jumped down. He picked up the TV remote and turned on the local news channel.

A reporter stood outside what appeared to be a small town in a war zone. Smoke blackened the sky, and dozens of small fires burned in the rubble behind him. Jack did not catch the name. Old footage rolled, the town during last year's Harvest Festival. Bustling people jostled each other for room as they meandered through market stalls lining Main Street, a horde of vendors selling fruit, T-shirts, and memorabilia as a Bluegrass band played on stage. The place looked like every other small town in the area, as aerial footage rolled showing a short main street with a couple of blocks of businesses surrounded by small enclaves of wooded housing developments. As Jack watched, the aerial view shifted to more recent footage. Fire ripped through the nearby industrial park as yellow buses packed with people pulled out of the local High School. Burnt cars littered the streets among charred boards and bricks that had once been buildings. The town, whatever its name, quaintly nestled in the heart of the Pacific Northwest, was now a scene of utter destruction.

Jack raised the volume as he moved to the kitchen and started a pot of coffee. He leaned on the kitchen counter and watched the news as the coffee machine did its thing.

The Evacuation Map was up again, and Jack saw that his small part of Wasco County had been upgraded as he slept. He was now officially Set, prepared to leave at a moment's notice. He wondered for a moment whether he should go now, but had some small hope that the raging inferno in the hills above his ranch would die down.

The newscaster returned and introduced a video shot from a water tanker flying over the mountain. The tanker banked to the North after dropping its fire suppressive load. Through a small plane window, the mountain peak was backlit by the setting sun, its snow-capped summit sparkling with sunlight. One spot in the peak's shadow suddenly flared bright red, and smoke began rising to join the haze above the mountain.

"New flames have appeared below Eliot Glacier, which would be the fifteenth separate fire report this week," the announcer said over the video. "A state fire plane recorded this video as fire erupted on the mountain's Northern slope."   On screen, the clip from the plane played again. Jack watched flames pour up from a small section of wood, then spread in a straight line northeast. It reminded him of a video he saw once that showed a match being lit in slow motion, or those old napalm videos of American jets bombing Vietnam.

"Authorities have said," the reporter continued, "they will have to respond by air as the few access roads to the area are themselves blocked by fire as they struggle to get older fires under control. More than forty-eight million acres of woodland have been destroyed by wildfires this season, making it one of the worst seasons ever recorded."

The video ended, and a new announcer said, "And one of those response teams is with our own Blake Redly as they prepare to dive into the danger zone." Blake stood beside a female firefighter with a parachute strapped to her back.

Jack let the buzz of the news report fade from his mind as he considered the trophies at the back of his closet. The evacuation area was not more than fifteen miles from Fallen J. Should he have been more proactive about what he wanted to pull out if the fire was that close? He thought for a second, then shrugged his worries off. *Things are just things,* Jill's voice said in his head. *Everything can be replaced.* But the thought of losing his home again was a weight he couldn't shake off.

He looked down as Otter wandered out of the bedroom, his massive head held low as he stalked toward his water bowl. The dog's nostrils flared, and he raised his head and sniffed. A short "Chuff" came from his throat as he looked up at Jack, his soulful eyes questioning. In that moment, the bond between Jack and Otter was palpable, a silent understanding amid chaos.

"Well, good morning, Otter. Thank you so much for warning me about the smoke in the house," Jack said. Otter's tail began to wag furiously. Jack's sigh was a mixture of relief and frustration.

He moved to the coffee pot and filled his steel mug before he set a frying pan on top of the stove. The familiar routine of making breakfast helped him maintain a sense of normalcy in the chaos of his day. He pulled four eggs and a couple of cheese slices from the small fridge, poured some oil into the hot pan, and then started cracking the eggs.

Otter barked once from the doorway as Jack slid half of the scrambled eggs onto his plate and then scraped the rest into Otter's bowl.

"I won't forget you, Otter."

Jack picked up Otter's bowl and, balancing his plate and mug, moved toward the back door.

7

Ashley Ember smiled and rolled her eyes as Blake Redly groomed himself in the reflection from News 9's van window. Her team leader owed her a big thank you for this. After just three months on the team, they throw her in front of the camera like a mascot. She knew she was the token woman on the team, but that didn't make it any less disheartening when they flaunted her in front of the cameras.

Blake touched the earbud in his ear and backed away from the van until he was standing at Ashley's side. "Here we go," the cameraman whispered to her as a giant grin splashed over Blake's face.

"Thanks, Rick; I am here with the Madras Air Rescue Service's Smoke Jumper, Ashley Ember. Ashley, your team is preparing to jump as more towns around the National Forest are being evacuated; what are your feelings right now?"

"I can speak for my whole team, saying we are eager to help. Several additional fires have sprung up on the far side of the mountain, and there aren't many roads up that way, so our team..."

The camera panned out to show a group of firefighters preparing gear in the background, "...will jump in as close to this spot fire as possible and try to put it out before it can spread and join with the larger fire. This will help control the existing fire and limit damage caused by the new one."

"That's a long way to drag a fire hose," Blake quipped. Ashley rolled her eyes and flashed a frustrated look at the reporter. She bit her tongue, knowing what she wanted to say would probably get her in trouble. Instead, she took a deep breath. She used the voice she reserved for young children when her Fire Rescue squad visited schools or attended community events.

"Our biggest tools at this point are an ax and shovel, Blake," she explained, "we will cut down or dig up any fuel the fire can use to form a buffer zone between the fire and the larger forest. This will starve the fire while holding it to a smaller area."

"We have heard reports of wildfires starting seemingly out of nowhere this season. Have you seen anything like this before?" Blake said.

"Every fire is different, but there have been some challenging situations lately. Unpredictable fire patterns and rapid spread keep us on our toes. That is part of why we are being deployed now; if we can stop or delay these smaller fires, other teams will have a better chance of containing the larger ones. With our help and God's grace, we can save the forest around Lawrence Lake..." It sounded like a big deal when she put it that way, but she knew the truth: besides a few campground cabins, there wasn't much to burn near Lawrence Lake. This whole interview and jump were just a show for the media so the higher-ups could justify the Madras Unit's existence.

After three years in the Portland Fire and Rescue Department, she joined the U.S. Forest Service as a wildland firefighter. She thought the local politics and position jockeying in Portland had been bad, but the USFS made Portland politics look like grade school. The Madras Smoke Jumpers Unit was established only two years ago as a rapid response team to cover the Eastern Slopes of the Cascades and the Ochoco and Malheur National Forests. The original idea was to shift some of the workload from the team based in Redmond. Still, the longer Ashley worked with them, the more she realized it may have just been a political move by an Oregon Senator to gain more funding for his district's regional airport and to secure a government job for his youngest son. The son was appointed an administrator, and the Forest Service upgraded a significant portion of the airport's equipment to accommodate the Unit. Interestingly enough, that expanded runway was now large enough to accommodate the private jets of some of the senator's biggest donors.

Ashley considered her place in the unit; the job didn't pay all that well. In fact, she earned more as an EMT in Portland, but the job did offer some attractive perks. Downtime in the off-season, some of the best fire control training in the world, and a reason to jump out of an airplane and get paid for it.

Blake Redly finished his update on the fire and the crew's mission without asking Ashley any more questions, so she stood there and smiled and fumed. The foreman owed her big for this. Redly signed off and, without thanking Ashley, he moved to the back of the van, demanding to see the replay. The cameraman lowered his camera. "You looked great," he said. In a lower voice, he added, "Don't worry about Blake, he's an ass." He wore a bright yellow ball cap, the news station's call letters filling the space above the brim.

Ashley grinned at him. "Thanks, I noticed. Nice hat."

"Occupational hazard," he said. His smile enveloped his face. "You really going into that?" he asked, pointing toward the distant mountains where smoke rose to block out the sky.

"That's the job."

"Damn, you're a tougher man than me," he said with his brilliantly wide grin.

Ashley's eyes narrowed for a moment, but when she looked at the guy, she realized he didn't mean anything by it, so she took it as a compliment.

"What, you wouldn't jump out of a perfectly good airplane to fight a fire with a half dozen guys in the woods?"

"You couldn't get me into the plane, let alone into the fire zone." He placed the camera on the floor of the van behind him and extended his hand. "Charlie Bean."

"Ashley Ember." She took his hand and shook it. Unlike most of the men who met her in uniform, he didn't bother to squeeze her hand in some macho show of power. He shook it, as if he were genuinely happy to meet her.

"I heard an appropriate name for a firefighter. Is it actually yours, or do you just use it on camera?" He flushed and held up both hands in apology, "I'm sorry, that was a California thing to say. Forgive me, I spent too long working in Hollywood. I've started to believe everyone operates with a stage name."

Ashly laughed. His embarrassment seemed authentic.

"Oh, nice humble brag, does that ever work?" she asked.

Charlie laughed, "Not yet, maybe one day. My hope springs eternal."

Ashley gave him a second look. He had that effortless charm that said Hollywood. It was the kind of charm she expected from a used car dealer, but he pulled it off without seeming slimy. Sun-bleached curls fell into his eyes as he laughed, and she thought maybe that cheesy pickup line might work on her. He seemed like someone she could be herself with.

Probably not forever, she thought. *Who was she kidding? Probably not even next.* He seemed warm and easy to talk to, but maybe that's what she needed.

Ashley reined in those thoughts.

Slow down, cowgirl, you just met the man, don't go getting yourself hitched to another loser.

He's got a job, she told herself.

Yeah, but for how long?

"So how long have you been working the news?" she waved vaguely toward the van.

"Here? About a year."

Damn.

Told you.

"I worked in LA before that, same company I interned with in high school," he said as if reading her mind. "They shut down and moved to BC last year, so I came out here to visit my sister, got offered a job, and," he shrugged, the golden curls bobbing in front of his eyes again, "just stayed."

He talked to her like an actual person, not like someone with something he wanted. He was friendly, warm, and easy, real in a way she wasn't used to.

Blake Redly pushed by Charlie and got into the front seat of the van.

"Let's go Beaner," Blake hollered, "No time for a play date, we've got another shot to get."

"Beaner," Ashley asked.

"I told you he was an ass," Charlie said softly as he turned to get in the van.

"Sounds like someone needs a sit-down with HR," she quipped.

"Tell me about it," Charlie said.

With one foot up on the running board, he stopped and turned back to her. "Hey, uhm, you think we could get a drink sometime?"

Ashley actually considered it. It had been a while since Portland, since... She couldn't even get herself to think his name. The rage still burned inside her like a wildfire, one she couldn't seem to put out, despite all the time that had passed. She let it fade. She was about to answer, but the rage had crossed her face.

Charlie Bean stammered. "Hey, uhm, I didn't mean nothing by it. I'm kinda new in town and haven't had much of a chance to get to know many people."

38

It was Ashley's turn to raise her hands in apology.

"No. I'm just off a kind of bad relationship. I'd be happy to. Swing by the unit office when all this," she waved vaguely around her, "is over. We can have coffee and talk about what an ass Blake is." She said the last loud enough that Blake turned in his seat to look at them.

That smile exploded on Charlie's face, "You got it. I look forward to it."

He jumped into the van and slid the door shut as Ashley moved toward the hangar where her team was getting ready to jump into the latest wildfire zone.

8

Onyx staggered from tree trunk to tree trunk. He stopped to scan the sky above and the forest behind every few steps. His clothes were ragged, soot-stained, and torn. Great gashes striped his back. He could see the glow of electric lights and a small cabin in the valley below from the ridgeline.

Onyx was sure he was no longer being chased. He moved out from the cover of the trees and headed down the slope toward the glow of the cabin below. His every step was a struggle. He struggled to lift his foot and move it forward. It was a battle to stay upright as the slope pulled him off balance. He struggled to continue forward when every cell in his body screamed for him to stop--screamed for rest-- screamed for sleep--screamed in pain.

He strained to stay upright and waited for the pain to subside. He wanted to stop, clean his wounds, and rest, but he knew he didn't have time. He left Ellis on the mountain, wounded and unable to escape. He had distracted the beast and led it away, but suffered as a cost.

They had tried. They had failed. Doom would come, and millions would die. They would have to face that truth. His only concern now was not stopping what was coming. It was saving those he left behind. Those who had trusted that he could lead them and do what needed to be done. He had failed them. But right now, he could block out the pain to find them help. He could endure the pain, the exhaustion, and the crushing guilt he felt to save his friends, to save his brother. He had to.

Onyx took several deep breaths. He fought through the pain and moved forward. A half dozen more steps down the slope, he emerged from the rough woods and into a large clearing. He crouched as he realized he was out in the open. He scanned the sky above and looked back at the ridge he had just left. He saw nothing and felt relieved. His eyes darted around the clearing. He took in the buildings in front of him: two barn-like buildings and a small house. Onyx moved toward the closest barn and the house beyond.

Lightheaded and nauseous, he felt like he would pass out at any moment. The pain was intense; his shoulders and back screamed, and his legs shook at just the effort of standing, but he continued forward. Driven by concern for his brother and the guilt he felt at the unknown fate of his cousins, he kept moving forward. A juggernaut of guilt and determination, he refused to stop or even pause to catch his breath.

His heart throbbed in his chest. Each beat sent streams of pain down his back and across his shoulders. The pain increased with each step. He feared it would never stop. He feared this was his punishment for failure. To be caught in the pain and terror his kin had felt on the mountain.

It's fitting, he thought. *An eternity of suffering was a fair price for his failure, wasn't it?*

He had brought the ragged group to their deaths. He had convinced them that they could make a difference, save the world, and overcome the obstacles ahead. He had convinced them to follow him. They were woefully unprepared for the danger they faced. Unprepared for the battle that awaited them. They were unprepared and lost, all because he convinced them they could accomplish what the elders of their Ienheid would not even try.

Onyx took a deep breath, another, and then another. Calm returned to his mind. He swallowed his panic and continued forward. The world spun around him. He staggered as his weight shifted to his left foot. His leg buckled, and he felt himself fall. Dull pain crashed through his body as he hit the ground.

Darkness enveloped him.

9

Jack sat on his back porch, his steel mug filled with piping hot coffee. Beside him, Otter licked scrambled egg and cheese remnants from Jack's plate.

In the distance, the snow-topped peak of the mountain glistened in the light from the rising sun. The giant black cloud of smoke that had obscured it for days shifted south with the change in the wind, and a vivid blast of sunlight shone down on the mountain. The fires were closer. Jack could see the glow of flames over the ridge line behind his property. The smoke rose evenly across the tree-lined ridge, reminding Jack of old photos he had seen of the strip burning of the Amazon rainforests. He set his coffee down. When he opened his back door and saw the black ash that covered the ground around the bunkhouse, Jack decided it was time to go. The fire was a ridge away, no more than a mile. Once the scrub pines caught, his property would be untenable. The front-line firefighters reported the massive fires were only fifteen percent contained, whatever that meant, but it didn't sound good to Jack.

He was ready to go. Resolved in his heart that he would be okay. His insurance should cover the buildings and most of his things, but even if they called it an act of God and refused to pay, he could still sell the land. Maybe. It sat on the market for years before he bought it, but that was a cabin with no running water and an old, rotted-out bunkhouse; with the new well, he would be okay. The loss would hurt, but he could rebuild his finances and life. Again. He had done it after the accident. He could do it now.

Jack rose from the old wooden rocker. He walked to the edge of his porch and leaned on the rail. He stared for one last time at the impressive view of the mountain he had enjoyed for the last year. Jack was resolved to let the fire destroy what he had built.

Otter stood, woofed once, and sprang towards the stairs.

"Is that a kid?" he asked the dog as a small figure stepped out of the tree line.

A small form moved toward the ranch house. It took a few steps out of the trees, then stopped to look around. Jack got the impression it was scared. Its eyes seemed to scan for danger, its posture set to dash back into the tree line.

"It's a dude," Jack thought. Even at nearly a hundred yards, he could see the waist-length beard the figure sported. The figure took in the bunkhouse, then the old barn, and then settled on the main house. He moved toward the house as Jack stood up from his place at the railing. The bearded man staggered as he walked, making Jack think of drunks leaving a pub to meander across sidewalks as they headed home for the night.

After a few steps, Jack also noticed a defined limp in the guy's gait. He hitched his right leg with every second or third step; as he moved closer to the cabin, Jack realized the figure was not very tall. As he reached the split post fence surrounding Jack's small garden, Jack saw that the man was about as tall as the four-foot fence.

"He looks hurt or damn tired, Otter," Jack said.

The dog, already halfway across the field, made no reply. Jack turned toward the small stairs that led down off the deck. As his feet hit the grass, he saw the guy stagger and fall to the ground.

Jack was winded when he made the hundred-yard dash to where Otter sat, nuzzling a small compact form on the ground. The dog whined as he nudged the guy's neck with his muzzle, then sniffed at the long and intricately braided beard that cascaded along the ground beside him, its tips singed and smoking.

Jack knelt. He reached down and placed two fingers against the small man's neck.

"He's got a pulse, but what the hell happened to him?"

His entire back was covered in blood. The black leather jacket he wore was in tatters. Four diagonal cuts slashed down his back as if a Bear or Cougar had attacked him.

Jack moved his hand away from the man's neck. He grabbed his shoulder and rolled him onto his side. Two of the cuts extended over the man's shoulder and deep into the meat of his upper chest. Blood still flowed freely from the chest wounds. Jack pulled off his shirt and pressed the fabric into the seeping wounds.

"He must have pissed something off, Otter," Jack said as he looked back toward the ridge. The wind had shifted, and rising clouds of smoke once again obscured the mountain.

"Don't die on me; I don't want to spend the day explaining how a midget died in my yard."

He grabbed the man's arm and wrapped it around his neck. Jack's knees popped as he lifted the man. Otter ran ahead as Jack carried him into the house.

10

Jack pulled his cell phone from the charger next to his bed. The phone pulsed in his hand as the screen displayed a No Service message. Jack moved to the living room and through to the entrance room, where a reception desk had been set up for the Bed & Breakfast. He picked up the landline; the phone returned only dead air. Silence. Jack swore.

Jack jogged out to his truck. He swung down the tailgate and pulled the bright red first aid kit from the pile of camping gear he had packed the day before. He returned to the bedroom where the stranger lay. He tossed the red bag next to the man's head and rolled him on his side. He pulled off one side of his tattered leather jacket. He then rolled him onto his stomach and pulled the coat off. Jack pulled a small pair of scissors from the kit and cut through his thin cotton shirt. Jack wiped the wounds down with antiseptic and a large gauze pad. The wounds were long but not as deep as the ones on his shoulders. Most of the blood was dried. It pulled away from the man's skin as Jack scrubbed. Most of the cuts had already scabbed over.

Jack gently rolled the man onto his stomach and cut away the rest of his cotton shirt. The shoulder wounds looked far worse than those on the man's back. He wiped off the man's shoulders to get a better look behind all the blood. The cuts were deep; Jack could see the white edge of bone at the bottom of the wounds for a brief second, then blood welled back up and filled the gashes. Jack pulled a pack of coagulant powder from the pack and scattered it over the bleeding wounds, unsure if it would help. He removed another pack of gauze and an extra-large adhesive bandage from the kit. He tore open the gauze and packed it into the deepest parts of the cuts. The man moaned and shifted below Jack, but did not wake. Jack took another pack of gauze and laid that over the first. He ripped open the adhesive bandage and slapped it over the gauze.

Jack pulled a pressure bandage from the kit and wrapped it around the man's chest and shoulder. He wrapped it again around his patient's back and pulled it tight, then pulled it around twice more and tied it at his uninjured side. The injuries were ugly, but with the bleeding stopped, he was sure he was not in danger of dying right away.

With his unexpected guest's wounds taken care of, Jack walked into the kitchen, started a new pot of coffee, and picked up the kitchen phone. Still no dial tone. Jack pulled his cell from his pocket and walked outside. He held his cell phone out in front of him, turning left and right as he walked, he watched the signal strength bar for a tower signal. He turned west and looked up at the mountain, then south, where he knew the nearest cellular tower stood. The entire area was glowing orange as smoke poured up into the sky.

So much for the cell towers, he thought.

Jack walked around the side of the house to his truck. There was room in the cab; he could throw the little guy in and head down to the hospital in Wimac or up to Hood River General. Both were the same distance, but Hood River put him on the way to his bugout camp. If he left now, he might not have the opportunity to return if the emergency status changes. Jack considered whether anything inside was worth saving. He thought about his collection of weapons, trophies, and the cedar chest in the back closet. *What would be the point,* he thought, *dragging all that stuff out and keeping it around as a constant reminder of what he no longer had?*

Just things, Jill's voice floated beside his ear--*parts of a different life.*

My eighth, he thought as a sad smile spread across his face.

On their first date, after nearly getting hit by a bus, they joked that they must have the souls of cats. Jill suggested that every event they survived that might have killed them had instead taken one of their lives. They had spent the following few dates trading horror stories of things that had happened to them. He was hit by a car when he

49

was nine. She fell off a roof when she was seven. He was stabbed in the thigh during a high school fencing tournament. She was caught in the middle of an armed robbery. After they married, they joked that every near miss on the highway or trip on the stairs removed one of their lives. They often used it as an excuse to change how they lived, rearrange the furniture, or quit jobs they hated, as if each loss granted them the freedom to create another life. At least they did until the accident that claimed Jill's life. An accident that forced him into a new life, one without the companionship he had in the last one.

Otter jumped up onto the tailgate and nudged Jack's shoulder. Jack rocked back from the giant dog's weight and snapped out of his reverie. He scratched the dog's head. *Okay,* he thought, *maybe not no companionship.*

"Ready to go, boy?" Jack asked. The dog woofed deep in its throat in agreement.

Jack moved to return to the house, considering the multiple lives he had lived. Jack the fencer, Jack the Olympian, Jack the washout, Jill's boyfriend, Jack the husband, Jack the marketing manager, Jack the widower, and now Jack the innkeeper. *What's next,* he wondered.

11

Onyx woke to pressure around his chest. It felt like something gripped his ribs like an unasked-for hug, making him self-conscious. His limbs felt spent. He felt weak, without the energy to even open his eyes. He tried to sit up. Pain flared through his back and shoulders. A memory came with the pain — the run through burning trees, the creature chasing him. The talons dragged across his back--the fall from the waterfall.

The ground on his back was soft like he had fallen into a pile of soft, fresh-turned soil. *Ellis is alone on the mountain.* His eyes snapped open. He had to get up. He had to get back to him. He expected to see the sky. Instead, he found himself staring at a blank white ceiling. A fan spun above him. Onyx watched as it turned. He tried to place it in his memory, but failed. The smell of coffee caught his attention, and his stomach growled in response.

Onyx sat up. He was in a bedroom. His feet dangled from a high four-poster bed. Daylight streamed through a window to his right, and in front of him was an antique wardrobe. Scarred and dark with age, it towered above him. He looked to his left at a small doorway and wondered how anyone had managed to get that giant thing through it.

He slid down off the bed. Pain flared through him again as he landed. He stopped and took several deep breaths as the pain receded. His shirt and jacket, covered in blood and ash, lay in pieces on the floor. He lifted his hands to his chest, where a cloth strip was wrapped around his shoulder and torso. On the bed next to where he woke sat a red bag, a large white cross across its side; someone had patched him up.

He remembered the tiny house and barn he had seen through the trees. *Is that where I am? Can I get help returning to the peak here?* Onyx looked toward the small door he assumed led into the rest of the house. *Would they help?*

Most people prefer to stay out of other people's problems. Let someone else do it, they thought -- the law, the government, anyone but them -- someone else can handle it. Self-preservation was the norm. Humans, in general, are awful to each other, aren't they? Scammers, thieves, and plain, mean people would often exploit the kindness of those around them. So, people held back, even when it was apparent they should help. When the only right thing to do was to step in and lend a hand, they still held back.

They did not want to get involved. So, they did not help when they should have. Onyx shook his head at the thought. Someone did get involved; someone patched his wounds. They might be willing to help him get up the mountain.

He squeezed his eyes shut tight as pain raced up and down his back. He swallowed and ignored the pain as best he could. He inhaled to calm himself. The smell of smoke hung in the air. Memories of fire and blood flooded his mind. Nausea rolled over him, and he ran into the bathroom. He dry heaved into the sink. The mirror on the wall showed sunken cheekbones and dark circles around his once-bright eyes.

Behind him, Onyx saw the reflection of light on steel.

Onyx turned and stepped into a closet. A light turned on as he entered, illuminating a wall of weapons surrounded by shelves packed with fencing trophies. They were all covered in a thin layer of dust, the oldest dated back twenty years. The weapons around them shone as if they had been used and polished often. He thought some of them appeared dull and of poor quality, not Eardfolc work, but others looked like masterworks.

Onyx stepped up onto a cedar chest below the weapons. He reached up and took down a double-billed battle ax. Its bright blue handle faded to silver as it joined the steel axe head. Mirrored blades curved out from a central post. They flared at the top and tapered down to points like the wings of an angel.

Onyx hopped off the chest; his back and shoulders twinged in pain as he landed, but the pain was not as intense as it had been. He lifted the axe, held it before him as if he blocked an invisible sword blow, and tested its balance. He held the axe straight out in front of him. He gave it a swing, and the sharp pain of his injuries returned.

He ignored it and swung again. He pivoted with the momentum of the ax as he swung its weight across his body and missed a pile of boxes against one wall. He brought the weapon back into a block. He swung up and then down. Then, up and down again in a mock combination blow. Pain flared through his back and right shoulder as the weight of the axe pulled at the muscles of that side. He sighed and lowered the axe.

The pain was excruciating, a result of his recent battle. However, it was bearable, not as intense as when he first woke up. He was sure he could manage to fight with the axe. He had buried his knife in the beast's side, but the creature had pulled away, taking the blade from his hand. He would need a weapon if the beast returned. This one was within reach; it'd do the job just fine. *But, will I?* Onyx thought as tiny shivers of pain ran across his shoulders.

He dropped his right arm to his side and made several one-handed swings with just his left arm. He was not all that accurate left-handed, but it would have to do. Ellis needed his help. He was sure that he could handle the weight of the thing left-handed. He looked at the steel axe blade. He raised a hand and flicked the steel with a finger. A crisp, solid note rolled through the room. Onyx nodded, satisfied. He scowled, leaned the weapon on his left shoulder, then moved out of the closet and toward the door, ready to face whatever lay ahead.

It was time to get his brother. Onyx's determination was unwavering, and his mind was set on the task.

12

Jack poured coffee into his steel mug.

He considered how his day was going to go. Get the guy to a hospital, head to the campground, set up camp, and head into Broadman for dinner. Settle into the camp, do some fishing, try, and forget his world might be turning to ash around him. Again.

In the living room, he could hear the news drone repeating the same stories they had been going over for the last several days. Fire and politics dominated local and national news.

Jack moved to the doorway and glanced at the map, which tracked the fire's progress. He was still in a yellow zone. Fire close, be set to go.

Jack heard movement in the bedroom. His guest was up. It's time to bug out. He looked around the room one final time. The first aid kit needed to be repacked and put back into the truck; the weapons and trophies were not as crucial as this injured dude.

Just things, he thought as he picked the truck keys off the coffee table.

Jack turned as the little guy walked out of the bedroom.

He held the teardrop battle axe Jack had bought at a gun and knife show in Atlanta years ago. It was a pretty blade, but Jack found it impractical in a fight. The weapon was top-heavy. Its handle was too small, which threw off the indexing, which caused Jack to hit with the flat edge of the blade more often than not.

None of this concerned the short man as he hefted the blade at chest level.

"Thanks for the first aid. I am borrowing your axe," he said. "I'll return it, if possible, but my brother's still up on the mountain, and I intend to get him back." His voice was a strong baritone, his accent a Midwestern drawl.

Jack blinked.

Why had I expected a Scottish accent? Has Hollywood made me assume all short people with beards sound like either Ewan McGregor or Warwick Davis?

Jack stayed silent, unsure of what to say to the little guy's declaration. His house guest continued.

"I could use a ride up to the peak," he said, "I appreciate what you've already done, and I'll return the favor if ever you need it, but my brother's up there, and I need to get him down."

"Look, you should see a doctor," Jack said. "Those cuts are deep, and a couple of bandages will not stop infection. I can run you up to the hospital in Hood River and get you checked out. We can call the authorities from there; they can send help for your brother."

"I am fine. My brother is injured and is still up there with the thing that did it."

Jack was silent for a long moment. He seemed unable to process what was happening. A little person had shown up injured on his doorstep and was...what? Hitching a ride?

When Jack did not speak, the man nodded and scowled.

"Okay then," he said. "It's a long hike back up the mountain. I'd best be leaving." He moved toward the door.

Don't just stand there, Jill's voice rang loud in his ears.

"Look, I can't let you leave like this," Jack said.

This, he thought, *is why I never get involved with people. Complications.*

Jack considered his predicament. He helped the guy and did what he could; it was not his responsibility to do more than he already had. *Or is it,* he thought, *what kind of asshole lets a wounded man hike up a mountain.* On the one hand, he did not know the guy or his brother, but on the other, he was not too thrilled about the idea of letting him wander off to die.

The truck keys bit into Jack's hand.

Dammit.

"Look," Jack said as the guy reached for the door handle, "we'll take the truck up to get your brother, then I can run you both down to Wasco General."

The man thought for a minute as he eyed Jack, suspicion clear on his face. After a moment, he seemed to relax. "Okay, but you'll need a weapon. The beast that sliced me is still out there."

Jack nodded, "Yeah, not a bad idea. What is your name anyway?" Jack asked as he moved to the front office.

"Onyx," he responded, "Ellis is my brother; we...uh, live up on the West side of the mountain."

"Jack," Jack said as he opened the coat closet. "I didn't know anyone lived deeper into the National Park than I do," Jack pulled out a plastic rifle case. He set it on the desk, opened it, and pulled out the Remington 870DM Shotgun nestled in its foam liner.

"Well, my people were there long before it was a national forest," Onyx said.

Jack looked at the little man. With that impressive beard, he looked more like Swamp People than First People. Jack could not help himself and said so aloud.

See, he thought, *this is why I have no friends.*

Onyx laughed. "I would prefer Mountain People. I would say we are Native, but we aren't Native American, though there may be some Modoc blood in my taller cousins; some of them are almost five feet tall."

Jack stopped and looked at Onyx. The man's scowl was still firmly in place, so Jack was unsure if he was joking. Afraid to offend him, Jack kept his mouth shut.

Jack removed a six-round magazine from the gun case. He thought about the giant slashes he had seen on Onyx's back and slid out the birdshot rounds. He dropped them into the case. He pulled a dozen 3-inch slugs from a box on the top shelf of the closet and slid them into the magazine. With the magazine full, he clipped it into the box receiver on the shotgun. He racked the slide and checked the safety. Placing the gun on the desk, he pulled another magazine from the case and repeated the load change with a second, a third, and then a fourth magazine. He grabbed an ammo pouch hung on a hook on the closet door and slipped it onto his belt. Jack dropped the three magazines into the pouch.

He turned toward the front door. Onyx stood bare-chested in front of him. The bandages were still white, so his bleeding had stopped. "Don't think you should go out like that," Jack said as he returned to the closet.

"I'll be fine."

Jack rustled through the closet. In the back, he found a cardboard box of clothes left by various vacationers. He pulled out a plaid shirt and saw what he was looking for below it.

"Here, see if this fits you," Jack said. He held a child's leather bomber jacket in one hand. "I'm pretty sure the kid who left it forgot it on purpose."

Onyx eyed the jacket. "I can see why." It looked new. The leather shone like a wet lollipop. The inside, cuffs, and collar all sported a thick padding of wool-textured yellowish fur. If asked, Jack could only describe the color as poop brown. "It'll be cold uphill," Jack said, "you'll want something when we get there."

With a sigh, Onyx thanked Jack, took the jacket, and slid it over the bandages. He was surprised to find it fit him.

"So, how big was this cat that attacked you?" he asked.

"Huge," Onyx replied.

Jack thought for a moment, then returned to the closet. He pulled down an ammo box with a stylized dragon breathing fire on it. He pulled a half dozen white phosphorus shells from the box and slid them into an empty magazine. He filled a second, then shoved them both into his jacket pocket. As he closed the closet door, Jill's voice echoed in his head, *Hat, mister, you don't want to be dealing with sunstroke again.*

Jack reached up and grabbed an old hat off the shelf.

"Grab the first aid kit off the bed; I'll start the truck. Where did you say your brother was?"

"I didn't, but it is a stone house below the Glacier. We stumbled on it as we ran from the beast."

Jack had skied the glacier the previous winter, when he discovered that skiing wasn't his thing, and he had hiked parts of the trail leading to it several times.

"I know the place. That's a long haul on foot; how long ago did you leave him?"

"Yesterday at dusk."

Jack looked up toward the mountain.

Could I make a trip that far in twelve or thirteen hours?

"You got here just after sunup, damn good time," Jack said.

"I was being chased," Onyx said as he joined Jack, the first aid bag in one hand and the axe in the other.

"Good motivator."

"You can't imagine," Onyx said.

Jack pulled his cell out. He clicked on the net app, but received the "no signal" message again. Navigating back to the main screen, he clicked on his GPS app. A spinning wheel appeared on his phone as the app started. A small silhouette of the United States came on screen with the message, "GPS not found, map data unavailable. Connect to the Internet for real-time data."

Jack slammed the phone down on the kitchen counter. "Damn, guess you'll have to navigate," he said as they headed out the door.

13

Ashley Ember's stomach spun and tumbled as always when the plane left the runway. She was unsure whether the feeling was a result of the flight itself or the anticipation of the jump ahead. Phil had constantly teased her about jumping out of a perfectly good airplane.

Just one of the many red flags I missed, she thought.

She loved the thrill of the jump. From the air whistling past her as she dove to the serene drift to the ground after her chute opened, everything was perfect when she jumped. She could leave all her problems behind as she concentrated only on the task at hand. That was one of the reasons she had joined Portland Fire & Rescue, originally to leave Phil and his raging narcissism behind as she concentrated on a job and did it well.

As the plane banked, she looked out the porthole window beside her. The clean, clear air of the Columbia Plateau spun below her. As the plane began to level out, she got a glimpse of the Cascades to the South and west.

Smoke filled the early morning sky above the not-so-distant mountains. Spots of red and orange flickered on the mountainsides. The sky swirled with tornadoes of smoke and fire as the Cascades burned. At last report, nearly a million acres were burning fiercely along the mountain range, and now several fires had sprung up along the base of Mount Hood.

The pilot eased the plane northward as he jockeyed around the worst turbulence caused by the rising heat and smoke of the burning countryside. The mountain came into view. From this side, it looked like someone had dropped a giant ice cream cone on the landscape and then covered it in trees. Lots and lots of trees, she thought.

She remembered how much she loved the sight of the snow-peaked mountain on those rare sunny days she could see from their apartment in Portland. Phil was never impressed, though. That should have been the brightest of the many red flags she had missed in their relationship.

Shouldn't you find joy in what makes your loved ones happy?

Before heading out, the topographic map they had reviewed showed a snow-covered starfish, with each of its arms forming a ridge that headed up to join the snow-covered peak. The glacier's edge glinted in the smoke-hazed distance. Three glaciers, Ashe thought, or was it four? She could never remember. Several different glaciers, anyway, met at the peak of the mountain. Ice and snow laid down millions of years ago, which were only now beginning to melt off, revealing acres of land that had not seen the sun in millennia. She heard there were ice caves and mile-deep ice crevasses all around the summit, but she had never made it up there. For the last eight months, she had thrown herself into work.

After the breakup, she joined the U S Forest Service, hoping to restart her life away from Phil. She felt like some ghost of her life with him haunted every place she went in Portland. She could not go anywhere without an echo of their time together, destroying the safety of the city she loved. The new smoke jumper unit seemed like the best choice. Her time with Portland Fire Rescue and the hours she logged as a skydiving instructor provided her with enough experience to be considered by unit command.

She always loved the view of the mountains from the city and found that they were even more beautiful up close. Although she had uprooted and changed her life, she was still somewhere familiar — close enough to the city to visit and far enough away that memories of the bad times did not haunt her.

An alarm blared in the cabin, and a yellow light on the ceiling lit up.

Jim Deevers tapped her arm. He held up five fingers and mimicked checking the belts on his jump harness. Ashe nodded and began going through the pre-jump checklist in her head. She rechecked to ensure that all her gear was in the right place and that all her belts and buckles were secure. The jump leader had the side door open.

Air rushed through the small plane's cabin as the yellow light went out and a red light went on.

All queasiness ended as Ashe fell into the sky. Her body rigid, she dropped out of the plane. Feet pointed to the ground. Arms crossed on her chest like a mummy. In the near distance, she could see Lawrence Lake, a vast expanse of blue in the otherwise unbroken greenery. South of her, the glistening glacier sparkled in the feeble sunlight that broke through the smoke-hazed sky. Between the two, a thin stretch of forest was ablaze. The flame was tiny compared to that of the fires burning further south. It looked like a cone of flames, a quarter mile long. Not as big as she expected, the fire seemed contained within a valley of pine and maple, surrounded on both sides by bare cliffs. It spread out in a V-shape that pointed back toward the lake.

Ashe was jarred to one side as an updraft grabbed her chute and bounced her around. She reached up and grabbed the control lines above her head. She prepared to dump air to move back into line with the jumpers below her.

Ashe's head snapped back. She felt weightless as something pulled her up and sideways, away from the landing zone. She looked up to check her chute. She could not see anything above her. She continued to drift up and back toward the peak.

Oh my God, she thought, *my chute line didn't release. I'm still connected to the plane. Do they know?*

In her head, she saw herself being dragged along behind the plane as it returned to the airfield. Her movement up and toward the peak continued, and she got further away from the drop area with every second.

Why haven't they cut the line? They must know I'm still connected.

With a rush of speed, she was suddenly above the glacier line, rising toward the peak.

What is it? Eight thousand feet, she thought. *Jeez, why haven't they...*the thought was cut short.

She saw the plane cruising sedately away from the mountain, a mile to the South, away from her.

What the hell?

Ashe began falling. The chute was no longer fully open. It caught air, but barely enough to keep her aloft. She spun as she fell. She could see jagged tears in the fabric as if someone had dragged a knife through it. She pulled at the control lines. Neither responded. The trees rushed toward her. She dropped her jump pack, hoping to gain some altitude. Her descent slowed, but the trees in front of her were too high.

This is going to hurt, was all she had time to think before the branches of a giant pine tree smashed into her.

14

The door slammed shut behind them as Jack and Onyx walked out of the cabin. As Onyx crossed the yard, his eyes drifted to the peak behind the cabin. The mid-morning sun pierced through a gap in the layer of smoke that blanketed the sky. It glinted off the snow-capped mountain. The rest of the smoke-covered sky glowed with an orange abandon that made the thin beam of sunlight seem like a candle in comparison.

Ashes whirled around their shoes like the hope that swirled in Onyx's chest. He had found help and was on his way to his brother; all would be well. The countryside still burned. The smoke still rose, blocking the sky's blue, but Onyx had hope. Hope that he'd reach his brother. Hope that all would turn out for the better. Hope that allowed him to ignore the pain pulsing through his back and shoulders.

Onyx sighed. Not long now, Ellis, he thought. Onyx turned and continued to follow Jack. His vision caught Jack's oversized truck parked just a little too close to the fence. The thing was massive. Not a monster truck, but bigger than your standard work truck. It had tires that looked to Onyx like they could roll over boulders. Its black paint gleamed in the mid-morning light. Its cab stood well above Onyx's head.

"That's one hell of a truck," he muttered.

"Yeah, not really a ranch truck. But I've had her since LA and don't have the heart to give her up and get something more practical." Jack said, his boots kicking up ashes as they walked.

Onyx watched as Jack stopped, straightened his jacket, and glanced over at the cabin, a wistful look on his face.

Onyx could not take his eyes off Jack's truck. A twisted knot of anxiety rolled through him, a sense of unease far beyond any he had felt before. He had never liked trucks. He preferred a motorcycle or small car, something close to the ground that made you feel like you were flying along the asphalt. In trucks, he always felt disconnected from the road, a particle with no control, swept along by an unstoppable current, unable to determine his own fate.

The truck itself did not intimidate him. The oversized tires were taller than he was, but they were just tires. It was the passenger seat that felt miles away from his place on the ground that piqued his anxiety. He worried about how he would hoist himself up into the cab. On any other day, a climb into the truck would have been no problem, but today was no other day. His muscles felt fatigued, his back burned, and his right shoulder radiated pain in sharp pulses that matched his heartbeat as they ran down the length of his body.

Onyx's thoughts raced with feelings of self-doubt. He did not want to appear weak or incapable. This guy, Jack, had helped him. He needed Jack to trust him. Looking like he wasn't strong enough to perform even the simplest of tasks, might convince Jack he needed a hospital more than he needed to get to Ellis. He must present an image of confidence and capability in front of this Reuzin, but the weight of his self-doubt was heavy.

The last thing he needed was to seem weak or inept. He did not want Jack to feel inconvenienced. He did not want to make him feel like he was dealing with an invalid. He needed him. Onyx could not risk alienating him; he had to get to Ellis, and this was the fastest way.

Onyx checked his pockets, stalling to buy time. His physical strength had always been his pride. His ability to do the challenging task without help was something he knew others admired in him. Right now, it was not about getting into the truck; it was about what being unable to get in it meant. Needing help, worse, showing weakness, felt like admitting defeat. And defeat was not something he was willing to face. His heart pounded as he grappled with his pride and the reality of his situation.

Just go for it, he told himself.

With a deep breath, Onyx stepped onto the sidebar below the passenger door. He reached over his head for the door handle. He hopped back as the door swung open, pain blasting down his right side as he dropped to the ground. The door missed hitting him by inches. Despite the searing pain, Onyx was determined to overcome it and get into the truck.

Alright, step up, grab the door handle, and pull yourself up like you've done a hundred times.

Onyx did not move. The more he thought about it, the harder it seemed.

What if I miss the step? What if my hand slips and I take a tumble? What if it takes too dang long to swing up and in?

He clenched his fists. Anger simmered within him. He was better than this. He was stronger than this. He was not some simpering invalid who required help just to get in a damn truck. Onyx had spent his life leading others. He was the strong, capable, and invulnerable one, and he did not want anyone, not even this Reuzin, to think that he was not.

Onyx drew in a breath. His anger faded. He knew he had to get to Ellis. He was not going to let anything stop him. Not the creature that had wounded him. Not the man opening the driver-side door, and not this damn truck. His determination was unwavering, a beacon of resilience in the face of adversity.

Onyx unclenched his hands, stepped up, grabbed the door, and pulled himself into the truck.

15

Jack opened the driver's side door and carefully placed the shotgun between the two front seats. As the passenger side door creaked open, Onyx struggled into the truck. Jack hesitated, torn between offering assistance and respecting Onyx's pride. He averted his gaze, pretending to be engrossed in the view of the house to avoid making eye contact with the struggling man.

Jack ran the numbers in his head: two hours to reach the peak, figuring they would have to stabilize him, get him down the hill, and into the truck. The trailhead was not too far off the State Road that runs straight north into Wasco City, so maybe an hour to the hospital, then to the campground in Broadman, two hours. Five hours tops, six if they had trouble getting Ellis down or at the hospital. He couldn't just ditch the pair at the ER entrance; he'd have to stay until they settled. Either way, he would have plenty of time to set camp by sundown. And he could say he did the right thing — no regrets or guilt from inaction.

I can say I did the right thing.

"If I remember right," he said after they settled in, "it's like an hour trip; sit back and relax. We'll be there in no time."

No problem, Jack thought. His mind raced with uncertainties. He could not remember how far the shelter was up the trail from the closest parking area.

I'll have to add a couple of hours; I don't remember the hike being too bad, but hiking with Otter and bringing a guy down off the mountain is a big difference; it might get rough. When is sunset? he thought; *eight, eight-thirty? Can I still make it, or do I sleep in the truck?*

Jack whistled out the truck window and swung his door back open. Otter trotted out from the barn.

"Let's go, Otter. Truck."

The dog looked up at Jack and barked.

"Come on, boy," Jack swung his door out a bit further. Otter squeezed through behind Jack's seat. He jumped onto the back bench and barked again.

"Why are you bringing a cow?" Onyx asked.

"That's Otter," Jack said.

"Never seen an otter that big or with curly hair," Onyx leaned tight against the passenger window as Otter stuck his head over the back seat and sniffed at the man's face and chest. Jack reached over and pushed Otter into the back.

"He's a Newfoundland, kind of like a water-loving St. Bernard, except without the keg of liquor."

"Too bad," Onyx said, "I could use a drink about now."

Jack shut his door and twisted the key in the ignition. He looked back out at the Fallen J Ranch, *maybe for the last time,* he thought, before he said, "You and me both."

As he started down the gravel drive, he looked at his passenger and asked, "How long have you and your brother been up on the mountain?"

They passed under the wrought iron arch that marked the entrance to his ranch. At the top of the arch was a small shield and a Fleur-de-lis, the family crest of some past ranch owner. In the crest's center was an Iron letter J hanging upside down from one rivet.

Onyx looked up as they left the drive. "Your J's falling."

"Story of my life," Jack said. "It was like that when I bought the place; I felt Fallen J was as good a name as any. Describes me and the ranch."

The Mountain lay in the distance, wreathed in flame and smoke. From his back porch, the ridge behind his property obscured the fires in the southwest, but the flames on the mountain were clear here, up above the valley. Swaths of fire covered the land ahead of them.

Can we even get past all that? Jack thought.

"My brother and me, we've been up on that mountain our whole lives," Onyx said. His words broke Jack out of the mini panic attack that had gripped him at the sight of the fires. "Our people've been livin' up there for near a hundred generations."

"I thought you said you weren't American Indian."

"We ain't."

Jack laughed, "So you're telling me a tribe of midgets has lived on the mountain since before Columbus, and no one has ever noticed."

"Midget's not a term you should be usin', y'know," Onyx said. He looked at Jack, his eyes cold and disapproving. "Historically, folks used that word to put down small people. It isn't very respectful, and it ain't somethin' you should throw around. 'Little Person' or even 'person with dwarfism'--those are more respectful terms for folks like that."

"Sorry, I meant no disrespect," Jack said as he leaned back into his seat and concentrated on the road.

"I'm considered average height for my people," Onyx declared with pride, "And before you ask, no, we ain't little people, and we sure as hell ain't midgets. You can call us dwarfs if you must, but we're the Eardfolc--the hardiest of the Sidhe--crafters, artisans, protectors of all that lies beneath the soil. Long before the Reuzin came along, we lived among the hills and mountains of the world. We've served this land since its creation." His words resonated with a deep sense of belonging and duty.

"Reuzen," Jack asked, not recognizing the word.

"Onhandige Reuzen," he said slowly, pronouncing each syllable as if to a child, "It's from the Old Tongue. Our name for your people. Humans."

Is he suppressing his disability? I am not short; I'm a fairy tale dwarf, Jack thought. *What have I gotten myself into? Am I on a rescue mission with a lunatic? Is there even a brother?*

"So, like a tribe of miners in caves?" Jack's voice betrayed his growing uncertainty. The situation was becoming more bizarre by the minute, and he couldn't shake off the feeling of being in over his head.

"Don't be a racist. Some of us mine, just like your people, we dig, and we build. We've got farms on the mountain and all around the area. We own businesses, we've got our own markets, our own homes. We're part of the communities here. It ain't dank tunnels and dusty mines. We've got modern conveniences: electric lights, running water, computers, the Internet, solar, and geothermal power. We don't live much different than you do. Like all Sidhe, a lot of us live right among you. We pass as humans, and our days of hiding under the earth have long passed."

"Computers, where do you get computers?" Jack asked.

"Amazon, mostly," Onyx replied.

Jack stared at Onyx.

He must be putting me on.

16

Onyx wondered how he could explain the beast to this man, who couldn't accept that the Eardfolc existed, let alone something so far beyond his limited experience. Would any human believe him, though, he wondered. Just because a thing is true doesn't mean people will accept it.

He considered how Jack would react when he told him the truth. Will I even be able to tell him the truth? He considered his options: say nothing and get to Ellis as quickly as possible, or tell the truth and lose his only chance at help. Ellis is hurt, but he would be okay a little longer if the beast had not returned to his hiding place. His injuries weren't life-threatening. Ellis was in more danger from the fire and exposure than from his injuries if the beast didn't return.

The mountain peak rose in the distance, smoke rising around it like a veil.

They drove down a narrow road into a low valley. Rows of trees whipped by so close Onyx felt like he could reach out and grab the branches--the only sound was the trees' whoosh and the large dog's panting in the back.

"What's with all the hardware in your closet?" Onyx asked as he patted the axe. "You've got some fine work in there and quite a few trophies. Why hide them away?"

"Old college trophies and things I picked up along the way," Jack replied.

"I saw the Olympic Medal. Quite a feat. Gold, was it?"

A smile flickered across Jack's face. "Bronze, but thanks."

"Why hide it in a closet? It seems like something most people would brag about."

Jack's shoulders raised and lowered in an awkward shrug as he gripped the steering wheel. "Not something I think about anymore. It's something I did once. A distant life," he said as echoes of Jill's voice surrounded him. A different life. Seems like a hassle to have to explain it every time someone new comes along, so I keep it private."

"Seems like it'd be somethin' to be proud of," Onyx said.

"Don't mean much," Jack said. "My wife still died, my 401k still tanked, and I still need to bust my ass to pay the mortgage." Jack sighed. He relaxed slightly as Onyx watched. Then, he began to speak, his tone melancholy and distant. "We struggle to reach our dreams and still end up in the monotony we call life. You have a dream, you fight to make it happen, and when it does, when you have made it, when you've reached that thing that you thought would make you so happy and change your life, you find it's no different than anything else. You did it, but you are still you, still grinding away to pay the rent."

"Payin' the rent is the guarantee of shelter, a place where you can catch your breath and plan your next move."

"You make it sound noble."

"Isn't it?"

"Anyway," Jack said after an awkward pause, "my point is dreams get buried under what we do to get through life. The past passed. It is over. Move to the next dream, and let's hope this one makes you happy. Or makes a difference."

"Don't discount the significance of success or even failure, Jack. The things you've done are the building blocks of who you are. The things you do, your failures, and your wins--they're the foundation of your character. And that character, well, that's what'll help you reach new dreams."

Jack lifted his foot from the gas pedal. As the truck slowed, he looked at Onyx. "That's a hell of a piece of wisdom there. What did you say you do for a living?"

Onyx grinned at Jack, "I might be small, but that don't mean I've seen any less of life, ya know."

Jack smiled back and let out a short laugh.

"Look, I don't like talking about my fencing years because I don't like the questions they bring up. The scrutiny, the expectations -- people look at those trophies, then look at me now; it gets overwhelming. They inevitably ask why I quit, why I don't take it back up, and why I would waste all my talent by not doing the thing I did so well."

"And you don't have answers."

"Oh, I have answers, plenty of answers, but not any that don't show me out as a failure. Nothing I have done since will ever measure up to what I did then."

"The discipline, dedication, and hard work it took to get that far-- they ain't just in the past. Those are tools you keep with ya, carryin' 'em your whole life. Maybe it's not about what's behind ya, but findin' a way to channel those same talents into your life right now."

"I guess that is what I was trying to do with the Fallen J: build something successful. Something that will last. Something other than faded newspaper articles that say Jack Season was here, he existed, he was worthy."

"A worthy goal, sure, but even without it, your worth is more than those old, faded newspaper articles. Beyond them headlines, I'm sure you've made an impact on people. Not just the ones around you, but those who might only know you from those stories. How many young folks did you inspire? How many lives you'll never know about were changed just because you were out there, doin' what you did?"

"It doesn't matter," Jack said as he looked down into the valley below. They had just turned onto Old Forest Road and rolled to the top of a large hill. They looked around at the charred, still-smoking landscape around them, "The Fallen J will be ash by this time tomorrow, and I'll be paying the mortgage on a hundred-acre ashtray."

Onyx sighed. He turned in his seat to face the window. After a few moments, he said, "That may be, but a ranch can be rebuilt; rebuildin' a spirit, well, that ain't so easy.."

Onyx sighed.

How do you explain the fantastic to someone so beaten down by the everyday? How do you give hope to those who have lost it

17

Ashe couldn't move. Her arms were tangled in the control lines above her head. She looked up. Her parachute was shredded. What was left of its billowing cloth was caught in branches high above. Paracord hung around her like limp snakes that swayed gently in the breeze. Ashe wiggled and yanked at the lines that trapped her arms. Instead of coming loose, they only got tighter. Soon, her hands began to tingle. Tiny lightning bolts traveled up and down her fingers. The entrapping rope was cutting off the blood supply to her hands.

Ashe looked down. Her head spun as vertigo overwhelmed her. The ground stretched far beneath her, an impossible distance that made her stomach flip. She took several deep breaths and closed her eyes until the spinning feeling eased. She stopped struggling, aware that the control lines above her were the only thing keeping her from falling to her death. The nearest branch was more than half a dozen feet to her side. Get to that branch, she thought as she planned her way out of the tree. Get to the branch, take the weight off the ropes, and untangle yourself, then find a way to climb down. Easy-peasy, she thought.

She reached her foot out and tried to catch the branch below her. No luck. The branch was just out of reach of her toes. She stretched her leg as far as she could, but the lines tied around her arms kept her from reaching the branch. Well, she thought after several more attempts, that won't work.

Ashe looked at her surroundings again. It looked like she was caught in a giant ponderosa pine high up on a ridge below the mountain's peak. Across from her was another ridge, its trees blocking her view out of the deep ravine she had landed in. She blinked. That can't be right. They had jumped over Lawrence Lake. That was far below the peak. But there's the peak, I can spit on it from here; she thought as she looked toward the glimmer of glacial ice above. She swiveled her hips and kicked her feet to slowly spin herself around and get a better view of her surroundings.   To her left, she could see branches and, beyond them, the glacier-rimmed peak of the mountain. Behind her was only the trunk of the tree and the branches of the trees behind it. She could see the mountain's slopes below her as she spun three-quarters of the way around--a road cut through the carpet of trees far below. If I am near the peak, that must be East, and that must be the state road. She followed the twisting line of the road toward her ridge, where it met a thin blue line that could only be White River. Her mind whirled. I am on the wrong side of the mountain.

She must be mistaken, though; either that was not the peak, or it wasn't as close as it seemed. Terror suddenly filled her as she realized her predicament. They won't look for me here. She was supposed to be on the lower northern slopes. That was where any rescue would search, not here. Not only that, she thought, they would not even look for her right away. That was a scary thought, but she knew it was right. For some reason, the plane headed back to the airstrip, so they thought she had made the jump. As the last out, her crew would not have seen her jump and would think she could not, so they would not worry. At least not until they checked in by radio tonight. Panic gripped her by the throat, her realization of the direness of her situation intensifying her fear.

She began pumping her legs like a child on a swing set. She had to get out of this tree. She arched her back as she swung her body toward the closest. She stretched every muscle in her legs, torso, and shoulders toward the branch. Her toes passed mere inches above it. Again and again, she tried. She could not get to the branch. But she didn't give up, her determination shining through her repeated attempts.

The sun peeked through the leaves, casting dappled shadows that flitted across her face. She looked up and squinted through the maze of branches that made up the forest canopy. Her parachute was a mess. The billowing balloon of cloth she expected was nowhere to

87

be seen; instead, strips of fabric wrapped around several branches, like garland on a Christmas tree. Its paracord hung limp like a shattered spider's web. The strands swayed with the breeze coming down from the peak.

Below her, the forest floor seemed miles away. Ashe swallowed. She tried not to think about the damage such a fall would cause if she did manage to escape the swirl of paracord. She swung halfway up the ancient pine tree as the frigid wind from the glacial peak streamed down the mountain. She stopped trying to reach the branch. Her body swayed and spun now from the force of her attempts.

There was a soft tearing sound, and Ashley dropped as the cloth of the parachute above her tore.

A single breath later, her body came to a jolting stop. Ashe looked down. The ground was not much closer, and the branch she had been trying to reach was now above her. Below her and to the other side was another branch. This one was just as far away as the last, but she could reach it; all she had to do was try. The branch was right there, not far from her. If only she could stretch her leg or swing herself over, she could hook onto it. The ropes held her firmly, leaving her to spin and sway in the open air. Again, Ashe kicked her feet out. Again, she swung and stretched toward the branch below. Again, she was disappointed; the branch was inches out of her reach.

Realizing it was hopeless, Ashley Ember let out a scream full of rage and frustration that echoed across the mountain.

18

Jack pulled up to the stop sign at Old Forest Road. The fires were out of view, hidden behind ridges to their south. The sky still glowed orange with the reflected firelight off the low-hanging clouds of smoke.

"So, how did you get torn up," Jack asked Onyx.

"My brother and a few cousins were on the glacier when the beast attacked us. We fought it off, but my brother's leg was broken. I grabbed him and headed down the mountain, trying to get away from the beast. It must have finished off or gotten tired of the others because soon I could hear it behind us. We stumbled over a rise and saw a small stone shack. I moved Ellis inside and waited for the beast to get close. I attacked it and drew it away from the shack when it did. Luckily, it followed me. I tried to lose it several times in the woods, but it stayed tight on my tail. It caught up to me early this morning, and," Onyx sighed, looking embarrassed, "it sliced open my back as I dove into a creek, hoping it wouldn't follow. It didn't."

"What happened to the others?"

"I don't know when I know Ellis is okay; we'll look for them."

"What were you doing up on the mountain," Jack asked.

"We were looking for the campsite of a clan member that disappeared up there a decade ago. He had a family heirloom with him, and we intend to get it back."

"Bad time for a treasure hunt, with the wildfires and all."

"It's important to us. Worth the risk, you'd say."

"Wow. What is this heirloom?"

"A sword from the homeland, brought by my people when they first came to the mountain. It is the property of one of our greatest warriors and explorers. Rumor is it has the power to protect its wielder from fire, even stop these fires altogether."

Jack stared dumbfounded at his passenger. Just because I did not see a head wound does not mean he does not have one, right?

Jack looked back at the road just in time to swerve left to avoid going off the road and into the trees.

"A magic sword," Jack said.

"Sure, if you wish to call it that," Onyx said.

Jack stared at Onyx again; he searched the man's face for any hint of deception. A twitch of the lips as he held back laughter, a looseness around his eyes, a chin quiver, anything to show he was pulling Jack's leg. He saw nothing. The small man sat stoically, as if all he said was, 'The sky is blue.' He wholeheartedly believed the story he was telling.

He really believes what he is saying, Jack thought.

The wheel jerked in Jack's hands as the truck began to edge onto the shoulder; the thin gravel scree of the shoulder pinged off the wheel wells. Jack blinked and looked back up at the road. The truck drifted right toward the wall of trees. Jack jerked the wheel. The truck careened back to the center of the road.

Onyx held up his hands. "Watch the road, please; I'm too small to wrap around a tree."

Jack concentrated on the road for a few moments without a response.

Behind them, Otter let out a low whimper, then a woof. His tail beat a short tattoo on the seat vinyl.

"Really, Otter," Jack admonished. Looking back at the canine, he said, "You should have gone before we left." The dog whined and lowered its head to its paws.

Jack pulled onto the shoulder; small stones of the shoulder pinged off the truck's frame and created a plume of dry dust behind them. Jack shut down the truck and turned to face his passenger. Behind him, Otter sat up, his tail wagging in anticipation of a walk. "Gimme a sec, Onyx," he said.

Jack opened his door and slid out of the seat. Otter followed. The dog looked up at Jack and whined.

"Go on," Jack said, "stay close." Jack pointed toward the trees along the road, withered by the heat. Even from here, everything looked dry as tinder and ready to go up in flames. Otter bound off into the trees, sniffed for a moment along the ground, and soon disappeared behind the rows of trees.

"So," Jack said to Onyx as he climbed back into the truck. "You were looking for a magic sword."

"It can save your ranch," Onyx said.

Jack stared a moment. "The sword can save my ranch."

"Yes, it can stop the cause of the wildfires. The creature that attacked me is causing the fires. The sword can stop it."

Jack eyed the axe in the foot well beneath Onyx.

Is he dangerous? It's too late for that. Is he going to get violent if I question his story? He is really caught up in this; what is it called, a psychosis? He believes every word. But what about the back wounds? Those were real. Jack was sure of it; he had dressed the wounds. You couldn't fake something like that, could you?

93

Onyx stood in the chair, his head grazing the roof. He faced Jack straight on, his face a mask of concern.

"For the past decade, wildfires have gotten worse every year. They've grown large enough to destroy cities and kill hundreds of people. But this year, the fires are different. These fires will continue to get worse until everything is destroyed. They get worse every hour. Humans can't stop them." Onyx paused to take a long breath as if steeling himself for an unpleasant task. He bowed his head and then faced Jack once more. "There is a way to end these fires. We have a chance right now to put an end to the destruction. Maybe not everywhere, but right now, we can make a difference. Save your ranch, save some lives."

Jack was not sure how to respond. He stared into Onyx's eyes, still looking for some sign that this was all an elaborate joke.

"There are risks," Onyx said. "I knew that when I started, my family knew it when they decided to join me. You should know it before we go any further. I intend to stop these wildfires by ending their cause. I may die, my brother and cousins may die, but we went into this knowing the risks. You have a right to know the risks before we go any further. I can get out here and get to my brother on my own. You have no reason to help me or even believe me. I want you to know that I am grateful for the help you have given me. But I can't drag you along without telling you the real risks. The creature that attacked me is still up there and will try to stop us."

"You talk like this thing is hunting you," Jack said.

"It is."

19

Onyx took a deep breath. The time of truth had come. He had to tell Jack just what he would face on the mountain. To do otherwise would just be wrong. A trickle of doubt passed through Onyx at that thought.

Was he less responsible for his brother's injuries just because Ellis agreed to help? This whole expedition had been Onyx's idea. When he convinced his cousins to come, didn't he become the cause of all that would happen to them? If not for him, they would still be safe at home, complaining about work and arguing over politics. *For how long,* he wondered. *Suppose the fires were not stopped here; how long before his community would be destroyed? How long before the fires were at the Eardfolc's doorstep? How long before his community was lost, like many human towns had been?* It would be too late by the time the Ienheid decided on a course of action. That was why he and his cousins had come and why they were trying to find the sword and stop the beast. The Ienheid was broken, indecisive, and weak. His people needed a leader who could stand up to the old men of the Ienheid and convince them to work together, convince them that their duty was not just to the Eardfolc but to the entire land. They needed someone who would restore the honor of their past to the Eardfolc and take them back to being the stewards of nature they had once been. The sword would prove the worth of such a person; no one would doubt the one who bore the blade of his grandfather. No one would dare question the sword bearer or the one who stopped the flames.

The flames weren't stopping; they weren't even slowing down. The entire West Coast was ablaze if he heard the Human's news channel right. Fires burned from San Francisco to Calgary. He was sure that if the fires were not stopped, they would consume the continent. His people's leaders claimed it was a human problem and claimed they were the ones who caused it, so they should fix it, but Onyx knew better. His ancestors had stayed behind; they had become mortal to restore the land, heal it, and protect it. He could not allow their sacrifice to be in vain.

They were Eardfolc; it was their sacred duty to protect the land. *When did we forget that? When did we stop looking out for the land and start looking out for ourselves?*

Jack's voice broke into his thoughts. "I'm sorry, Onyx, I'm having trouble buying into this idea that mythical dwarves are real. Throw in a magic sword, and it's even harder to believe."

"Eardfolc," said Onyx, his voice firm with determination. "Believe whatever you like; I need to get to my brother. I appreciate your help, but I'll make it alone from here if you don't want to help."

Onyx reached for the door handle as he spoke and started to open the door.

"Don't be like that," Jack said, his voice filled with compassion, "I'll get you up to the shelter, but magic swords that fight fires aren't in my reality set. We'll get your brother, then we can get you both to a hospital."

Jack opened his door and whistled. A high-pitched rise and fall filled the truck cab, and there was a bark in response out in the trees.

"Otter. Truck," Jack yelled. The dog came bounding out of the trees and jumped up into the back seat, the entire truck bouncing as the dog's weight hit it.

"Good boy," Jack said, reaching back and scratching the dog behind its ears. The canine's whip-chord tail slapped back and forth, a drumbeat of happiness against the vinyl interior.

Onyx shut his door and settled back into the seat as Jack closed his door, started the truck, and rolled back onto the highway.

"So, this Creature that attacked you," Jack said, then paused until Onyx picked up his explanation.

"It woke in Australia," Onyx said. "Started fires there as it began to feed and eventually made its way here. Australia, California, Canada, and now here.

"You're telling me the wildfires in Australia and the ones that are burning in Canada are all from this thing?"

"Not all of them, wildfires occur naturally every year, but most of the fires burning up and down the West Coast now were started by her."

"Her," Jack asked.

"Yes," Onyx said, "She is looking to lay her eggs; that's why she's chosen an active volcano. She burrows to the molten core of the mountain, lays her eggs, and reignites the volcano to incubate her clutch."

There it is, Onyx thought, *one more step, one more sentence, and there goes my chance to get to Ellis quickly.*

He looked out the window. Trees swept past in a blur, a green mirage that flowed past as the truck sped by. As they rounded a bend in the road, the distant peak came into view. *Not as far away as it was,* Onyx thought. *This truck may not get me all the way there, but I am closer than I was. Maybe I can stall this out a little longer. Perhaps I can just avoid it altogether. There's no reason to tell him all of it. Isn't it enough that he knows there are risks to helping me? Isn't it enough to know there is something out there after me? Something that can't be stopped, something that will destroy everything in its path.*

Onyx already knew the answer. He could not fool himself. If he was going to drag this Reuzin into his troubles, then he had to tell him the whole truth. Jack had helped him when he staggered onto his ranch, bleeding and broken. Without being asked and without any thought of a reward, he helped a perfect stranger. Jack deserved to know the truth. All of it. He earned at least that after all he had already done. Jack deserved to know what he was up against. Even if he did not believe it or thought Onyx was insane or a liar, he deserved to know what they were facing. Onyx knew that, but he could not bring himself to say it. He could not bear the thought of taking one moment longer to get to his brother if Jack decided he would not help, but Onyx knew he had to tell him.

Onyx sighed. There it was, with the truth on the table, the dice would be in the air. How Jack reacted would determine the success or failure of his attempt to reach his brother. He didn't expect Jack to help much, past getting to Ellis, but at least Onyx's conscience was clear. He would know the real risks, whether to help or not, that would be on him. Onyx's conscience would be clear if anything were to happen to Jack.

Wouldn't it?

20

Onyx spoke in such a matter-of-fact manner that Jack had trouble remembering that his passenger was a lunatic.

.   He studied the small man beside him, considering his words. *The dude is serious.* Jack thought again. *His story is consistent; his tone is natural and concerned, not manic or overanxious.* The axe next to Onyx glinted as a random ray of sunlight broke through the smoke and clouds. Jack wondered again if this guy would be dangerous if confronted with reality.   *What the hell have I gotten myself into?*

"Why here, though? Why this mountain?" he asked.

"It seeks the one thing that can destroy it. It knows the sword exists, it knows it's near here, and it wants to control it, possibly destroy it if it can. Its presence here proves the sword is still somewhere on this mountain."

Jack's disbelief grew as he listened to Onyx's story.

"So, it's here to find the weapon you can use against it?" he asked.

"Yep."

"And you're here to find the sword before it does?"

"Yep."

Dwarves. Magic Swords. Sword hunting monsters. Secret battles under the glacier. Onyx's story began to sound like something from the pages of a fantasy novel. Jack decided to play along. He even forced a smile and nodded. "And you and your brother were up on the peak looking for it?" he asked.

"Yes."

The monosyllabic responses started getting to Jack. *How do you break someone out of their delusion when they refuse to give more than yes as an answer?* Jack decided that his questions were the problem, so he switched tactics.

"Where did it come from?"

"It's been trapped in the glaciers far to the north for millennia. My people fought it when it escaped and tried to lair in a volcano to the North. That must have been more than fifty years ago." He looked out the window as the burnt forest passed by. "It endangered the Milesians living nearby, and our king saw it as our duty to stop it. We fought the beast under the mountain, and using the sword, we wounded it, and it fled the continent. Unfortunately, we didn't stop it in time to prevent the mountain from erupting, but we did limit the damage it caused."

"Wait, fifty years. Are you talking about Mount St. Helens?"

"That's what Milesians call it."

Jack's eyes flicked over Onyx's face, searching for any sign of humor. *This must be some kind of joke. Or am I the one losing it? This is--this is nuts. There's no way he believes this, right?*

"And what happened to the creature?"

Onyx spoke with such unwavering belief that Jack couldn't help but start to believe the story. His gaze never wavered as if he were daring Jack to believe. The sheer intensity of that stare unnerved him. With a sinking feeling, Jack realized this wasn't just some weird fixation. *Onyx truly believes this.*

"You're saying there is a creature that lives in volcanoes and spreads fires, and that's why you were looking for this sword."

Ok, why not? Jack thought, *'I've accepted that he is an Eardfolc and not human; may as well believe in monsters living in volcanoes too.'*

No, it was too much; Jack couldn't believe it. He couldn't even pretend to. *A little person who thinks he's from an ancient line of mythical creatures, I'll go along with that, but this is too much.*

"Yeah, it lives in..."

Jack shifted uncomfortably as Onyx talked. He barely heard what the man was saying. He struggled to keep his disbelief from showing. He grasped for rational explanations — *stress. Or a breakdown. That happens to regular people all the time, doesn't it? It could happen to someone who ran all night down a mountain in terror for his life.*

Jack couldn't hold it in any longer. Even if the guy was delusional, Jack was not responsible for it; he didn't have to humor him. He took a breath, his hands gripping the steering wheel, before interrupting.

"Oh, come on," Jack shouted, "You expect me to believe this. A battle under Mt. Saint Helens. A magical sword. Come on. What kind of creature can live in fire anyway?" Jack laughed and saw Onyx glare at him from the corner of his eye.

"A dragon," Onyx said.

"Onyx," Jack started, he chose his next words carefully, "you've been through a lot today; maybe it's affecting you more than you realize. I mean... dragons? Come on, that's... That's not real."

Jack smiled as visions of silk-clad dancers waving dragons on poles rolled through his mind. A laugh burst from his lips as he remembered the Lunar New Year parade he attended with Jill.

"So, like a winged fire-breather or one of those silk Chinatown dancers," Jack asked, his voice breaking with laughter.

Onyx's response to Jack's ridicule was chilling; his voice turned cold as he spoke.

"Soon, the mountain will be wreathed in fire, and the volcano will revive. An eruption on this mountain would cover the sky in ash and dust, plunging the world into winter."

Jack went quiet at Onyx's tone.

"It's happened before," Onyx continued, "in the 1800s, Mt. Tambora blanketed the Earth in ash. It altered worldwide weather patterns, leading to crop failures. Millions starved."

The small man turned and stared out the window as he continued to speak.

"This mountain is far larger than Tambora; this entire region, possibly the world, is in danger. With the sword, we can stop it. I don't need you to help; I just need a ride up the mountain."

He didn't want to hurt the guy's feelings, but this was far beyond anything he was equipped to handle. "I--uh--I don't know, maybe we should talk to someone about this. Maybe a professional, you know? Just to... make sure you're okay."

Jack's voice trembled as he spoke. He felt trapped between wanting to help and being terrified of what help would mean.

Could he somehow contract the man's delusion? He stared at the road ahead, hoping that, somehow, this whole situation would start to make sense.

21

Tangled in a web of paracord, Ashley Ember spun in slow circles. The parachute above her was shredded and snagged in the upper limbs of an ancient pine. The lines from the chute coiled around her arms like vines that tightened with every movement she made. She watched as the ropes above twisted like ribbons, then reversed. The momentum created by her attempts to reach the branch below had twisted the ropes and transferred the momentum to her body, slowly spinning her. She spun left until she faced the peak, and then the twisted cord spun her right.

Left.

Right.

Again and again, each spin slightly slower than the last. The landscape around her rolled lazily by.

Peak.

Ridge.

Road.

Tree.

Peak.

Tree.

Road.

Ridge.

Again.

And Again.

And Again.

Soon, it became a familiar blur.

Ashe closed her eyes. That did not help; it just made things worse as a bubble of nausea welled up in her gut. The spin slowed as the cords unwound. Soon, they hung straight down and held Ashe stationary above the deadly drop.

She opened her eyes and looked up.

She cursed under her breath and shifted her weight, hoping to loosen the grip of the cords. The lines that had guided her descent were now her captors. Tightly wrapped around her hands and arms, they held her dangling in the open air. Desperate to free herself, she wiggled and strained against them. She was careful not to spin too far around, sure that if she started spinning again, she would throw up. Just what we need to die covered in this morning's breakfast, she thought, and the image of spewed steak and eggs rolling down her jumpsuit flashed through her mind. She gagged and swallowed back a thin stream of acidic bile. *Good move, Ashe,* she thought, *make yourself sick.*

She hung motionless as she fought the rising bile. She stopped trying to get loose. No matter how hard she tried, the ropes only tightened, cutting into her skin. Her struggle only made her situation worse.

Below her, the ground seemed a world away. She felt like she was hanging over a canyon; the forest floor was lost beneath her. A dizzying drop. A hundred feet down, maybe more. She could not tell. With the sudden clarity that only near-death experiences bring, she realized that the lines that held her prisoner also kept her from falling. If she did get loose from the parachute lines, she would fall. If she fell, she would break something. From this height, she realized that it might just be her neck. She gritted her teeth. There had to be a way out of this. She scanned the branches above and below, trying to plot her next move.

Every slight adjustment caused the ropes to pull tighter, like a finger trap tightening around her.   She could no longer feel her hands. The ropes succeeded in cutting off her circulation. They bit painfully into her wrists as the tingling feeling of a thousand pins poking her skin began to disappear. She tried to flex her fingers to keep the blood flowing, but she couldn't feel them. She swayed with the breeze as it came down the mountain. The gentle sway back and forth soothed her.

The morning light filtered through the trees, casting soft shadows across her face. Her mind drifted, wandering through the memories of her time with Phil. She could still hear his voice, that cold, belittling sarcasm that filled his every sentence, that quiet rage always beneath the surface. His compliments had hidden barbs that left unseen wounds she still struggled to heal—her days had been consumed with trying to avoid setting him off. She had gotten used to walking on eggshells and the constant anxiety that came with it.

She knew she had stayed with him for far too long. At first, she thought she could fix him, but later, well, she had no excuse for that. At the time, she believed it was her fault that things turned out the way they did. It was her fault that he was unhappy, her fault that he was angry with the world. She knew now that the only thing she was at fault for was not leaving sooner. Thinking of the time she spent enduring all that made her heart ache. How had she let herself believe that it was love? What made her think that was how love was even supposed to be?

But she was no longer that person. She had made something of the life she had once given up on. She had clawed her way out and created her own life, one separate from his. It had taken time and a strength she had not known she possessed. Now, when she was finally free but not entirely healed, she hoped for something better.

Someone better. Someone who saw her as a partner, built her up, and did not tear her down. She let out a slow breath, and the knot in her stomach loosened just a little. She shook her head, trying to push the thoughts away. Maybe it was time to stop looking at the past.

Isn't this my luck, though? she thought. *Leave Phil, start a new life, get my dream job, meet a nice guy, then die in a tree.* She was unsure whether to laugh or cry. This had to be some twisted irony, a sick cosmic joke. With a small scream, Ashe began to pull herself up by the cords that fettered her hands. She kicked out with her feet and pulled at the cords above her, but they only tightened as she strained to get free.

Panic flickered at the edges of her mind, but she pushed it back. She stopped struggling momentarily and took several deep breaths to calm herself. Okay, think. There must be a way out of this. She worked with Portland Fire and Rescue, where she received training to assist people in challenging situations like this. She just needed a plan.

Her heart pounded as she looked around. No plan came. All she could do was stare down at the forest below and watch the shadows of the trees move with the wind.

The branches of the ancient tree crisscrossed above her, blocking her view of the smoke-filled sky. The branches below seemed to mock her. Like a mean joke, they formed a ladder down to the forest floor below. A crooked ladder, but a ladder nonetheless. Each of the tree's branches stuck straight out from the trunk in a swerving arc that wrapped itself around the trunk as it stepped toward the ground. All she needed to do was get to the first branch, and then she could use the lower ones, like steps, to get to the ground. She had lost count of how many times she had tried to reach that first branch. It was just out of reach. She stretched, swung, and did everything she could to touch it. Nothing worked. She would not reach that branch unless she could unwrap some of the rope that trapped her hands.

She thought about pulling herself up by the ropes around her hands, but they were twisted around her wrists and fingers so tightly that she could not grip them. She hung there, unable to do anything. Her heart raced. She did not want to die up here. Forgetting her nausea, she spun herself again. She stretched her toes toward the branch below her. The branches above her groaned. The sound of tearing cloth rent the air. Ashe fell. Her head smacked against a thick branch, and the world went black.

22

Jack pulled the truck around a curve in the road and was met with the flashing light of emergency vehicles. A beat-up antique firetruck and a shiny new police car blocked the roadway behind several orange barricades. A single police officer leaned against the hood of the police car. As Jack pulled the truck to a stop, he pushed himself off and raised his hand. Blue and red lights flashed off the mirrored glasses covering his eyes.

"Roads are closed on the mountain. You'll have to circle around and grab 225 to the north," he said as he removed his shades and slid them into a pocket.

Jack rolled down his window and spoke urgently, "We've got a friend caught up near the peak. We need to get him down."

The police officer peered up to look at Jack and Onyx. Jack noticed he did not step any closer. He stayed just out of the range of a swinging truck door, one hand resting on his gun.

"All the roads up have been closed because of the wildfires. Call Emergency Services; they can divert a team to get him."

Jack raised his cell phone and waved it back and forth in the window. "No service since yesterday. We can't get through."

The officer nodded, "Where'd you say he was?"

"That old shelter on the east side of the peak. He may have a broken leg." The officer nodded at Jack's words and raised the microphone on his lapel to his mouth. He spoke into the mic and waited.

A garbled response came through; the officer thanked the responder and mumbled back into the mic. He stopped, looked at Jack, and said, "You said the old shelter," he asked. Jack nodded. "You have a description." Jack looked at Onyx. He stood on the truck seat and leaned across Jack as he spoke to the officer.

"He's this high," Onyx held his hand an inch above his head. "Got a beard," he tugged at his beard, "carrying a backpack, and if our cousins catch up with him, he is with five more guys roughly the same height."

The officer's face twisted from suspicion to disbelief. He pointed at them, His voice rising, "This is a serious situation. Half the mountain is on fire, and half the towns have been evacuated, and you think it's a joke to send us running around looking for the seven dwarves. Turn that truck around and get back to the State Road before I arrest you for drunk and disorderly."

Jack looked at the officer's name tag. "Officer Brownlee?" The man paused, his disbelief evident. "I understand your disbelief. Believe me, I do, but my friend's family is up there, and they do need help."

Officer Brownlee sighed and dropped his hand from his shoulder. "Step out of the truck, please." Brownlee's voice was cold and steady. It reminded Jack of Jill's no more bullshit voice.

Jack complied. "Look, he's distraught; his brother got hurt hiking yesterday and is up on the mountain. He is determined to get up there and rescue him. If the mountain's been evacuated, no one is up there to help him. We just want to help his brother." Jack knew he was babbling as he stepped out of the truck. He only opened the door a few inches as he slipped out, worried that the officer would see the shotgun lying between the seats and jump to conclusions. He closed the door as soon as he was out and stepped back to stand at the edge of the truck bed. "If we can get someone to check on him, I can calm my friend down."

Officer Brownlee held out his hand.

"I.D.," Brownlee said.

Jack removed his wallet. He pulled out his license and handed it to the officer. Brownlee read Jack's details into his radio.

"Connley Creek Road." Brownlee asked, "Isn't that the old Johannson place?"

"It's the Fallen J Ranch now."

Officer Brownlee looked Jack over, then glanced up at the sleek black truck. "Yeah, that fits. I heard some city boy overpaid for it. Guess that's you then," he said with a chuckle.

"Yeah," Jack said. He was unsure if this was the right time to defend his real estate expertise. "I poured everything I had into the place; now I'm going to lose it," Jack said.

Brownlee looked up at the smoke-filled sky. A response blared from the radio. Brownlee nodded and spoke into the mic, his voice soft and muffled. His stern face softened as he looked back toward Jack.

"I'm in the same woodpile. My place isn't too far downriver from yours. Lord willing, the fire will be contained before we get burned out."   He sighed as he handed the ID back to Jack. "I sent my wife and kids to her mom's in Springfield. I'm going to hate staying there if things go sideways."

Jack was at a loss for words. *What do you tell someone about to lose everything they had worked for?*

What would you want to hear, Jill's voice whispered in his mind. *Nothing would help,* he thought, so he kept his mouth shut.

"Look, I'll call in your friends' location. I can't guarantee anything, but if we can get someone up there, we will. Back the truck up and head to Wasco General. If he's injured, that's where he will be taken. I'll send word there if I get any word on a search."

Jack climbed into the truck and backed away from the barricades. As Jack completed a three-point turn, Onyx leaned over to stare him in the face.

"What'd you go and turn around for? We need to get up the mountain. I've told you what's up there. We can stop it."

"I'm sorry," Jack said. "I'm not going up against a cop so you can fight some mythical beast."

"Ellis is still up there. You agreed to get me to him."

Jack sighed. Rescuing his brother at the peak was one thing, but getting roped into some delusional quest was entirely different. He did not owe this guy or his brother anything, and it was not his responsibility to rescue anyone, especially someone obviously in the throes of a serious breakdown. His best bet was to get Onyx to a hospital where he could get professional help, and hope that Brownlee would keep his word and send someone up to check on Ellis.

They drove on in silence.

23

The roadblock was disappointing, but Onyx was right. Jack had offered his help. He could not just back out now.

If there is a brother, Jill's voice said, *you can't just leave him stranded on a burning mountain.*

But what if there isn't?

Could you live with yourself if you're wrong?

I hate it when you're right.

I'm always right, remember.

Jack recalculated the time he would need to get to the campground, and he was pretty sure he would be sleeping in his truck that night. There was no way they could make it up and back before dark if every main road was blocked. Jack went over the routes up the mountain in his mind. There were only a few, but he was sure they would be blocked off like the Old State Road where Brownlee was stationed.

Jack saw an old, weather-beaten billboard on the right side of the road.

The sign was shaped like a giant saw blade, and the faded paint declared "Arkona Mill" ahead, one-quarter mile. Jack had a vague memory of the place. His neighbor's son mentioned it several times while discussing weekend plans. It was the local hangout for the more bored teens in the area. They told each other it was haunted and dared each other to spend nights inside. More critical to Jack right now was that the old gravel road to Arkona Mill connected this road with the Old State Road a mile or two beyond the roadblock.

Jack nearly missed the turnoff. The old logging road was overgrown with weeds and new saplings, but a thin set of tire tracks could still be seen. The truck fishtailed, and Onyx let out a curse as Jack slammed on the brakes and turned off the main road. The truck bucked and rocked as it rolled onto the worn gravel path. Onyx grabbed the panic bar as he was tossed around, trying to keep from being thrown into the wheel well by the rough road.

"I thought these things were all about off-roading," he yelled.

"I lived in East LA. I didn't spring for the suspension package. She'll be alright," Jack said. "The road should smooth out soon." Before the words were out of his mouth, the bucking eased. They traveled a still-overgrown but not as rutted gravel path and soon came to a wide opening where an old mill stood.

Jack could understand why the local kids thought it was haunted. In the smoke-shrouded morning light, the mill stood desolate and decayed in the far corner of a vast, empty lot. The once proud building was now a grotesque caricature of a turn-of-the-century mill. Its walls appeared to sag under the weight of time. Its dark windows seemed to stare back at him. The shadows surrounding it suggested light itself was afraid to approach. Jack could imagine it in its heyday; overall-clad men dragging logs in through the great barn doors to one side and hauling two-by-fours and cut lumber out the other. Now, though the atmosphere was so eerie, it sent shivers down Jack's spine. He could imagine the restless spirits of days past wandering through the empty rooms.

"Hope you don't need nothing in there," Onyx whispered.

"Locals say it's haunted," Jack said.

Onyx grunted, "I can see why; I'd rather face the dragon bare-fisted than get any closer."

Jack agreed and sped the truck down the gravel road.

Soon, they were driving up a steep slope. The trees disappeared beneath the roadway, and the distant peak of the mountain was visible. Covered in a haze of smoke, the snowpack of the glacier still glistened in the late morning sun.

Jack slammed on the brakes as the truck hit the paved surface and sped forward on the Old State Road. Jack laughed aloud. "Ha, you aren't keeping us off the mountain." Jack spun the wheel and headed upslope for another half mile.

The road rolled by houses that looked no different than any of the thousands of homes in Los Angeles: lawns neatly trimmed and well-maintained, but the carports and garages were empty, and the swing sets abandoned. If Jack remembered the fire map correctly, the area had been evacuated several days ago.

They reached the top of the long rise, and the road opened below them. Through the smoke filling the air, they could see the valley below. The town of Arkona, once a thriving community, was now a smoking ruin. The houses behind them, untouched and undamaged by the fire, were the exception. The desolation was overwhelming. Nothing in the town below still stood.

Jack drove down into the town. The truck slowed as they approached the remains of the once-busy downtown area. The air was silent. Only thick ribbons of smoke rose from the ruins, starkly contrasting what Jack remembered as a prosperous community.

The buildings that lined the main road through town were leveled; beyond them, Jack could see the blocks of several hundred homes that once made up the town. Skeletal frames of blackened timber stood like silent sentinels among the charred remains of ancient pine, fir, and maple trees. Streets that once bustled with the daily rhythm of human life were now littered with the burnt-out remnants of that life: twisted metal, the charred husks of cars, and the occasional fragment of a child's toy, all covered in still-smoking ash.

Jack wanted Onyx to be correct. He wanted something tangible, something solid he could blame for this. Something he could fight. Fire was a force of nature, an intangible power. It came from nowhere and consumed everything it touched. This town, his ranch, and who knew how many places were or would be destroyed because of a natural occurrence.

How do you blame fire for this? It was not to blame; it just was. Who do you blame, then, Jack thought, *the town leaders who plopped a city in the middle of a forest without considering how fire would sweep down the bowl of the valley? The builders or homeowners who didn't consider how the trees and vegetation they planted around their homes would catch and move the fire? The change in weather that caused prolonged droughts that dried out the vegetation so badly they burned like kindling, or do you blame the factories, companies, and industrial societies that contributed to the pollution that caused that change in the first place?*

Jack didn't know. All he knew was that he needed someone to blame. He needed something to make sense of the devastation around him. But as he looked at the charred remains of the town, he couldn't shake the feeling that this wasn't just a natural disaster. It was a manufactured catastrophe, a result of human decisions and actions. And if that was the case, then perhaps there was something that could have been done to prevent it. Perhaps there was someone to blame after all.

The silence was only broken by the wheels rolling over ash and the occasional creak of cooling wood.

The town will be rebuilt, Jack thought. *People will return and rebuild their homes and lives, like he did after the accident. But would they build it back smarter? Would they consider how fire spreads and how future fires could be prevented?* Jack doubted it. *We have no one to blame but ourselves,* he thought. *How much of this is our fault?* Jack rolled the truck to a stop.

The town's placement within the forest put it right in the path of any fire that rolled down from the ridges above, he thought. *And how'd the fire start? It surely was not a dragon, like Onyx kept telling him. A carelessly tossed cigarette or an unattended campfire was the most probable cause. Not to mention the weeks of unseasonal heat that arrived earlier and lasted longer every year. We are destroying the planet one wildfire at a time,* Jack thought. Unregulated industry, carbon emissions, fossil fuels, and deforestation all piled Carbon Dioxide in the atmosphere, leading to rising temperatures and changing weather patterns. Jack shook his head as he started the truck back down the road.

"We are our own worst enemy," he said.

As they drove up the slope out of the valley, they saw the deep red glow of the distant hillsides. Red-orange peels of color illuminated the smoke-laden sky.

24

As they neared the turn-off to the peak, the smoke thickened, creating a dense blanket of haze that obscured the mid-morning sky. The urgency of the situation was palpable, the air heavy with the impending threat of the raging wildfires.

The four-lane road wound its way around the mountain, a path of uncertainty in the face of the unpredictable wildfires. To the left, Jack saw the line of distant mountains covered in smoke and flame. The treetops burned like kindling, the flames reaching high into the sky, their jagged tongues licking at the smoke above, a sight both terrifying and awe-inspiring.

The flames, like a living entity, rose into the sky, their twisting beauty a stark contrast to the destruction they wrought. Their flickering tongues licked at the sky, as if trying to consume the very atmosphere. The super-heated air around the burning treetops shimmered, as though reality itself was bending to the fire's will. Sparks and embers spiraled up into the sky like fiery confetti, carried by the hot currents created by the inferno. They floated higher and higher, sometimes disappearing into the smoky haze that darkened the sky. The fire's glow reflected off the billowing smoke, creating an eerie, blood-orange sky like an early dusk had fallen. The blaze raged on, untamed, its flames flickering higher and higher as if trying to conquer heaven.

"Well, Jack," Onyx said beside him, "still think a lightning strike caused all that?"

Jack looked over at the man, "Wildfires have always happened. They are a natural part of the forest ecosystem."

"This big," Onyx said with a wave to the left. "The dragon was imprisoned under the ice caps; most of that ice is gone. The dragon is free."

"Under the Ice Caps?" Jack said, holding back laughter. "Why the heck would a dragon be under the ice caps?"

"That's where it was imprisoned long ago," Onyx said. "One of your human heroes fought it and buried it in Ice. Now it is free to burn and breed."

"Wildfires have burned out of control for the last several decades. Each year, the fires are worse than the last." Jack waved south, "This is just the latest in the pattern, the largest fire ever to burn through the Pacific Northwest."

"So far," Onyx said. "The world is heating up. Longer droughts, bigger fires here, stronger storms, and higher flood waters back East. Snow in Texas. The polar ice caps are shrinking. The Arctic zones that once held hundreds of miles of permafrost are now marshlands. Like it or not, weather patterns are changing; the climate is changing."

When Jack did not reply, Onyx sighed and said, "Why do you think the fires are getting worse every year?"

"Longer dry spells," Jack said. "More human encroachment on forest spaces and less forest maintenance. Dry, overgrown forests hinder firefighting efforts and accelerate fire spread. That leads to larger fires."

Onyx shook his head. "You, Reuzin, will come up with anything to avoid responsibility."

Jack let out a long laugh. "I mean, we're talking about the warmer weather; that's a scientific, real-world problem, but magical dragons? Can't you see how insane that sounds?"

They rode on in silence. Smoke hung about the truck like a shroud.

"Okay," Jack said, "Climate change is real. It's happening because of carbon emissions and deforestation. I'll give you that much, but dragons are a different story."

"You admit climate change is happening," Onyx asked.

126

"Sure," Jack said.

"That change has melted the ice caps. Below one of those glaciers was the dragon. That dragon is now intent on igniting this mountain."

"Dragons are fictional. They don't exist."

"That's what humans have said about Climate Change. Just because you have never seen it doesn't mean it doesn't exist." Onyx took a slow breath.

Jack laughed. "So, climate change somehow unleashed a dragon on the world."

Onyx nodded. He turned and looked out the side window. Trees swept past in a blur of green as they continued in silence.

The road was less claustrophobic than the last. A wide shoulder let Jack relax a bit. He tried to ignore the glowing red hellscape in his rear-view mirror and the idea that his passenger was delusional and might be dangerous. Shrubs and scrub brush lined the side of the road for a good dozen feet in most places, making the trees seem less immediate a danger. Jack felt like he had room to breathe and relaxed his grip on the steering wheel.

Soon, guardrails appeared on the side of the road, and Jack relaxed a bit more; he felt like he was back in civilization, and the familiar road, guardrails, and broad shoulders calmed him. He could imagine himself on a simple supply run to Parkdale or hiking to one of the glaciers, instead of a questionable rescue mission with an insane dwarf at his side. *Little person,* he thought. *No. Eardfolc,* he corrected himself again.

As they moved further north, the smoke, a constant reminder of the danger of the wildfires, settled lower and lower. A small parking lot appeared on the right. Jack slowed and looked at the bare gravel lot. He thought it was familiar, then remembered the hike to the waterfall he had taken when he first moved out here.

Jack slammed on his brakes as four deer jumped across the roadway. They broke from the tree line near the parking lot. Smack in front of the truck. Jack caught their movement through the thick smoke. Three bound down the slope to the right. The fourth stopped right in front of the truck. Jack figured the truck lights had distracted them, and as often happened on these roads, it froze as tons of steel barreled down on them, but the deer was not looking at the truck. It was looking back and up into the trees.

A line of fire flared out of the tree line. Burning liquid splashed across the road like napalm from those old Vietnam movies Jack used to watch. The burning liquid covered the immobile deer in flames. Sheets of fire roared up from the roadway as the asphalt caught fire, deepening the surrounding smoke in black billows. The deer stumbled and fell to the ground, burning like a candle. A deep rumbling roar echoed off the surrounding hills as a huge shape dropped from the sky and perched beside the burning corpses of the deer.

25

All Jack could see through the smoke was the silhouette of what looked like a large, winged reptile landing in the fire in front of him.

Is insanity contagious? he thought.

Half of the burning deer disappeared as a giant mouth stretched open like a snake's and closed around it. The head lifted in the smoke, neck straightening as it chomped twice and swallowed a mouthful of venison like some twisted seabird.

If Jack had seriously considered Onyx's tale, he would have thought the creature would look like something out of one of the movies he had seen, Smaug-like or even a winged Godzilla. What he saw in front of him was a creature from a nightmare. It looked like someone had added wings and a beak to a Komodo dragon and then crossed it with an armadillo.

The creature's entire upper body was encased in segmented scale plates, while its lower body and wings looked like the pair of snakeskin boots his wife had given him one Christmas. The creature stood amid the smoke, surrounded by flames.

No, that isn't right, Jack thought, *it's wreathed in flames as if it's on fire.*

Tongues of flame licked up from beneath the plates of the segmented scales on its torso and head. They whirled along the smooth skin of its legs and tail. They flickered up the single line of ridged protrusions that rolled up its back like a deformed crocodile.

Behind Jack, Otter growled deep in his throat. A steady rumble shook the dog's body as he stared into the smoke.

"Easy Otter," Jack whispered.

The dog ignored him and barked--an echoing, full-throated challenge.

Beyond the wall of burning asphalt, the beast turned toward the truck. A head poked through the flames and swirling black smoke. Teeth the size of Otter glistened in a beak-like face that filled the truck's window. The smoke still hid most of the body, but Jack could see the flaming red and orange scales covering the beast's head and neck.

The dog stood between the two front seats, its paws on the dashboard, barking its heart out. The mouth pulled back into the smoke, then opened and lunged forward. Otter was silenced as the beast roared back a challenge that shook the truck.

"What the hell," Jack said. The dragon stalked from the flaming asphalt. It approached the truck and sniffed several times.

"That's the dragon," Onyx said.

"No shit," Jack said as he dropped the truck into reverse.

As the truck slid away from the beast, Otter resumed barking.

Smoke swirled above the dragon's head as its wings beat, and it rose slightly off the ground. A claw trailing fire burst out of the smoke and slammed into the side of the truck.

Jack lost control as the wheel jerked out of his hands. The truck rocked with the blow and slid toward the shoulder, where a low wall sat against the slope.   The truck hit the wall. Jack slammed on the brakes and shifted into drive as the beast stalked forward and slammed its claw into the truck again. Something hit the side of Jack's head. Otter squealed as Onyx swore in a language Jack didn't recognize. The truck rocked against the wall. It wobbled, close to its tipping point, then settled back onto four wheels.

The engine stalled.

Raising its head, the dragon roared into the sky and slammed a claw onto the truck's roof. Cracks spider-webbed the windshield. The dragon leaned close and ran its beak along the side of the truck, stopping to pause and sniff at the back window, then above the truck bed loaded with Jack's possessions.

Satisfied that its enemy was defeated, the dragon turned back toward the deer. More of the smoldering carcass disappeared into the toothed maw. The head rose, and the neck stretched again.

Otter whined beside Jack. The creature's head swiveled toward the truck, a low growl reverberating across the road.

Jack watched in awe as the massive creature stared at him through the rising smoke and cracked windshield. Jack blinked and checked the road ahead. The dragon was straddling the center of the road, its hind legs and tail jammed up against the guard rail that started a dozen yards ahead of the truck. The shoulder was blocked. Jack saw a small gap between the guardrail's start and the low stone wall the truck leaned against. If he could get through that gap, a short section of gravel extended behind the guardrail. It looked wide enough for the truck to swerve around. They could dash through it and rejoin the road past where the creature stood.

Jack pumped the gas and restarted the truck. As it roared to life, he shifted into drive and slammed on the gas pedal. The truck rumbled in response and heaved forward as the dragon swung its head back to roar another challenge. Jack steered the truck down the shoulder toward the dragon, aiming for the small gap between the distant guardrail, the tail, and the stone wall.

"Hold on," Jack screamed.

Beside him, Onyx let out a short scream. "We're not going to make it."

133

Swaying on a sprung suspension, the truck rattled forward. The steering wheel was pulling fiercely to the right; Jack fought the pull to keep the vehicle straight, aiming for that narrow gap where the curve of the guardrail met the end of the low stone wall ahead. The dragon spun to follow the truck's progress; its rear end whipped away from the guardrail. Jack spun the wheel to aim for the new gap and smashed the pedal to the floor. His body rose off the seat as he half stood. His rational mind knew pressing the pedal further would not make the truck go any faster, but he kept his foot pressed to the floor in his desperation and panic.

"We aren't going to make it," Onyx screamed as the dragon's head emerged from the smoke again, striking toward the truck. In his peripheral vision, Jack saw the beaked maw hurtling toward him. He spun the wheel left, and the truck fishtailed as the dragon's beak slammed into the truck bed. The truck spun on the flaming asphalt, and the screech of tearing metal ripped through the air. Jack leaned into the turn and kept the wheel pegged left. He slowly eased out of the second spin, facing North again. He stomped on the gas pedal.

Hot tires spewed burning asphalt as Jack barreled back up the State Road. In his rearview mirror, he watched the dragon shake its head and roar. Beating its wings, the beast took several steps forward and launched into the air after them.

26

Onyx felt himself pressed against the passenger door as the truck followed the curving road up the mountain. He gripped the seat belt, crossing in front of his face as Jack barreled down the road. The slope to his left was a wall of brown and green, where the last rows of pine and fir reached up toward the bare and broken landscape of the peak above them.   Memories of his mad flight down the mountain the day before flashed through his mind and stopped his breath. His heartbeat staccatoed in his chest as the still-raw wounds on his back pulsed in time. Terror filled Onyx, but like the evening before, he swallowed it; he concentrated on what was important: his brother Ellis, injured on the mountain. Behind him, the black dog barked and growled as it pressed its face against the back window. Onyx pushed himself off the passenger door and looked back through the gap between the seats.

All Onyx saw was the giant dog's black fur. The dog's teeth occasionally hit the glass as it challenged the creature chasing them. The window shook with each enameled blow, rattling in its frame as the cracks lengthened. As the truck followed the curve of the road, the dog, still barking and growling, moved to the opposite side of the seat as if moving to that side would get him closer to his enemy. Onyx got a clear view of the scene behind them as the dog moved. His throat went dry.

The asphalt was a winding river of grey that curved back around the mountain, backlit by raging fires in the distance that colored the sky in red and orange licks of flame amid the swirling black of rising smoke. Behind and above the truck, the dragon beat its wings, surging forward with every downbeat. Soon, it was only yards behind the truck.

The truck's engine roared as it hurtled up the winding mountain road, tires screeching with every turn. Jack's knuckles were white as he gripped the steering wheel. Onyx looked out the rear window again. The dragon, a massive beast swathed in fire, was only feet behind them, its eyes glowing with primal fury.

"Come on, come on!" Onyx shouted, his eyes darted between the road ahead and the monstrous creature behind.

The dragon swooped low to swipe one giant claw at the truck. Its claw scraped the asphalt in a shower of sparks. The truck lurched as its back tires lifted off the ground for a terrifying second before they slammed back down. The truck fishtailed, swerving across three of the road's four lanes before Jack regained control.

Onyx saw the bend in the road ahead--a tight curve hugging the cliffside. Less than a quarter of a mile ahead was their turn-off, a five-mile stretch of winding road known locally as the Serpent's Tail. With more than two hundred curves and hairpin turns in its first two-mile run up the side of the mountain, it was a favorite of bikers and hot rod enthusiasts. The turnoff was a black spot among the greenery where a small bridge crossed a ravine, the raging White River more than a hundred feet below. The turn would be tight. Onyx knew they would overshoot the turn if Jack did not slow down. If he did not speed up, the dragon would catch them before they made it.

"Faster," Onyx yelled as he pounded Jack's shoulder, "faster."

"This is all we got," Jack screamed, his right leg stretched to the floor, his foot solid against the pedal.

"It's going to breathe," Onyx screamed as he watched the dragon's mouth open. The creature's wings stilled in a glide as it inhaled for a long second. Its neck and head reared back, and with a sudden downbeat of its wings, its head shot forward. The dragon exhaled, and a torrent of flame erupted from its jaws; a blinding, searing light filled the air. Onyx closed his eyes as the light blinded him. He blinked several times to clear the spots that floated in his eyes. The fire roared like a furnace, igniting everything in its path--trees, rocks, and asphalt. The stream of burning liquid flew straight at the truck. Onyx screamed. The dog whimpered and dove into the foot well as fire hurtled toward them.

Onyx heard Jack scream, "We aren't going to make it."

Onyx closed his eyes again and waited for the searing pain the fire would bring, his only hope that his brother would somehow survive without his help.

The truck's front bumper struck the guardrail on the far side of the bridge. There was a scream of tearing metal, and the truck lurched as sparks flew past Onyx's window, and the side of the truck dragged along the guardrail. The curved piece of steel kept the truck from hurtling into the river far below as they whipped around the corner onto the twisting road up the mountain.

A blast of fire scorched past behind them. Jack stomped on the gas pedal, and the truck responded with a screech and a lurch. Its engine roared as it struggled up the mountain.

The dragon, unable to bank fast enough to follow, soared past the turnoff as the truck struggled up the new road's incline.

The dragon banked away from the mountain. Its wings beat as it rose higher, circling to come back at the truck from behind once more.

"Holy shit," Jack said, "We made it."

A roar shook the windows of the truck as Jack spoke. In the valley behind them, the dragon had settled on the crumbling smokestack of a burnt-out factory, its wings outstretched and its muzzle to the sky as it screamed in frustration.

"So," Onyx said as he settled back into his seat. "Still think I should seek professional help."

Jack looked over at the Eardfolc.

"After that, I think we both need therapy."

27

Ashley woke up still in the tree. A thin stream of liquid heat trickled down the side of her head. The warmth crept over her scalp, pooled in the curve of her neck, and slid down her collarbone. Sticky and uncomfortable, it sent shivers down her spine.

I'm bleeding, she thought. Pain radiated from the side of her head, her right side, and under her left arm. She remembered falling, remembered hitting her head. She looked up at her still-trapped hands. Above her, she saw broken branches that formed a tunnel through the treetop. She imagined her unconscious body bouncing from branch to branch as she fell. The arm of her jumpsuit was ripped, and a small branch full of pine needles poked out of it.

How hard did I hit to tear the Kevlar, she thought.

She counted more than a dozen broken and bent branches above her. *And how many times?*

She stopped that train of thought before it sent her over a cliff. The only important thing was that she didn't hit the ground. The chute, the ropes this time, she thought, stopped her before she smashed into the ground. She could see no sign of the shredded fabric that held her up earlier.

She looked down. Thirty feet below her lay a yellow helmet, its chin strap broken, its face shield shattered.

I think that thing just saved my life, she thought.

She stifled another scream of frustration.   She knew there was a way out of this. There had to be.

The ground appeared to sway, shifting in rhythm with her own spinning body. *Wait. I'm not spinning.* The distance to the ground seemed to stretch further when she tried to focus on a single point. *How hard did I hit my head?* The yellow helmet and its shattered faceplate spun on the ground beneath her.

Pretty darn hard. She closed her eyes until the feeling stopped.

Ashe's breath came in short, panicked gasps. She was helpless, dangling from the tree like an abandoned marionette.

She struggled to remember the map they had studied before the jump. The State Road to the east traveled up the mountain in a long curve that brought it within a mile of the peak. She thought she was somewhere near White Lodge Road or Spur Ridge, but had no landmarks to compare to the map in her head. All she could see from her position was the peak rising above her to one side and a short strip of the highway in the distance to the other side. The tree she hung from blocked her view south, and the slope of the ridge in front of her blocked her view north.

She shifted, twisting her body to get a better view of her surroundings. That's when she saw it--from the corner of her eye, a flicker of movement down the slope. A tiny dot, barely a speck on the distant highway. She squinted, heart racing. A truck. Far below, it sped along the thin line of asphalt, moving within the billowing black smoke that hung over the roadway.

A flare of fire burst in the vehicle's path, barely a speck on the thin line of asphalt; it raced away from the new line of flame. At first, it was hard to make out, just a tiny dark shape among the smoke blanket covering the four-lane road far below. The truck swerved across the roadway as if the driver was drunk, trying to avoid obstacles in the road or maybe just blinded by the smoke around it.

Ashe kicked her feet back and forth as she attempted to spin herself to get a better look. To the South and West, thick and ominous smoke was tinged with orange flames, stretching toward the horizon and covering the distant peaks. The truck hurtled toward her like a lone survivor out of the chaos of fire and smoke.

Maybe they'll see me, she thought, her pulse quickened with hope. *How could they? I'm buried in these trees. They'd have to be looking up, and even then, I'm practically invisible at this distance.* She gritted her teeth, frustration and desperation building inside her.

The sun was rising higher, casting long shadows through the trees. She clenched her jaw and fought the panic that threatened to overtake her. She had to act.

That truck means something. I can't just hang here and hope. I need to get out of this tree. Now.

With renewed determination, she began twisting her body again, searching for any possible way to free herself. None of the branches around her were close enough to reach.

The truck was headed up the mountain, though. There's a chance it's headed for the peak. She might be rescued.

Maybe they'll come looking; doubt gnawed at her. *What if they don't? What if no one comes?*

I'm going to die here.

No one knew she was here; no one was coming. They wouldn't look for her. Not for days. She was too far off course.

I'll die in this tree. No one will find me until it's too late. What if I never get down? What if I just...

The image of her body, cold and limp, swinging from the branches, filled her mind. Her vision blurred as tears stung her eyes. Her breath hitched. Her mind raced with a thousand dark thoughts, each worse than the last.

She followed the truck's journey up the mountain until the ridge across from her blocked its path. To get anywhere near her, the truck would have to take one of the few turn-off roads that came closer to the peak, turn-offs she could not see from her place in the tree.

Unconcerned with the thirty-foot fall getting loose would bring, she started kicking her legs again, desperate to get loose and move. The paracord dug deeper into her hands. The pain was nothing compared to the terror in her chest.

"Help," she screamed several times before she realized there was no way anyone that far away could hear her.

28

Onyx fought against the truck's momentum as it careened through sharp curves at breakneck speed. His body swayed from left to right, the turns threatening to slam him into the passenger door.

He knelt on the seat and turned to look out the back window. A ragged row of forest blocked the smokestack on which the dragon had roosted.

Onyx scanned the sky--no sign of the beast.

"I think it lost interest in us," he said.

"Maybe," Jack said, "but I wouldn't place any bets."

Onyx turned forward. He plopped into his seat and looked out the passenger window. All he could see were trees. A gap opened, and he saw dark smoke rising beside a blue lake in the distance. A pit of despair welled within him. The once grand forest he had walked in only days ago would soon be a graveyard of crisped trees. He was supposed to prevent this. Recover the sword and stop the dragon before the land suffers. He sighed heavily.

What was the point, he thought, *if the land was going to be destroyed anyway? Why had he risked his life, his brother's, and their kin if fire was going to consume it all anyway? Why had he dragged this perfect stranger into his quest?*

He checked the sky. A smoky orange haze filled the air as far as he could see.

It is hopeless, he thought. *The dragon is going to win. It'll nest in the mountain, and the volcano will awaken. The towns around the peak would be destroyed, and those who hadn't fled would die. Those who had would lose everything. His failure would cast his people from their lands as magma buried everything they had built over generations.*

They ascended another ridgeline, and Onyx looked out Jack's window to get a clear view of the sky to the South. Smoke glowed with the orange of the fires on that side of the peak. Tall stands of smoking, burnt pine covered the next several ridges. Onyx's despair increased. Behind him, the dog whined. Onyx looked back and saw nothing but healthy trees filling the near distance behind him. Tall, proud trees stood in defiance of the flames, their green branches swaying gently, unconcerned with the chaos and destruction that burned just hundreds of yards away. The entire mountain had not been consumed. There was still green on the mountain. The sight hit him like a hammer. There was still a chance. Onyx's clenched jaw eased, and his grip on the panic bar relaxed. *Not everything was lost. There was still life here, still something to fight for.*

There was still hope.

He felt his weight shift again as Jack spun around another curve.

"You can slow down. We've lost it."

Jack ducked down to look up through the windshield at the sky above. "You sure?"

"Looks like it."

They drove on in silence. The road narrowed as they edged toward the northern cliff face once again. The trees thinned. Onyx had a clear view of the northern horizon. Smoke still filled the sky in all directions like one massive cloud hanging low on an Autumn Day, but only one small stream of smoke rose to the north. Orange light flickered below the smoke. Onyx glanced back along their route. The smokestack at the center of the small town they passed was silhouetted against the smoke on the horizon. No dragon roosted on it.

Onyx rolled his window down and leaned out of the truck to scan the sky.

"The dragon's gone."

"Gone. What do you mean, gone?"

"Gone. Not where it was. Not where I can see it. Gone."

The truck slowed as Jack leaned forward to look up through the windshield.

He turned around to glance out the back window.

"I don't see anything," Jack said.

"Me neither."

The truck slowed to a crawl.

A low growl came from the back of the truck. Otter stood in the center of the back seat, his hackles up and his tail tucked low. He stared over the cliffside. Onyx followed the dog's gaze. He had no time to shout a warning.

Without warning, the dragon's head emerged above the tree-lined ridge, its fiery breath aimed directly at the truck, a sudden and terrifying sight.

The fire scorched across the pavement a few feet in front of the truck.

Onyx was thrown into the window frame as Jack swore and slammed his foot on the gas pedal.

Jack fought to maintain control as they skidded through the burning line of dragon fire.

Onyx folded onto the truck seat as they sped off, tires trailing smoke and burning bits of rubber. Flames licked up the side of the truck cab as the burning wheels spun. Jack cursed, and Onyx grabbed the panic bar over his head with both hands.

"Drive, drive, drive," he yelled.

Jack took another curve at speed. The truck hugged the side of the cliff. Onyx looked out the window at the sheer drop as they edged the road's soft shoulder. The only thing between them and the chasm below was a thin strip of grass and an already bent and twisted guard rail.

Jack yanked the wheel left, and the truck surged back onto the pavement.

Onyx looked behind them. The dragon's head filled the back window as it winged toward them. The massive dragon was behind them; its flames surrounded it, licking the air.

The beast's breath had turned the mountains into a hellscape; its fire burned through towns, trees, and brush, devouring everything in its path. Onyx had come here to stop it. He had placed those who followed him in danger to stop this thing's rampage. He had enlisted Jack's help to end the dragon's reign of terror. He owed it to all of them not to give up hope. Whether his brother lived or not, Onyx owed it to him and all of them to complete the task they set out to do.

The truck bounced and skidded as the pavement ended, and they turned onto a dirt road. The dragon, unable to turn that fast, passed them, circled, and was soon back on their trail.

Onyx's heart pounded in his chest. Not everything was lost. There was still life here, still something to fight for.

"Hold on," Onyx's voice rang with newfound determination, "We're not giving up yet."

The dragon banked into a dive, and the flaming beast plunged toward them like a spear.

29

Jack's grip on the wheel was so tight that his knuckles turned white as he veered the truck off the road and onto the rugged path leading to the campground. The truck jolted and jostled over the uneven terrain, kicking up clouds of dust that concealed the enraged dragon hot on their trail. Jack could sense its presence--furious, scorching, and dangerously close.

The dirt road twisted sharply as it hugged the edge of the mountain. Gravel crunched under the tires. The truck skidded as Jack took the curves faster than he should. There was no time for caution. He could hear the dragon's wings beating the air behind him. Each downstroke shook the trees and rattled the truck with a terrifying rhythm.

Jack's heart raced as he saw the dragon's silhouette rising above the treetops in the mirror. He was desperate to gain speed on the rough terrain, knowing the campground was just beyond the next rise. But the dragon was too close, flying just above them. Its gleaming talons swooped lower, clawing at the truck's roof. The sound of tortured metal screamed through the cab as Jack fought to stay ahead of the dragon.

The campground was his only chance. The trees or terrain might offer some cover if they could make it.

The truck spun into the campground parking lot. The dragon, unable to make the turn, shot past them once more and rose into the sky.

Jack scanned the parking lot. He hoped to find some cover from the flaming beast, but his luck was not holding out. A deep gully ran along the left side of the lot, a drainage ditch, Jack figured. It ran around half the lot and angled toward lower ground ten or more feet below. The slope was steep, and Jack was sure the truck would flip if he tried to drive down it. The tree line to the right was packed; he would not be able to get the truck through there. The trail ahead looked wide enough for the truck to travel, but a large information board blocked it. "Dead end," Jack yelled. "Everybody out."

The dragon circled above, its shadow rolling ominously across the parking lot. In the mirror, Jack watched the beast plummet. Its neck kinked back in flight as it inhaled. "She's going to breathe," Onyx screamed as he pulled at the door handle.

Jack opened his door, grabbed the shotgun, and rolled onto the gravel-strewn lot. His hat rolled beside him; he caught it as he gained his feet. He sprinted toward the gully as heat seared his back. He hit the edge of the gully and tumbled down the steep embankment.

Definitely would have flipped the truck, he thought, as he rolled to a stop against a young pine tree; his weight and momentum bent the tree in half. He looked up and saw nothing but open, smoke-shrouded sky. *I'm exposed here*, he thought, *got to move.*

Jack rolled to his hands and knees and scuttled across the gully and into a stand of thin fir at its edge. He flattened under the lowest branches and looked back up toward the parking lot.

The dragon stood above the burning truck. Its head dipped down as it grabbed the side of the truck and lifted it, and it flipped to its side. The cab facing Jack was empty.

Good, he thought, *everyone got out.*

The dragon slammed one of its claws down. The truck buckled. The dragon's beak slammed down and worried at the back side of the truck. The tailgate came away in its maw. The beast swung its head. Jack winced as the tailgate smashed into the ground, feet away from him. The claw came down on the truck again and smashed it flat. The dragon's snout dug into the vehicle's undercarriage. Metal screamed as it was pulled apart.

There goes our ride home, Jack thought.

Jack watched the dragon tear into the underside of his truck. The beast was so focused on destroying the truck that it never glanced up. He crouched and moved through the small copse of fir and maple. Where gaps in the trees appeared, he sprinted across to the next group of trees. He kept the low-hanging branches between him and the dragon as much as possible as he made his way toward the trailhead. Jack kept a wary eye on the dragon as he moved, conscious of the beast's attention. The dragon was focused entirely on the ruined truck, its back foot standing on the rear axle as its jaws continued pulling apart its underside.

Jack's eyes were fixed on the trailhead. A wide path led up the mountain to a high ridge covered in pine. If the whole trail were like that, they would at least have cover from the dragon. Using the tree line as cover, Jack moved toward the trailhead with a single-minded determination. He had to find Onyx and Otter. The space under the trees was thick with shadow. The scent of pine and damp earth almost drowned out the ever-present smell of burning timber.

Jack moved cautiously through the underbrush, half his attention on the path, half on the giant flaming beast tearing apart his truck. He stayed close to the trees to use the deep shadows below them as cover, his every move calculated to avoid catching the dragon's attention. His first instinct was to run and get out of there, but he could not abandon Onyx.

The guy wasn't crazy after all.

Jack froze as the dragon roared; a primal cry of triumph echoed through the valley.

30

Onyx jumped out of the truck. Pain flared in his back and shoulders as he hit the gravel and rolled. Fresh abrasions appeared on his forearms and cheeks as the gravel cut into his skin. He scrambled toward the tree line, desperate to escape, as the dragon's shadow filled the sky above him. He heard a sharp yelp from the truck and turned to see the dog caught in the back seat, unable to squeeze between the front door frame and the seat. He lunged back toward the truck as it erupted in flames. The dragon landed with a crash as it plunged its beak down, grabbed the truck, and flipped it to one side. Onyx turned toward the tree line and ran.

Onyx met Jack a hundred yards up the trailhead. They both ducked low and peered down the trail toward the lot they had just left. The crackle of flames and the long, low growl of the dragon filled the air. The sound of metal ripping away from metal pierced the air as Jack watched the rear bumper of his truck fly across his view. He could not see the truck or the dragon. He turned to Onyx and pointed up the trail.

"She can't see us if we can't see her," Onyx said as he turned to move up the trail.

"Otter," Jack said with sudden realization; he stopped and looked around the trail, eager to see his old friend. The dog was nowhere in sight. He turned and started to move back toward the parking lot.

Onyx grabbed his arm. "He was still in the truck when the fire hit. I don't think he made it."

Jack looked at Onyx, dazed. He had lost everything. The truck flipped over and on fire. The truck that held everything Jack cared to save, including his dog. Jack blinked. Otter was all he had left. The only thing in his new attempt at life that mattered to Jack. He had to go down and get him. Jack tried to pull away, but Onyx held tight.

"Jack the dog was trapped in the truck. He didn't make it out."

Jack refused to understand what Onyx was saying. If he did not acknowledge it, it would not be real. There was a roar and the screech of metal as the dragon continued to tear into the truck's undercarriage.

"That thing just destroyed everything I own," Jack said. "Everything worth keeping was in the back of that truck."

"If Otter is dead," Jack said, as understanding broke through the fog his thoughts had become.

Jack shook Onyx's hand away. "That bitch just destroyed everything I own and killed my dog. It's time she goes down." Jack tore his arm away from Onyx. He flipped the safety off the Remington and returned to the parking lot.

When Jack charged out of the trail, the dragon did not look up from tearing the truck to pieces. He ran toward the beast, pulling the trigger as he went. There was no need to aim; the dragon was a wall of scaled flesh in front of him. The lead slugs flew from the shotgun and slammed into the dragon's flank. Jack watched scales shatter and holes appear in the dragon's flesh. He watched flames pour from those wounds. What looked to Jack like molten lead oozed out of the wounds and down the dragon's skin. The fire around the wounds flared bluish white.

In two heartbeats, the bloody, gouged flesh was gone, replaced by pristine scales covered in fire.

The beast swung away from the truck. Its neck slammed into Jack as it did. The shotgun flew out of Jack's hands as he slid across the gravel lot, his coat smoldering. The dragon's maw pulled back to snap Jack in half. The jaws of its beak-like mouth opened. Jack saw rows of serrated teeth inside, like a shark's. As the dragon's head moved toward him, Jack heard a scream from Onyx as the little man jumped onto one of the dragon's legs. The winged axe rose and fell.

The dragon spun to bite at Onyx as Jack scrambled for the shotgun.

Onyx slammed the axe home again. It bit through the thick scales of the dragon's hide. As he pulled the axe out to slam it in again, flames spurted from the dragon's flesh and writhed around the wounds. The flesh gashed open by Onyx's axe was suddenly whole, the skin unmarred as if never injured. Onyx screamed as he slammed the axe into the beast's side again. And again, and again. Each cut sprouted flames that healed the injuries in seconds. The fires that seemed to form the dragon's flesh ate into Onyx's clothes. The bomber jacket began to smolder as Onyx slid down the leg of the beast.

He saw the dragon's head swivel toward him from the corner of his eye. Onyx tensed his legs as the toothed beak rushed toward him. At the last moment, he pushed away from the beast. Onyx flew out from between the dragon's jaws as they slammed shut. He hit the gravel on his back and rolled several feet back toward the trailhead. Intense pain flared across his back, and he lay motionless as the dragon's head moved toward him.

Jack pointed the shotgun at the beast above him. He pulled the trigger. The hammer fell on an empty chamber. Jack pulled out the empty magazine and fumbled at his belt. He slammed the new magazine home and racked a round. He pulled the trigger, and hot lead slammed into the dragon's side. The dragon swung its head back toward Jack. It leaned in toward him. Jack could hear the beast inhaling. The wind rushed past Jack. Ten feet in front of him, the dragon opened its maw. Jack raised the shotgun, took two fast steps forward, and pulled the trigger. The round slammed into the back of the dragon's throat. Fire flew from the dragon's mouth as the round struck. The dragon's eyes went wide. Its mouth opened in a roar of pain, then snapped shut tight. The dragon sprang into the air.

"It shrugged off my axe blows; they just flared up, and bang, they healed," Onyx said as Jack helped him to his feet.

"My shotgun blasts too," Jack said as Onyx brushed himself off, "They healed within seconds."

"Then what the hell was that?"

"I shoved the gun in its mouth," Jack said, unable to remove the grin from his face, "guess she doesn't like the boom-stick down her throat."

Onyx looked up to the circling dragon, "I don't think it did more than piss her off."

Above them, the dragon banked and dove. Fire wreathed its skin, and smoke trailed from its mouth. The flapping of its wings paused as it drew in a breath.

"Shit," Jack said as both men dashed toward the trailhead. Behind them, a new blast of fire scorched the still-burning parking lot.

31

The two men moved up the trail, their eyes locked to the heavens.
The dragon's shadow crossed the trail several times, but the beast did
not see them. They moved from tree to tree until they reached the
top of the ridge line they followed. Jack looked over the ridge and
down into the valley behind them. The maple and cedar seemed to
have been left back at the trailhead. The trees around them were
mostly fir and pine, with the occasional Hemlock poking through
what looked like a giant Christmas Tree lot.

Less than a mile ahead, the trees thinned out. He could see where
the tree line ended. The thick forest of trees began to thin out,
gradually giving way to broader and wider gaps of scrub and small
brush, until only rock and sand could finally be seen creeping to the
edge of the snow-covered glacier far ahead. Jack and Onyx,
determined to survive, wondered where they would find cover from
the dragon circling above in that near-barren wasteland.

The menacing shadow of the dragon passed above them, a stark
reminder of the peril they were in.

"This isn't going to work," Jack said, "the trees thin out ahead; once we are out in the open, she is going to see us."

"Then we stay under the trees," Onyx said as he pointed toward the valley before them. "If I remember right, that ridge," he pointed to a crest that rose on the valley's far side, meets up with this one before the shelter. More trees over there, and they go higher up and closer to our destination."

Jack looked at the sky. The dragon circled high above. It seemed to follow the ridge they were on; it soared up to the line of trees and then back to the parking lot.

"Better to use the trees for cover; let's head down. It will take us longer to get there, but so will getting roasted."

Onyx nodded and started moving downhill.

The trees here were close together, their branches casting deep shadows that wrapped around their bases. The scent of pine and damp earth mingled with the ever-present smoke and the charcoal and sulfur smell from Jack's still-hot shotgun. Now and then, the beast's shadow skimmed along the ground as the predator hunted them from above. They pressed themselves against the thick trunk of pine trees, held their breath, and waited for the dragon's shadow to pass. Jack stayed low and blended in with the environment as best he could, the rough bark of the tree against his cheek, the sound of his own heartbeat in his ears.

Hopefully, it will be enough.

The crunch of dry leaves beneath their feet made Jack nervous. *How good is a dragon's hearing?* He stopped and scanned the sky for any movement; his ears strained for the flap of wings he expected any second. The dragon was still above them, its shadow a constant reminder that it searched for them. Their path under the trees would only buy them time. At some point, they would have to move out into the open. It had not spotted them yet, but Jack had little hope they would make it across the barren wasteland below the glacier.

Jack kept to the denser parts of the woods, where the trees grew close, and the underbrush was thick. He hoped the dragon would not find them through the branches above. They slid between underbrush and over tangled roots, eyes glued to the sky, hoping beyond reason that they would evade the beast or it would grow bored with trying to find them.

As the sun rose higher, it cast long shadows across the forest floor. Jack found himself wondering how far they had traveled. He looked back toward the ridge they had come down, but the thick wall of trees blocked his view of the path they had taken. His legs ached with every step. He had walked the trails around this mountain hundreds of times, but the trek down the valley was far different than the smooth, well-maintained trails he once walked with Otter.

Those hikes had been on clearly marked paths, peaceful meandering strolls on gently winding trails. The ground beneath their feet was smooth and packed firmly. Otter beside him, they would share the trail in companionable silence, the only sound the rustle of tree branches in the wind. Occasionally, Otter would dart into the trees to sniff out something interesting or chase some critter he spotted. At Jack's call, he would always return wearing that carefree grin so common to dogs. It was a simple escape from the noise and worries of the world — time for Jack to unwind and enjoy the outdoors.

Every step in the valley with the dragon hunting them felt like a struggle--no gentle slopes up a clear trail here. There was no path, just steep inclines in the general direction they were going. The ground was littered with unseen rocks and tree roots under a carpet of slick pine needles. Any step would likely send Jack tumbling to the ground or twisting an ankle. More than once, he slipped on patches of pine or loose stones. Their movement through the trees required constant focus to avoid falling and stay on course toward their goal. Every step was a battle to stay on track, a testament to their physical endurance.

Jack glimpsed the peak several times through the towering trees, only to realize they were not heading toward it. He would change his course and aim for the peak, but he found he was off course again when he caught another glimpse of it through the trees.

The easy days of walking with Otter seemed like a lifetime ago. Every step Jack made in the valley made his loss more acute. Jack's grip tightened on the shotgun as the dragon's shadow passed over them again. His heart was racing, not from the terror of the dragon but from the loss of Otter. The memory of Otter's bright, trusting eyes, wagging tail, and familiar presence pained him. Otter had been his only constant since the accident. He was all Jack had after the loss of Jill. All Jack needed. The dog had become more than a pet, more than a dog. He had been family. The thought of losing him to the dragon was unbearable.

Jack swallowed the lump in his throat as a memory returned to him.

Otter had saved his life when the accident took Jill's.

Why hadn't I made sure Otter was out of the truck? How could I have thought only of myself as fire speared toward them?

Jack's chest tightened with grief and anger. He missed Jill. Her absence was a weight he carried with him every day, a weight heavier than anything else he endured.

God, I miss her. But she isn't here. She never will be again. And now Otter is gone, too. I am truly alone. Jack leaned back against the nearest pine, slid down it, and leaned his head against his knees as the tears came.

32

The air was heavy with the scent of smoke and the crackle of dry leaves as Onyx stepped through a thick patch of underbrush. Thin rays of sunlight, tinged gray by the ever-present smoke, floated across the underbrush. Onyx scanned the trees ahead of him. Jack sat against the rough bark of a towering pine tree. His shoulders were hunched forward, his head resting on his knees, his arms wrapped tightly around them as if to hold himself together.

Onyx stood frozen. He was not sure what to do. The sight of the man like this was jarring. Jack was not sobbing aloud, but tears streaked his cheeks in paths that glistened in the feeble sunlight. The man had jumped in and helped a perfect stranger without a thought for himself. He handled the trip up the mountain with calm competence. Even after being attacked by the dragon, he showed himself to be a steady and effective leader. He had seemed unshakable, in complete control of any situation, but now, seeing him like this, Onyx was shaken. Onyx had felt the cold grip of loss, but seeing Jack like this tore at his heart. He recognized grief when he saw it.

Onyx stepped closer. His mind raced as he considered what he could do or say to help, but nothing came to him. He was not good with this kind of thing. Emotions were not his strong suit, not dealing with his own, and definitely not dealing with other people's. What could he say? Words seemed inadequate. So, he said nothing. His first thought was to pretend nothing was happening. To give Jack some space, some time. So, he stood there and watched as the man who helped him when he needed it broke down in front of him.

Say something, he told himself, *offer some kind of comfort.*

Jack might not want anyone to intrude on this private moment, but Onyx knew he would rather have been alone at such times. He sighed, rubbed the back of his neck, and considered what comfort he could give. He knew grief was not something he could fix, and he should make sure Jack did not go through it alone. But his mind was blank, his words caught in his throat. He did not know what to say. He did not know how to help.

The silence of Jack's grief under the majestic pines hung like the smoke from the millions of acres burning around them, thick, cloying, choking off life and killing laughter.

Onyx knew grief. He had felt its weight and knew its burden, but he had been able to move past it. He had not ignored it; instead, he had learned to use it. The loss was a solid pain he always felt, but that pain pushed him forward when he would rather stop. It motivated him to make the most of his life, if only to prove that the loss he endured was not in vain. It drove him to live the best life he could live, to be the best person he could be, *but how do you tell that to someone in the middle of their grief? How do you communicate that the pain does not lessen but becomes bearable? How do you tell someone they would emerge stronger from their pain?*

Onyx was engulfed by a feeling of helplessness, a sensation he despised. His jaw tightened, a physical manifestation of his inner turmoil. He was a man of action, comfortable with tasks, challenges, and battles. Emotions, comfort, and feelings were not his forte. He was at a loss when it came to comforting a friend in need. The gnawing feeling of uselessness in his gut was impossible to ignore.

Onyx approached Jack and placed a comforting hand on his shoulder. He tried to find words of solace, but they eluded him, caught in his throat. Instead, he settled for a reassuring pat on Jack's shoulder. He stood there for what felt like an eternity, hoping that his mere presence would bring some comfort to his friend.

Onyx began to pace among the trees. He could not stay still; he needed to do something. His heart pounded in his chest. Ellis was still on the mountain. He had to get to Ellis. Jack had chosen the wrong time to have a breakdown. Onyx could see the final line of trees from where he stood. Maybe he was fooling himself, but he swore he could see a dark smudge on the snow-covered glacier, the stone hut where he left his brother. Ellis was within sight, and Onyx was stalled here by Jack's meltdown. He considered just pushing forward without Jack, but he knew he could not leave him behind. The man had helped him. He could not just abandon him now. Onyx's sense of duty to his friend was strong, even in the face of his own emotional struggle. He wanted to panic; he wanted to rage; he wanted to shake Jack and get the man moving again. He needed some distraction to snap Jack out of it so they could get moving again. The sunlight flickered across his path, and he stopped his pacing. It had been a while since he had seen the flicker of the dragon's shadow skimming the ground. He moved toward a small clearing among the tightly packed trees. He crouched in the underbrush at the clearing's edge and scanned the sky. They were halfway across the valley, on the upward slope of the ridge. The smoke-filled sky above them was clear of flying reptiles. He waited and watched for several minutes while deciding his next move.

Onyx sighed and moved back toward Jack.

"The dragon seems to have moved on."

Jack did not even lift his head. He stayed curled up, silent tears falling from his cheeks.

"If we move quickly, we might be able to get across that bare patch ahead before it returns."

Still, Jack made no response.

Onyx's jaw clenched. He shifted awkwardly on his feet a few times before sighing, setting his axe on his shoulder, and turning back into the trees.

Onyx returned to the clearing. He followed its edge, keeping to the shadowed underbrush, and he stopped frequently to scan the sky.

33

On their fifth anniversary, Jill handed Jack a small box. He raised an eyebrow, intrigued by the tiny package. "What's this? Jewelry?" he said as he shook the box.

"Not quite. Open it!" Jill said. She bounced on the balls of her feet, eager to see him open the box. Her excitement was infectious. Jack lifted the lid.

A photograph was on a soft foam cushion. A tiny black shadow with floppy ears and enormous brown eyes sat in a small puddle of water.

"You got me a picture?" Jack teased. He lifted out the picture and turned it back and forth in the light.

"Where are the buttons?"

Jill smacked him on the arm.

"Don't be dense. Come on," she said, "He's outside." She grabbed his arm and pulled him toward the back door. "Since I'm working weekends now, I thought you could use a hiking buddy."

They stepped onto the back patio where a cardboard box lay tipped to one side, its open flaps revealing a very empty interior.

"Oh, no, no, no," Jill cried as she released Jack and searched the yard.

Jack picked up the box and helped in the search. He was checking under the hydrangea when he heard a splash from the Koi Pond. He turned toward it in time to see a little head break the surface. A tiny black dog paddled energetically toward the grass.

Jack called to Jill as the dog finished its swim and walked confidently over to sniff at Jack's shoe. He knelt and scratched the puppy behind the ears, his heart melting.

"He's like a tiny otter," Jack said as the little pup rolled playfully on the ground before it ran back and dove into the pond.

Otter was small at first, but he grew — and grew. His once oversized paws soon became massive. His body thickened; his gleaming black fur stretched over a muscular body that dwarfed all the other dogs in the neighborhood. By the time he was a year old, the black fur ball weighed more than 160 pounds and looked more like a bear than a dog, but he still loved water. Every stream, lake, or puddle they passed would have Otter dive in, emerge dripping and ready to shake water all over Jack. Jill joked that when she had picked him out, she had no idea she was bringing home a miniature horse. No matter how big he got, Otter was always the same affectionate and playful pup.

After the worst morning of Jack's life, the dog was the only reason he was still around.

On that day, as they returned from a trip to the farmer's market, Otter let out a soft whine and refused to enter the house. No matter what Jack tried, the dog refused to enter; Jack finally had to drag him into the kitchen to get the door shut.

As they started putting things away, Otter nudged Jack's leg. Thrown off balance by the dog's weight, Jack laughed and patted the dog on the head as Jill unpacked their bags.

"I got another one of those candles from that little Amish lady," Jill said. She held a glass jar up to Jack's nose. "Smell."

Otter whined again and pushed his head against Jill. She staggered back, recovered, and scratched absently between the dog's ears.

Jack sniffed at the candle. "Smells like rotten eggs," he said, "mixed with lavender."

Jill punched his arm, "Not funny, mister." She placed the candle on the table. "Just for that, I'm lighting this one first."

As Jill opened the kitchen drawer to get matches, Otter barked and ran toward the back door.

"Looks like someone wants to go back out," Jack said. When Jack did not move toward the door, Otter ran back to him and bumped his head against Jack. He reached out and scratched the dog. Otter woofed and ran to Jill. He bopped her with his head, and she pushed him aside with a groan.

"Take Otter out, Jack, so I can put the rest of this away without getting knocked over." Jill laughed and rubbed the dog's back. "Go on out, boy."

Jack rose and moved toward the back door. Otter led the way but stopped to look back at Jill as they reached the door. The dog barked, a loud, insistent sound that echoed through the quiet house. It was not his usual playful bark--this was urgent, insistent, almost demanding.

Jill moved toward the table, a long barbecue lighter in her hand.

A tinge of unease shivered through Jack.

The dog was acting weird; he ran back to Jill, then to Jack, and back to the door. It was like he wanted them both to follow him outside. Jack swung the back door open and called to Otter as the dog nudged Jill away from the table.

"Jack," Jill said.

Jack called the dog. Otter ran toward him as Jill flicked the lighter.

Jack realized what the rotten egg smell had been and turned toward Jill. Jill clicked the barbecue lighter. Jack's shouted warning was drowned out by the explosion that ripped through the kitchen. Jack had not connected the bitter smell of sulfur to a potential gas leak until it was too late.

The new stove hissed for days, an imperceptible sound over the quiet hum of the house. Not yet recalled by the oven manufacturer, the faulty valve failed and began spilling gas into the house. The gas gathered in pockets around the stove, in the cabinets, and along the baseboards. The faint sulfuric smell that hung in the kitchen went unnoticed by the occupants until Jack sniffed the candle.

Jack woke to the wail of sirens. Red and blue lights flashed around him. Otter's heavy weight was on his chest. The dog whined, and Jack shoved him off. Pain flared in his chest and head as he struggled to his feet. He looked around, dazed. Thrown across the yard by the blast, they were both on his neighbor's lawn. Otter's fur was singed and still smoking; one leg was twisted at an odd angle. The dog tried to stand but fell to the ground with a whimper.

Jill was all Jack could think of as he sprinted back toward his house.

34

A woman's cry for help cut into Jack's memory.

Jill hadn't screamed for help, had she?

No. There wasn't enough time.

He was sure she had not screamed.

This was something else. Someone else.

Jack sat up as Onyx moved out of the trees toward him.

"Did you hear that?" Onyx said.

"Hear what?" Jack asked.

"Hey," called a voice. "Over here," louder. "I could use a hand." This time, Jack heard it.

Onyx and Jack looked at each other, unsure of what to do.

Jack stood, ducked under the line of trees to their left, and moved slowly toward the voice. He emerged from the trees into the small clearing beyond.

"Oh, thank the heavens," the voice said, "I knew I saw someone moving through the trees. Can you help me out? Up here."

Jack looked toward the voice. His gaze moved across the clearing and the trees to where a shredded parachute was tangled.

"What the hell," mumbled Onyx.

A woman dangled from the end of the parachute, her hands tangled in the lines above her head.

"Don't just stand there staring; give a girl a hand."

Jack scanned the sky.

"It's clear for now; move and get under cover," Onyx said.

Jack gripped the shotgun as he moved through the clearing. He sprinted for the far side. As he reached the stand of trees, he dove beneath the branches, spun, and scanned the sky.

"Okay," said the voice above him, "a little dramatic, but I'm not in a position to complain."

Convinced the sky was clear, Jack stood and considered the dangling woman.

He couldn't tell much through the tree branches. Her red hair was cut short in a military-style cut. The high collar on her jacket protected her neck and face, but her forehead was streaked with blood. Shouldn't she be wearing a helmet, Jack thought, just as he noticed the cracked and broken yellow helmet on the ground below her. She looked familiar, though he was not sure why. He didn't know many redheads and certainly not one who would be parachuting in Oregon.

The shredded chute was tangled in the upper branches of a Ponderosa Pine. A good twenty feet of bare tree trunk was between Jack and the lowest branch--another ten to fifteen feet to where the woman dangled. Jack hefted the shotgun and considered, *well, no,* he thought *that wouldn't work.* He circled the tree and scanned the lower branches, but none of them were low enough to get to without some climbing gear.

As he rounded the tree, he saw several broken strands of paracord that dangled to the ground. He grabbed one and tugged at it. It came away from the tree and coiled to the ground. He tugged at the others and found three that were firmly tangled in the branches above.

"I don't like what I think you're thinking," Onyx said as he walked up next to Jack.

Startled, Jack scanned the sky above. "I haven't seen it in a couple of minutes. In fact, I don't think I've seen it since we started uphill," Onyx said.

Jack nodded and resumed tugging on the paracord. Satisfied that these cords were not coming down like the first one, he wrapped the cord around one arm, leaned back, and pulled. He put his whole weight into the pull. The cord stretched slightly but did not slip. Jack stood, reached up, and pulled himself off the ground. He dangled for a moment. Then dropped to the ground.

"I don't suppose you'd climb up there and cut her down," Jack asked.

"Sorry, I don't do heights." Onyx replied, "The Fates put me close to the ground for a reason; I intend to stay here."

Jack sighed. He looked up at the woman dangling in the tree above. She smiled down at him. Jack's heart melted. Okay, maybe it hadn't melted; maybe it had thawed slightly as he considered future possibilities.

After all, what was the loss of everything he owned, his truck, and his dog, compared to finding a hot redhead in a tree? Jill's voice said in his mind.

Okay, not hot, Jack thought, *but at least interesting.* Jack let go of that chain of thought and grabbed the bundle of paracord.

He hadn't free-climbed a rope since middle school, but was rather good at it back then. It was a bit easier now because he could use the tree to walk himself up the trunk. It took only a few moments before he could swing one leg over the lowest hanging branch.

He let go of the rope and climbed the branches around him like a ladder. He made it level with the woman, then climbed above her. He reached out, grabbed her harness, and pulled her toward the branch next to her. Her feet did not reach the branch. Jack let her swing back slowly. He reached into his front pocket and pulled out a small pocket knife. He flipped open the knife and sat with both his feet around the branch. Jack leaned out to grab the woman's harness, then he sawed at the rope trapping her. As the rope split, the woman began to fall. Jack held tight and swung her toward the branch. She landed sitting on the branch, her hands still tied above her. Jack tied the rope tightly to the branch he was on and swung down to stand next to her.

"Well," she said, "fancy meeting you here. I'm Ashley Ember; my friends call me Ashe."

"Jack Season," Jack said as he reached up and untangled her arms from the parachute cords.

"Thanks," she said, shaking her arms as Jack got them loose, "My arms went numb hours ago."

"How long have you been up here?"

"Don't know, we jumped just after sunrise, but I was in the air a lot longer than I should have been."

"After you," Jack said as he pointed toward the ground.

"Sure, let me fall first so you have something soft to land on," she said, as she slipped off the chute harness.

Jack smiled, "That's the plan. You do have more experience at falling."

She smiled, and Jack reconsidered his earlier thought.

Jack followed as Ashe climbed quickly down the ladder of branches. When she got to the last branch, she looked down, anxiety obvious on her face.

"That's a bit of a drop," she said.

"Naw, just follow me." Jack sat on the branch they stood on. He grabbed the branch and dropped his feet out into the void. Hanging by his hands, he let go and dropped to the ground.

35

Ashe followed the cowboy's lead. She sat on the branch, swung down, and dangled like a gymnast. She dropped to the ground. As she set foot on solid ground, a small, bearded man spoke, "Not the safest place to go skydiving," he said.

"It is for me; usually, when I land, stuff is on fire."

"On fire?"

She introduced herself, "Ashley Ember, Smoke Jumper." The man's handshake was hesitant, as if he had just stumbled into a world he didn't understand.

"Onyx Eisenhart, Eardfolc."

Ashe eyed the large axe he carried, then glanced at Jack as he picked up a hat and shotgun leaning against a nearby tree.

"Are you guys some kind of Cosplayers? Or LARP-ers? Bad time to be playing on the mountain." The situation was becoming more bizarre by the minute.

Jack shook his head. "Onyx's brother is up near the peak; he's injured, and we are going to get him. Emergency Services is kind of busy."

"I bet. Half the state has been evacuated or is about to be, but" she pointed at the axe in Onyx's hands, "you expect rogue trees to try and stop you?"

Onyx harumphed. Ashe had seen the word in print a hundred times but had never actually heard someone do it. It was like a sigh, a huff, and a growl all rolled into one. Ashe was impressed; he was quite good at it.   So much disapproval and annoyance was expressed with one simple sound that she could tell he used it a lot.

Ashe moved to the helmet. She picked it up. The cracked face shield was witness to her strike against the tree. She dropped the helmet and wandered through the copse of trees. She searched the ground. Now and then, she looked up into the trees.

"Lose something," Jack asked, concern in his voice, also looking up.

"Yep, my gear bag."

Jack and Onyx scanned the sky before they followed.

"I dropped it, hoped to gain height and make it over the trees before getting tangled up in the chute."

"Guess it didn't help," Onyx said.

"Nope. Just hit higher up and got stuck. I should have aimed for that dry creek bed." She pointed down slope as she spotted an orange flash among the dried-out bushes.

She let out a short squeal of delight as she ran down to the bag.

"Got it," she shouted. The two men cast nervous gazes toward the sky.

She pulled a large pack with a short shovel and an axe tied to its sides from a small clump of bushes. Squatting, she checked that everything was secure, then rummaged through the various pockets. She pulled a block of plastic out of an outside pouch. Plastic shards, wires, and electronics fell from her hand. "Damn. So much for radioing for help."

She eyed the little man with the axe and the cowboy beside him. Her dazed mind finally caught up to the situation she was in. Worry gnawed at her. These two were strangers only moments ago; just because they had gotten her out of the tree didn't mean they were harmless.

Why are they armed? Am I safe, or have I just dropped into another problem?

Trying to shake off her anxiety, she grabbed a pack of hand wipes and the first aid kit from her bag. Her fingers trembled as she wiped at her neck. Jack stepped up and offered to help.

She glanced up at him; his broad shoulders filled the space above her. She had no reason to trust him, but there was something grounded about him. Like the mountain around her, he seemed patient and steady. His brawny frame spoke of someone shaped by necessity, not vanity. The cowboy hat was a bit weird, but she could let that pass; not everyone had good fashion sense. The tight cords of muscle in his chest and arms were not the excess of a bodybuilder, but rather the result of someone consistent and dedicated.

A runner, maybe, or a swimmer, she thought.

His hands on her neck were surprisingly gentle as he scrubbed at the dried blood. His touch was that of someone who had done this before. The damp cloth was cool on her skin, but did little to soothe her nerves. The nagging worry lingered in her mind. He touched her scalp, and butterflies of pain fluttered across her head.

"Sorry," he said as she flinched away from him. "There's a lump on your head and a cut, but it's not bleeding." He rummaged through the first aid kit and pulled out a small bandage.

"Better in than out," she said, suddenly flushing as the words left her mouth. *Oh my god, that sounded pervy.* She rushed to recover.

"Isn't that what they say about hits to the head, " she said, trying to recover. The short man snorted out a laugh.

The cowboy didn't seem to notice.

"Yeah, swelling means there probably isn't any structural damage, maybe. A cracked skull is pretty dangerous," Jack said as he glared over at the short man.

She tried to ignore the tightness in her throat as he bandaged her head; his hands were a pleasant distraction.

Ashe swallowed and pulled a water bottle and a granola bar out of her bag. She flipped the top of the water bottle and chugged the contents. "Damn, that's good," she said when she finished. "I was dying of thirst up there."

She pulled a second bottle out of the pack and tossed it to Onyx. He caught it and offered it to Jack. Jack shook his head, so Onyx popped the top and drank.

"Did you really head up this mountain with nothing but an axe and a shotgun?"

Jack shrugged, "We kind of lost everything else along the way."

Onyx let out a gruff laugh, "That's an understatement." Jack flashed him a dirty look; Onyx just laughed again.

"What kind of idiot skydives onto a burning mountain?"

Ashe glared at the little man, "What kind of idiot hikes a mountain with no gear?"

"Like Jack said, we lost it all."

"Like I said," Ashe said slowly, as if talking to a child, "I am a Smoke Jumper. A group of wildfires started near Lawrence Lake. My team was sent in to put it out."

"You're a long way from Lawrence Lake," Jack said.

"After I jumped, some crazy updraft from the fires caught me and blew me off course. It seemed like every time I started down, another updraft would grab me and drag me up again. I'm not even sure which way the fire is anymore." Ashe spoke in a nearly continuous stream. "I can't be more than a couple of hundred yards off course, though."

"Couple hundred yards," Onyx said with that same gruff laugh, "Lady, you're on the wrong side of the mountain."

"Yeah, right," Ashe said as she hefted her gear bag onto her back.

"See anything burning nearby?" Onyx asked with a laugh.

A look of concern crossed Ashe's face as she turned in a circle and scanned the sky for smoke. She stormed past the two men and headed up the hill.

Ashe reached the top of the ridge line. Flat ground covered in trees ran up toward the peak. To the south, the ridge edge dropped into a steep sand-covered slope that ran down to another dry creek bed. The opposite slope was covered in trees that rose to the snow line. In the distance, she could see two columns of smoke, a few degrees apart, rising from the trees. The Lawrence Lake Fire. Behind her, the sky glowed orange as distant fires consumed the countryside south of the mountain.

She shook her head as Jack approached.

"No way. This is impossible," she pointed toward the two columns of smoke. "I jumped over Lawrence Lake. There is no way. No Way an updraft pushed me this far off course. A mile, maybe, in the worst circumstances, if that's even possible," Her hands waved in the air toward the columns, toward the peak, and down toward where she had landed. "But that's got to be four miles, at least."

"Six, probably," Onyx said as he caught up to them.

"Six," Ashee repeated. "No way. It can't. It's not possible."

"The news said the fires have been doing weird things," Jack said.

"Weird, yeah, but not impossible. Starts and flare-ups during heavy rain, blow-ups with no apparent cause, upwind spark fires. This thing," her hands waved toward the smoke-covered horizon to the south, "is so big that everything you can see in a fire has happened. But this," her hands swung toward the smoke again, then back toward the copse where she had crashed, "is not possible. Six miles. No way. There's no way an updraft pushed me six miles off course."

Onyx shrugged. "Either way, you are here. Lawrence Lake is that way," he pointed North. "Enjoy your hike," Onyx pointed toward the peak, "But my brother is that way." He began walking along the ridge. After a moment, Jack followed him.

Ashe shook her head, took one last look toward the two columns of smoke miles to the north, then turned to follow the two men.

36

The ridge opened onto a high-altitude desert below the Glacier. They passed the last row of trees. Only sparse groves of fir lay ahead of them. The path they traveled on became a bleak landscape of grass and rocks. Large boulders tumbled by glacial movement millions of years ago lay strewn about the empty landscape.

Jack gasped as he caught up to Onyx.

"Wow," was all Ashe said as she left the cover of the trees.

Wow is one word to describe it, Jack thought. *It's a weak word, but a word, nonetheless.*

Jack looked back at the way they had come. The trail twisted out of view a few hundred yards back. The ridge they had traveled broke to the northwest, becoming a tree-covered valley with the winding sparkling blue of the river cutting through it. A bare spot in the trees far below still had a thin line of smoke rising from the still-burning Michelins on his destroyed truck. Ahead, the mountain peak rose out of the ice, the glacier surrounding it covered in a layer of snow, even this late in the season. The smoke and glow of fires along the western and southern slopes made the peak seem to be rising from the fires of hell itself. Onyx, unable to hold his tongue any longer, turned to Ashe.

"Ashe, this is no ordinary wildfire. There's a dragon at the heart of it," Onyx's voice was grave, his eyes reflecting the seriousness of the situation.

A laugh burst from Ashe's throat as she stopped and turned toward Onyx. "A dragon? You're pulling my leg, right?" She turned to Jack, "This some kind of sick joke." She pointed South toward the rising smoke in the distance. The orange glow seemed to roll toward them in the thin air of the afternoon. "Half the damn country is on fire, and you two want to make jokes about a dragon. Thanks for getting me out of that tree, but I'd appreciate it if you kept the bullshit to yourselves."

"Wish we were kidding." Jack spoke calmly, his head down, "I've seen it. It's real. I don't know if it started," Jack threw his arm out toward the glowing fires in the distance, "all that. But I do know it's real, and where it goes, fire follows."

Ashe rolled her eyes and threw up her hands, "of all the tree lines on all the mountains in all the world, I had to get stuck on the one with the two lunatics." She stormed toward the peak; her boots crunched over the icy scree as she left the cover of the last remaining trees.

"Come on, guys. Let's find Onyx's brother and get the hell off this mountain. The two of you are hallucinating from all the smoke."

Onyx's voice was firm as he called after Ashe, "I understand it's a lot to take in, but we've seen it, faced it. It's not a hallucination. We're not crazy, Ginger. We're determined to stop this."

Ashe spun around and stomped up to Onyx. She bent until she was eye-to-eye with the man. "Do not call me Ginger," she said in a cold, slow voice. "My name is Ashley. My friends call me Ashe. You can call me Ms. Ember."

"Look," Onyx said, "my people have been fighting this creature for decades. It has returned here to nest. It plans to ignite the volcano to warm its clutch." His words carried the weight of years of struggle and determination.

"Your people," Ashe asked.

"Dwarves," Jack said, "er, I mean Eardfolc," he corrected when Onyx glared at him.

"No, my people. The Talamh Sidhe, the people of fae," Onyx said. "When the world was young, we fought humanity over control of the natural world. We struggled to keep your people from destroying the world we all inhabited. We created soldiers to help us destroy humanity. Creatures that used the weapons of nature against man, but we failed; man became dominant, and most of our people fled. But some stayed. They stayed to protect the land, heal the damage caused by the war, and tend to the world's hidden natural places. But Man's need to always have more has poisoned far too much of the planet. The glaciers that once imprisoned the creatures have receded. The dragon is free because the permafrost she was once buried under has melted."

"Lord," Ashe said, "you LARPers take your backstories way too seriously."

Onyx stomped a foot and glared at her. "This isn't a game. That thing," Onyx waved an arm into the air above them, "wants to burn the world. We can stop it. There is a sword that can do that on this mountain. We plan to find it."

Ashe looked at Onyx and then burst out laughing.

"So, what, we're on a quest to slay a dragon? Like some damn fairy tale? What's that make me the princess or the evil queen?"

Onyx, wounded by the woman's ridicule, shouted, "Right now, I'd say you're the cynical bitch."

"Onyx," Jack said. He turned to Ashe. "Look, it's not just about the dragon. It's about saving Onyx's brother and stopping any more destruction. We believe the mountain will erupt."

"Impossible, this mountain has been dormant for centuries."

"Actually," Onyx grumbled as he stormed past the two, "This is Oregon's most active volcano. The center of the Cascade Volcanic Arc. Volcanoes that range from Northern California to British Columbia."

Onyx stopped and turned back to look at them, "But you know what, don't worry about it. Think of us as crazy. My people failed the first time this thing appeared; there is no reason to think I can succeed at a second attempt just because I have your help. Let the damn dragon nest. Let it set off the volcano. Let every damn volcano on the coast blow. I don't care anymore. I just want my brother safe."

Onyx stormed along the ridgeline, his boots crunching in the ice-tinged volcanic ash.

"First time," Ashe asked Jack.

"Mount St. Helens," Ashe began to laugh, but the look on Jack's face stopped her. She wasn't sure whether it was concern for his friend or concern about the situation, but it stopped her humor.

Ashe sighed and started after Onyx. "Saving a brother from a dragon. That's a new one for me.".

"We don't need your help," Onyx yelled from ahead. "Head down the mountain. Join up with your crew. We'll be just fine."

"Got a first aid kit," Ashe asked with a smile as she hefted the orange pack on her shoulder.

Onyx remembered the red bag he stowed behind the truck's passenger seat and glared at the woman.

"So no, then." Ashe said, "Do you have any medical knowledge? First Aid, EMT, or Medic training?"

Onyx's glare deepened. He stopped. He turned to the woman. "Jack did alright patching me up; we'll do just fine with Ellis. without you." Onyx spun and stomped up the mountain.

"I know basic first aid. I was an unofficial medic for my fencing team in college, cuts, scrapes, sprains, nothing major." Jack said as he caught up to Ashe. "But we could use your first aid kit."

"Fencing team. Like swords and stuff."

"Yeah. I started in high school and fought Saber in college, but Schlager became my obsession." Jack sighed, "The first of many, I guess."

"Schlager?"

"A German dueling sword, I guess a type of longsword, but not used in Olympic fencing. I became obsessed with learning it and a couple of other weapons, and kind of backed off the official stuff."

"Not before medaling in the Olympics," Onyx shouted from ahead.

"Jerk," Jack whispered.

"Really," Ashe said, "The Olympics, for fencing."

"Yeah, it was quite a while ago," Jack said.

"And now you're hiking the glacier with a shotgun and a..." Ashe paused to consider her choice of words. "Little person."

"Eardfolc," Onyx shouted. "Bitch."

Ashe smiled, "and an Eardfolc bitch." she corrected.

Ahead, Onyx growled and walked faster.

Jack pointed at Onyx's back. "The little guy,"

"Eardfolc," Onyx shouted.

"...showed up on my doorstep this morning. Burnt and cut up. He said he was being chased, and his brother was up here injured."

"Chased," Ashe asked, "by who?"

"The Dragon," Onyx shouted.

Ashe scowled.

Jack grinned. "Yeah, I thought the same thing. I patched him up and offered him a ride up the mountain."

"A perfect stranger, injured, with a crazy story, and you offered to help anyway."

Ashe wondered what kind of man Jack Season was. Phil would have called the cops and had the guy arrested for trespassing. At the very least, he would have thrown him out on his ear. She wondered what it says of someone willing to help a perfect stranger with no promise of any reward. Jack looked like a decent guy, but so did Phil when they first met.

"What was I supposed to do? Let him walk back up the mountain alone." Jack said.

"So, you just walked up the mountain with him."

Jack turned and pointed toward the thin line of smoke rising from the parking lot below.

"That fire is what's left of my truck."

"So, you crashed it," Ashe asked.

"The Dragon ate it," Onyx shouted.

Ashe laughed and looked at Jack.

"He's not wrong," Jack said with a shrug.

37

Ashe took the lead as they reached the final line of trees. To their left, the ridge dropped away in a steep slope of sand and gravel. Ahead was a vast wasteland of gravel inter-spaced with worn boulders and spurs of rock that, even in the depth of summer, held rims of ice around their shadowed bases, the remains of the receding glacier that once covered this part of the mountain.

Onyx and Jack held back. They scanned the skies, took several steps forward, and then scanned the skies again. Jack picked out several boulders he could use as cover if the dragon returned. Beside him, he noticed Onyx doing the same. Clueless, Ashe continued forward.

This ridge joined with another as the slope of the mountain opened in its last run up to the peak. A well-traveled path ran ahead of them, merging with a path from the northern ridge. The glacier sparkled in the afternoon sunlight.

A small shack of stone stood at the edge of the snow, where ice and rock met.

"There it is," Onyx said. He quickened his steps and soon passed Ashe, the thought of the dragon forgotten in his eagerness to reach his brother.

The small stone building sat nestled among the rocks and ice of the glacier's edge, its tin roof covered in ten inches of snow.

Onyx sprinted up the trail. He burst through the little wooden door and called his brother's name.

Jack began to run as Onyx appeared back in the doorway. "He's not," he started as his eyes grew wide, riveted on the sky above. "Run," he yelled.

"Run," Jack shouted as he caught up with Ashe. He wrapped an arm around Ashe and dragged her behind him.

"What the hell," she yelled as she tried to keep up with him.

"Inside, inside, inside," Jack yelled as they reached the shelter.

Onyx dived away from the doorway. Ashe glanced back.

A line of fire grew from the sky. It hit the ground fifty yards in front of the shelter and rolled toward them. Ashe kicked the door shut; she grabbed Jack around the waist and pushed him on top of Onyx.

Her right hand snaked down to the side pocket on the leg of her jumpsuit. In a blink, she pulled a length of silver foil from the pack and dove on top of the two. She pulled the fire shelter over the top of them all and held it firm to the ground. The three lay coiled against the stone corner, the fire shelter above them. The tin roof screamed as the snow piled above it was super-heated, reduced to steam in seconds. The heat rose. Burning shards of the wooden door blasted through the shelter as the line of flame crashed into it.

Ashe saw the line of fire erupt from the sky in her mind's eye again. The creature behind it was impossible.

This is a day for the impossible, she thought. *They weren't kidding. There is a dragon on the mountain.*

Heat washed over them. The stone wall beside them began to warm. Ashe shifted her bare hands off the stone and wrapped the foil of the fire shelter under them.

There was a roar from outside. The stone cooled as the heat was drawn off by the melting snow outside. Ashe stood; the silver tent fell beside them. A small line of fire lit the shelter in flickering light. Like some fancy fire pit, it burned from the door to the wall.

The front wall of the shelter rocked as something large crashed into it. What was left of the still-burning door frame splintered. A second crash, followed by another roar, rattled Ashe's nerves. She backed into the corner behind the two men. Jack racked a round in his shotgun and raised it toward the door; beside him, Onyx hefted his axe.

Ashe could not believe what she was seeing. A giant reptilian head wreathed in fire filled the doorway. Teeth the length of her forearm crashed together as they tried to chew into the shelter. She stared, fascinated.

Fire sheathed the creature as if it had been doused in kerosene. The flames seemed like part of it, an aura of heat and light that swirled across its skin. It flickered and smoked as the beast moved. The skin, a muted shade of red, was smooth, like a snake's, from tail to torso, and shifted to thicker, separate scales as it reached the dragon's belly, head, and chest. They plated the beast, like armor, as flames sputtered between and around them, shifting like the flames of a gas log in a breeze.

You're dead, Ashe, she thought. *That's the only explanation. Impossibly pushed miles off course, facing an apparent flaming fucking dragon. I jumped, and I died, and this is the hell my final thoughts decided to torment me with. A dragon, a cute guy, and a dwarf. Why not? As final seconds go, it beats a tunnel with light at the end. But what the heck does it say about my mental state,* she thought. Concepts from her college psychology class rolled through her mind. *The fiery dragon is the monster of my career, putting out fires to please my overbearing parents. Right, isn't that what psychology's all about, how bad your parents messed you up?*

She looked at Jack as he raised his shotgun and pointed it out the door. Even the cute guy makes sense.

He was the relationship I avoided so I could concentrate on a career, only to be caught in a violent and destructive one. He's the nice guy I always thought I would end up with. A composite of all the things I wanted in a relationship. It's classic psychology, isn't it?

But the dwarf, she thought, *what does he represent in this twisted, mixed-up death dream of yours, sister? Is he my self-esteem,* she thought, *bitter and shrunken after years of being put down by Phil, desperate to slay the dragons of my insecurity?*

The stone of the shelter wall cracked as the creature pressed against the door.

Maybe I'm not dead, she thought; *maybe I'm in a coma or drugged up so my body can cope with all my injuries, and this is a drug-induced dream. Yeah, I like that one better; it's less final. I'll go with that. So, how's that work,* she thought. *You're in a coma dreaming, and you wake up by escaping from the dream, right? That's what they do in the movies. So, how the heck do I get out of here?*

Ashe looked frantically around the room. No windows, no back door. They were trapped. The creature's head pulled away as it roared — the air in the shelter filled with the scent of ashes and cooked flesh.

38

Jack stepped back from the cabin door. Ashley seemed frozen in place. Terrified. He couldn't blame her. He was about two steps from losing it himself. The giant maw of the dragon banged into the doorway again. Unable to get through the door, it roared its frustration. Its foul breath filled the small stone shelter. Jack realized it was bigger than it had been earlier.

We're all dead, Jack thought. The thing would breathe fire through the door any moment now, and they would cook and sizzle like bacon. The dragon smashed its face into the doorway of the stone shelter. Once, twice, three times. It drew back and opened its mouth. Jack expected it to breathe flame. He braced himself. The fire would not be a streak of flame this close to the doorway. The room would fill with it. Jack hoped it would be painless.

Maybe my impulse to help a perfect stranger, a stranger who seemed deranged at the time, wasn't such a good idea, he thought.

It's never a bad idea to do the right thing, Jill's voice said.

Jack looked toward the corner where Onyx stood, gripping the axe he had taken from Jack's closet. Jack closed his eyes as the dragon's head lurched forward, releasing a roar that shook the building. The echo of the beast's roar deafened Jack, but no flames rolled over him, just the stench of burnt meat and ash.

The creature pulled away from the doorway and turned to look at something behind it.

Jack heard shouts as his hearing returned. The dragon spun. The shelter's wall shook as the beast's tail slammed into it.

Jack moved closer to the door. Something white and wet smashed into the door beside him. He jerked back. A rain of snow showered down. Several more snowballs went wide of their target and splattered beside Jack.

The shouts turned to commands as one voice rose above the others. "Berry, Opal, move to the left, draw its attention away from the cabin so they can make a break for it. Bramble, stay in the snow."

Jack watched as the dragon lunged down a strip of stone where its fire had melted the snow. Jack saw a half dozen little men hurling snowballs at the dragon as it moved away. Every place a snowball hit, the fire that flickered over its skin went out. Jack saw several fire-free spots along the beast's back and tail where snowballs had hit. The skin in these spots looked dark green, a bright contrast to the flaming red hue of the rest of it.

Onyx moved beside Jack, "Ellis," he shouted.

"Get out of there, you damn fool, while we have it distracted," the voice yelled. "Get into the snow. It won't follow."

Onyx hurtled out the door and headed toward the sound of the voice. Ashe stood beside Jack; she looked confused as she stared into the back of the shelter. Jack grabbed her and shook her arm.

"Let's go," he said as he pointed toward the snow where Onyx ran.

The woman blinked and started running beside him. Jack quickly passed her.

As he cleared the back of the dragon, he saw Onyx leap a small snow drift to grab another man his size in a fierce hug.

Guess that's Ellis, Jack thought. He looked like an older version of Onyx, with a thick silver-shot beard and the same bulbous nose.

"Good to see you, Oni." He spoke in measured words, his voice deep as a mine shaft, carrying the weight of thought behind every syllable.

Ashe cleared the drift and slammed into Jack's back. He had stopped, frozen in place as a familiar bark rolled through the chill air. Jack turned.

Otter stood in front of the dragon. Teeth bared, the dog stood just out of reach of the dragon's snapping jaws. His hair was singed on one side, the skin below it raw and burnt. Blood matted his rear legs, but none of the injuries kept him from staring down the dragon as he walked backward in sync with five Eardfolc.

"Otter," Jack said softly; he was about to shout for the dog when Onyx hollered from behind him. "Get over here, Jack. The damn thing will be ready to flame any moment."

The Eardfolc hurled snowballs at the dragon as they backed away. They matched each step the dragon took forward with two steps back of their own. Each group in turn hurled snowballs at the dragon. One man scooped up snow while the other threw it. One snowball flew from the left. The dragon turned left. Two snowballs came in from the right. As the dragon shifted that way, the other side threw again.

The front legs of the dragon had turned a dull green as the snow dampened the fire that enveloped it. It roared as more snowballs hit.

"Ninety seconds," Ellis said, checking his watch.

"Beryl," yelled Ellis from beside Onyx. "Now."

As the dragon shifted its attention to the left once more, an eardfolc wearing a long blue scarf ran in from the right. The figure's hair was dark, wild, and sticking out in all directions, like the wind had tousled it. But what struck Jack most was the eyes: piercing blue, bright, and the clean-shaven face.

A dwarf without a beard, he thought. *He looks more like an elf than a dwarf, like he should be making toys for Christmas or baking cookies inside a tree.*

The figure, Beryl, rolled, came up on one knee, and plunged a long knife between two dull green scales on the dragon's chest. The dragon roared in pain, it pulled away from Beryl, and its head reared back as its attacker rolled away into the snow.

Beryl jumped to his feet and ran, moving to circle the dragon. The beast moved to follow, its front claw stomping into the snow. It roared in fury as it pulled its now flameless claw out of the snow.

"Time's up; everybody out." Ellis screamed as he looked at a silver wristwatch, "It's going to breathe."

The other dwarves ran toward Jack, Otter bounding ahead of them. Jack watched, transfixed, as Beryl ran toward the far side of the little cabin, the dragon's head reared back, then shot forward, and a line of flaming spittle flew toward the eardfolc.

Otter with patches of singed fur around his muzzle and a limp in his back leg, barreled toward Jack with all the joy his body could muster. Before he realized he was moving, Jack dropped to his knees, arms open. Otter slammed into Jack, whining and barking all at once, as if trying to speak. They both toppled back into the snowbank. Otter licked wildly at Jack's face.

Jack wrapped his arms around the dog, burying his face into thick fur that still smelled of smoke and pine.

He did not see if the flame hit Beryl.

"I thought you were dead," he choked, voice breaking. Otter licked his cheek once--slow, deliberate--then rested his head against the man's chest with a long, contented sigh.

The dragon could come. The world could end. But for a pair of heartbeats on that snow-covered glacier, all was right with their world.

39

Onyx watched in horror as the dragon unleashed a torrent of flames that roared towards his cousin. He instinctively moved to rush forward and help, but Ellis's firm grip on his arm stopped him.

"It's okay, he'll be fine. The dragon can only breathe fire every eight minutes. We've got to be out of here before it can flame again. This way." Ellis's voice was steady, his plan clear.

Ellis moved toward the peak. He kept low to keep the snow bank between them and the dragon. Onyx followed. He checked behind him to ensure the two humans followed, then turned to his brother. "The eight-minute thing, you are sure about that," he asked.

"Yep. It's been a heck of a day since you ran off on us, little brother." Ellis said with a smile, his eyes filled with a mix of relief and brotherly affection.

"I didn't run off," Onyx said, "I drew that great beast off of you." Onyx stopped. He threw a hand toward the two humans, "and I brought help."

Beside Onyx, Ellis chuckled, "A lot of help they were. They about got you all roasted in that little stone oven." The dwarves walking around them chuckled.

Onyx felt the heat rise to his face. He'd been wounded; he thought his brother was dead, and they said he abandoned them. His fist clenched around the axe, his muscles tense as he stopped walking, "Why you, I..."

A hand patted his shoulder, "Don't listen to them, Oni. They're trying to wind you up." Opal said as she walked beside him. "You saved us and your brother. If you hadn't led the beast off, we would have been hard-pressed to get to Ellis."

Opal was a wisp of a creature, no taller than Onyx's shoulder but with the presence of a calm meadow. Her wild brown hair was a nest of curls, adorned with tiny flowers and bits of twine, as though she had recently rolled under the pines. Her eyes shone dark and knowing, filled with the quiet wisdom of someone who has seen the wondrous workings of the world. She moved with the weightless grace of a falling leaf.

"Thank you, Opal, it is good to see you safe." Onyx knew she would ask for no thanks and expect none, but he said it anyway

Onyx looked at his brother and, for the first time, realized he was using a thick tree branch as a crutch. His leg was bandaged, wrapped in scraps of cloth and a splint of thin branches. He stopped and looked at the others. All of them had at least one bandage.

Berry's hand was swathed in so many layers of cloth that it looked like he was holding a snowball. With a wave of the bandaged hand, Berry noticed his gaze and said, "Hey, how do you like this? Lost a finger. Now everyone will be able to tell us apart."

Beside him, Bramble punched his shoulder, "Don't be stupid; everyone knows I'm the pretty one." Like Beryl, the twins were beardless, looking more like Santa's elves than dwarfs.

Onyx, used to the twins, ignored their antics and looked at Ellis. "How'd you figure the eight minutes?"

"The creature followed you downslope. It didn't come back until after sunrise. We had moved to the shadow of that spur of rock," Ellis pointed to a large boulder bare of snow that rose out of the wasteland opposite the shelter. "We saw the dragon flame something down near that ski lodge, then head this way," he waved downslope toward the south. Onyx remembered the lodge; they had spent a night there on their way up the mountain. He couldn't believe it had only been three days ago.

Ellis continued, "The dragon dropped down and sniffed around at the path but never moved toward the shelter."

Berry waved his giant bandage, "That's when Bramble realized that the lizard was avoiding the snow."

Bramble raised his hand and smacked his twin on the back of the head, "Quiet, Ellis is talking."

There was a roar from back the way they came.

"We should walk while I fill you in," Ellis said as he moved over the ridge.

"So, we moved onto the snow, and sure enough, it didn't follow. We threw a couple of rocks and riled it up. It tried to cook us, but it never stepped into the snow. It took to the air and tried to fly by roast us. That's when we realized there was a pattern; every eight minutes, it'd return and try again."

Berry leaned forward, "It'd land on the spot it melted last and blow forward like it was clearing a path."

Ellis nodded in agreement, "That's when we decided to bug out."

"That's when we found it," Berry yelled in excitement. Bramble's hand snaked up and smacked the back of his twin's head. "Shhh."

Ellis grinned at Onyx, "Oni, we found the cave entrance. You said it was here, and we found it." The relief in his voice was palpable. A shimmer of hope coursed through Onyx.

Hands patted Onyx's back as those around him congratulated him. Various versions of "you were right" filled his ears.

"While we searched the caves, the twins headed down to look for you." Ellis pointed to Berry, who just grinned until a hand smacked the back of his head.

"Now you can tell him," Bramble said.

"Oh, okay. We followed your tracks down the slope but then heard the dragon in that old campground, so we lay low until we saw it fly off."

Bramble picked up the story, "We saw smoke coming from the area, so we went to investigate. We found this truck that had been torn up and set on fire."

"And we heard a whining coming from the burning truck," Berry said in a rush, "and inside was a dog." The joy in their voices was infectious, spreading a warm feeling of compassion among the group.

"Otter," Onyx said, his voice filled with surprise. The unexpected reunion with the dog filled him with a sense of wonder.

Berry nodded. Hearing his name, Otter ran up and nuzzled at Onyx's shoulder as he walked. Onyx absently reached up and scratched behind the dog's ear.

"He was all beat up and burnt, but we got him out before the truck blew, and then he ran off, and we chased him, and then we saw your boot prints and realized he was following you. Is that your dog? Can we keep him?" both twins asked together.

"He's my dog," Jack said from the back of the group, "Thanks for rescuing him." Jack's mouth turned down as he looked at Onyx and said, "We thought he was killed when the truck went up in flames."

Onyx huffed, then said, "He was caught between the seats when the dragon landed; we couldn't get him out with the dragon standing right over him." Onyx scratched the dog's side, "But he's here, and that's what matters, isn't it?"

Ellis picked up the tale during the awkward silence, "We saw you heading to the shed and were on our way to meet you when the dragon reappeared."

"Yeah," interrupted Berry, "Then Bramble suggested we use the snowballs to distract it, and well, you know the rest."

"What, no mention of my heroic sacrifice?" said a voice ahead of them. Beryl stepped out from behind a high bank of snow. "Gee, what have you got to do around here to get a little respect?"

Onyx greeted his cousin and embraced him in a long hug. "I thought you were toast."

"Naw, no lizard is going to catch me. I ducked around the shelter and rolled down the slope. Circled around and came up that embankment there." Beryl pointed to a long track in the snow downslope.

There was a roar from above. Onyx looked up to see the dragon circling above. The creature paused midair and dove toward the group. "This way," Beryl screamed and pulled at Onyx.

Onyx followed him to another snowbank. A tunnel cut into the snow sloped down into the mountainside.

Ellis dove into the hole, followed by the others. Onyx paused at the lip, not sure what he would find below.

"Go, go, go," Jack yelled behind him.

Onyx clutched his ax and jumped.

40

As Jack disappeared down the hole, Otter whined and sniffed at the opening. Last in line, Ashe dropped down and pulled the giant beast into the hole with her, sending them both into darkness. The smell of burnt hair and wet dog made her gag.

"Dang boy, you need a bath," she said. Otter whined softly; his tail thumped twice against her leg.

They slid forward a few feet. Stalled just inside the lip of the tunnel, Ashe heard the flap of wings. She looked behind her. A dragon wing flapped above the opening as the beast hovered to align itself with the hole. Ashe panicked. She wiggled her backside forward and planted her feet flat on the icy tunnel to pull herself down the chute. The feeling brought back the memory of the time her parents replaced the metal slide in the backyard with a fiberglass one. They said the metal one got too hot in the summer, but the new one never worked as well.

Ashe felt the bottom drop out beneath her as they dropped a dozen feet. She felt her stomach roll as they began hurtling down the slide. The dog whined in the darkness as they shot forward like a ride at an amusement park.

There was a roar behind her. A blast of flame filled the tunnel. Heat wafted over them as they plummeted ahead of the fire.

The narrow slide twisted and turned as it became steeper, then leveled out only to pitch steeper again. The others were lost to sight in the darkness as the slide shifted around several snakelike turns. Ashe held tight to Otter. The dog no longer whined; its face was now inches from Ashe's, and its eyes stared into hers as if to say she had its complete trust. Otter's tongue flicked out and slapped across Ashe's chin and cheek.

"Ugh, Dog germs," she said. The dog's tail smacked against her toes as the dog leaned in for another lick.

Ashe looked into Otter's eyes, "No. Do not do that again," she said.

The dog whined, and then its tongue flicked out. Ashe felt the warm, wet tongue travel across her face again. "Ugh! Do that again, and I will let you go down this thing alone," she said, pushing forward on the dog's chest as if to push him down in front of her. Otter laid his head on her shoulder, knocking the breath from her with his weight.

Ashe scratched the dog behind the ears, her current predicament forgotten momentarily.

Yells and whoops reached her from below as the slope leveled out, and their speed began to slow. A light grew in the tunnel. Jack slid out of the chute a dozen yards ahead and stood, only to fall as his feet slid out beneath him.

As Ashe reached the tunnel exit, hands appeared on either side of the opening. Opal and Berry grabbed her by the arms and lifted her to her feet, holding her steady on the icy floor of the frozen cave. Otter slid out into the middle of the room. He slammed into Jack as he tried to stand, and they both slipped to the ice. The eardfolc's shared laughter echoed through the cavern.

"Welcome to the center of the mountain," Berry said as Ashe stood.

They were deep in the heart of the mountain, in a cave below the glacier with walls and stone floors covered in shimmering ice. Stalactites, covered in icicles frozen mid-drip, hung like rows of teeth from the ceiling above. The air flickered with red light. Thin cracks of glowing crimson spread through the frozen floor like tree roots. They all converged at a fiery pool on the far side of the cavern where a spur of rock thrust up from the frozen floor. A shining sword poked out of it like Excalibur; its blade thrust deep into the stone beside the pool of fire. The otherworldly stillness of the cavern was broken only by the voices of the dwarves as Ashe took in the scene around them.

Across the room, Ellis stood with Jack and Onyx in front of a giant curtain of ice that blocked access to the magma pool and sword. Onyx held a burning torch; its light seemed weak and inferior to the bright red light shining through the ice below them.

"Where are we?" Ashe asked.

"Depends on who you ask," replied Berry. "Opal thinks we are in the center of the mountain. If so, it should be a lot hotter. Beryl thinks we are at the glacier's heart, but why the stone walls? Personally, I think we've passed into the underworld and are doomed never to leave." The short man grinned up at Ashe.

Ashe grinned down at him. "Ellis said you found this place before, so you've already left once." She waved one hand toward the pile of packs and remains of a fire that stood on one side of the room.

Berry shrugged, leaned in conspiratorially, and whispered, "Yeah, but maybe that was just to lull us into a sense of complacency so we would return with more people." He waggled his eyebrows as he said it, and Ashe could not help but laugh.

Berry pointed to the pile of packs. "We had to break out the climbing gear." He pointed to the far side of the cavern. "The wall there goes to a crevasse nearly two hundred meters of sheer ice wall up. Ever climbed the center of a glacier?"

Bramble walked up and smacked Berry on the back of the head. "Stop being an idiot." Bramble pointed to a dark shadow of a tunnel leading off one side of the room, "That tunnel goes up to the surface; it's steep, but it can be walked and puts us out and far above the snowline where that slide was."

Ashe looked at him, amazed, "How'd you have time to dig that slide in, what, a day since you lost Onyx?"

"We didn't. It's how we found the cave," Bramble said. "Idjit here," he smacked Berry on the back of the head. Berry just grinned and waggled his eyebrows again, "Fell down it. That one", he jerked a thumb at the shadowy exit, "was blocked with snow at the top, but it only took us a few hours to dig out."

Berry's face turned serious, his eyebrows creased together, and he intoned in a deep, serious tone.

"The Tuatha De Danann has blessed me, for I have found the Icenforge. Fame and fortune will follow me all my days. I shall be known as Berry the Discoverer!"

Bramble smacked the back of his head again, and Berry's grin returned. "Berry the Clumsy is more like it. You aren't blessed. You tripped and fell in a hole."

Berry stuck his tongue out at his brother, "You're just mad you didn't find it."

"Idjit," Bramble sneered as he stormed away.

Ashe looked at Berry, a sad smile twisted her face, "Why do you let him hit you like that?" she asked.

Berry looked toward his brother. Bramble moved to the old campfire and began putting wood from one of the packs into it.

Berry lowered his voice, saying, "I don't mind too much. My brother is there when I need him, and that's what matters."

Ashe thought about it a bit. She shook her head. "That's not right, though; You shouldn't let him hit you. No one should demean someone they love. "

Berry set a hand on Ashe's arm, "If I thought there was an ounce of spite or meanness in my brother, I would agree. I know it's just how he shows his love."

Ashe winced as she remembered similar words she had used about Phil. *Is a brother different than a lover,* she thought. Nothing justifies placing your hands on someone else. But she knew from experience that simply saying that would not change anything. Berry would have to find his way through his relationship; all anyone could do was be ready and willing to help when he did.

Ashe clasped Berry's hand in both of hers. "Demeaning someone isn't love; it's control. You deserve better than that." She dropped his hand and moved toward Jack and Ellis.

Her feet slipped out from under her. Berry's arm grabbed hers and kept her from dropping to the ground.

"Careful, the floor is pretty much made of ice. It's a bit tricky to get around." He pointed his free hand at her feet. "Slide your feet; don't pick them up. Kinda like skating only without the skates."

Ashe nodded, "Thank you, Berry," she said as she slowly slid toward Jack and Onyx.

Berry nodded and looked over at his brother, his perpetual grin gone.

41

Jack, Onyx, and Ellis stood before a thick wall of ice that blocked passage to the pool of fire and the sword.

"So there really is a magic sword. You two aren't crazy." Ashe said.

"That's yet to be seen", Ellis said.

"So that's the Icenforge," she said, her voice tinged with curiosity and wonder.

Startled, Jack turned toward her, his eyes wide with curiosity, "The Icenforge," he asked, his voice tinged with suspicion.

"That's it," Ellis said, his voice carrying the weight of centuries, "Forge of the Winter King."

"I think I skipped a chapter," Jack said. He turned to Ashe, "You knew about this place."

"No, Berry just gave me the name."

Jack nodded, "Okay, so what is this place, and what's with the sword in the stone there?" he asked as they turned back to Ellis.

Onyx spoke from beside his brother. "It's the sword I was telling you about. Iismid, the Frostforged Blade. It's the way to slay the dragon."

Bramble came up behind them. When Onyx did not continue, he said, "The Icenforge was used to create the elements of creation, Fire, Earth, Water, Air, and Spirit. When the first Eardfolc came to this land, they were menaced by creatures of the desert to the South. The Winter King forged a magical sword with the powers of Spirit and Water to combat the fire creatures."

"Emberkin", Ellis said. He spat on the floor as if the word left a bad taste in his mouth.

Onyx nodded and continued, "King Villnar and his people fought to stop the creep of the desert lands. The sword was held in our family for generations until the debacle at Mount St Helens, where it was lost."

"Debacle?" Ashe asked.

"The dragon attempted to make its nest there," Jack said.

"Our kin fought to stop it," said Onyx. "The King was betrayed. He fell, and the remaining warriors fought among themselves to possess the sword. Ultimately, they defeated the dragon but not before the volcano erupted; many lives were lost, and the tribes were fractured."

Ellis picked up the tale, "Iismid was lost in the chaos and has not been seen since."

"Until now," Onyx said as he pointed at the sword in the stone. "I knew it would be here. Returned to where it was forged until it should be needed again."

"I'm confused," Ashe said, "If the sword was lost, how is it here?"

Ellis and Onyx exchanged a look.

"What?" Ashe asked.

Ellis stared through the ice wall at the sword as he spoke. "Our eldest brother was with the Winter King; he saw the power struggle that erupted after his fall. He feared a civil war among the clans. He told everyone it was buried under the magma." The small man grew quiet, his head low. "He must have returned it here."

"I told you he lied," Onyx said. His fists were clenched. He shook a fist at the ice wall. "I knew he was hiding it. He never directly talked about it, his travels, or his time on the mountain."

Ellis's head snapped up. His eyes fixed on his brother. "He did what he thought was best. That's all any of us can do. Do you think he

223

could have ruled the council? At that early age? Would they have listened? Those old men who care only for their personal power. Or would there have been war among us anyway?" He threw up his hands and yelled, "Yes, you were right. Will you lord it over us now? Crow about how our brother betrayed the clans, how you knew all along."

Jack flinched at the palpable anger in Ellis's voice. The tension in the air was thick, and it was impossible to ignore the strain on their relationship.

Jack saw a flicker of pain cross Ellis's face, betraying the storm of emotions he kept bottled up. Neither one wanted to admit how much the other's belief hurt. Instead, they let it gnaw at them, keeping them apart even as they stood side by side. Onyx bowed his head, unable to make eye contact with his brother.

Seeing his friend so dejected, Jack reached out and placed a hand on Onyx's shoulder.

"I am sure he chose correctly. The sword would not be here for us now if not for him."

Onyx looked up and nodded. "You're right." He looked at his brother. "I am sorry, Ellis. I did not mean to speak ill of the dead."

Jack reached out and wrapped a knuckle on the ice wall before them.

The knock echoed through the chamber. It seemed to resonate within the stone walls. The echo became a low rumble as Jack looked up at the ceiling and wondered if the entire glacier would come crashing down around them.

The ice that covered the wall on one side of the room shattered. It rained down in broken shards. Jack watched, expecting the ice to smash to pieces as it hit the ground. Instead, each piece seemed drawn to a single spot in the center of the room. They tumbled down and began spiraling through the air until they landed in a pile. As Jack watched, the pile shifted. It moved. Each piece of shattered ice slid into place and reformed into a smooth pile of ice. It stirred. An arm formed and reached out from the pile. It pressed down on the chamber floor as a knee emerged. The entire pile shifted. Then stood.

Jack stared as the largest ice sculpture he had ever imagined rose from the pile. A giant man in a kilt and knee-high boots carved of ice stood before them. Light gleamed from the smooth, bare chest of ice.

Arnold, eat your heart out, he thought, remembering the old Conan movies Jill loved so much.

The ice giant was three times as tall as Jack. Its head was just below the stalactites hanging from the ceiling. It reached up and pulled a hanging stalactite from the ceiling. The room was filled with the crackling and splintering sound of glass breaking as the ice-covered stone broke away, and a giant club was now in the hands of a giant made of ice.

It raised its club and stared down at them.

The club hurtled toward Ashe.

Jack was frozen in place. Ashe screamed.

42

The sound of shattered glass filled the chamber, but Onyx continued to stare through the curtain of ice. Beyond it was the sword they had come so far to claim. They had risked the cold and the fires on the mountain, battled and evaded the dragon, been injured, burned, and beaten, all to find this sword. All to prove himself worthy. He had endangered himself, his brother, his cousins, and two perfect strangers in the thin hope that the sword would be here. He had no proof the sword would be here, yet here it was. He had found it.

He had. He was right. It was here. Iismid, the historic blade of the Winter King, for millennia. The sword that granted its bearer the leadership of the Winter Court.

He had found it.

The sword would be his.

Another crash of breaking ice filled the air. No one screamed or called for help, so Onyx was not too worried. He had been right. His brother had returned the sword to the glacier. Now, Onyx would bring it out from under the ice and unite his people. All he needed to do was find a way through the ice curtain before him.

He ran his hands along the ice. It was perfectly smooth and perfectly clear. No cracks, bubbles, imperfections, or haze marked it.

If he took a few steps back, he couldn't tell it was there.

He leaned his weight into it. It was solid. His eyes scanned the edges of the curtain where the ice met the stone of the cavern walls. The curtain melded seamlessly into the ice-covered stone. No gaps, crevices, or seams showed at the edges. He reached down and lifted the axe. He gripped the handle and raised it to slam into the curtain. Behind him, Ashe screamed.

Onyx turned. The ginger girl stood face to belt buckle with a giant sculpted from ice.

An ice elemental.

Onyx kicked himself mentally.

Of course, the sword had protection. Why wouldn't it?

He looked up at the towering creature as it raised its club above its head and brought it down on the girl.

Jack leaped across the space between them and tackled Ashe just as a gigantic stone club slammed into the space she was standing in. The two rolled against the far wall as the elemental lifted its club off the floor and turned to follow them.

Ellis ran forward. He waved the torch above his head and yelled to get the elemental's attention. He slammed the torch against its back. The flame sputtered and died as it hit the slab of ice. The elemental spun from the hip. It's club smashed into Ellis, knocking him into the air and sending him flying into a stalactite. With a loud "Oof," Ellis collapsed to the cavern's floor, unmoving.

"No". Onyx roared. He gripped his axe and flung himself forward. All his wounds of the last day forgotten as he charged into battle. With an overhand swing, he brought the axe down on the wrist that held the club. There was a loud clunk. A chunk of ice the size of Onyx's hand flew from the elemental's wrist. The creature howled and swung the club back again. It struck Onyx square in the chest. The air blew from Onyx's lungs. He felt himself lifted as the force of the club knocked him across the room. He smashed into the curtain of ice. Every nerve in his body screamed in pain as he slid to the floor. He tried to inhale, but he couldn't. His vision blurred. Time slowed around him as he watched the elemental stalk toward him.

Beryl moved behind the giant elemental. He shifted his feet like a skater as he leaned his weight from one foot to the other, skating across the ice-covered floor. His long knife flicked out as he passed the elemental's legs.

Suddenly, Beryl held a broken knife hilt in his hand. A ding sounded as the fractured blade fell to the ice.   The elemental shifted its weight to one leg and kicked out with the other. Unlike Beryl, the creature did not slide on the ice-covered floor; it melded to it. One enormous leg merged into the ice floor as the other lashed out and slammed into Beryl. The bald man went flying.

Berry and Bramble charged the elemental. Bramble slammed a climbing axe from their gear into one leg as he skated by. Berry used it to climb toward the elemental's back and hammered a piton into it. The elemental swung around wildly, trying to dislodge the Eardfolc on its back. Bramble climbed up after his brother. They hammered more pitons into the elemental as they used them to climb to its shoulders. In moments, one brother sat on each of the elemental's shoulders. Together, they raised their ice axes. They each set a piton against the elemental's neck and hammered it in.

With a scream that shook the cavern, the elemental grabbed both eardfolc from his shoulders and pulled them away. The elemental slammed the brothers together and threw them across the room.

Onyx wheezed in a breath. He tried to rise. Pain scorched across his back and shoulders.

The elemental turned toward Onyx.

Opal and Flint skated into view. Each held the end of a long length of rope. The two skated around the elemental, passing each other as they wrapped the rope around the creature's calves. Startled, the ice elemental looked down and growled. It reached down, grabbed the rope, and pulled. The thick climbing rope pulled apart like a string. Opal was pulled sideways into the back of the ice giant's legs. The rope wrapped tightly around Flint's wrist; as the giant pulled the rope up, Flint went with it.

The ice creature held Flint dangling inches from its mouth. It opened its mouth and leaned forward to bite him in half. Opal reached up and cut the rope away. In the same stroke, her small knife flew out and stuck into the ice creature's nose. Flint fell to the ground. He landed on the ice-covered stone, the breath knocked out of him. Opal skated past, grabbed her cousin, and pulled him behind a stalagmite as the monster pulled the knife from its face. The ice elemental scanned the room. When it did not see its tiny tormentor, it moved toward Jack and Ashe.

Onyx inhaled. Pain stabbed into his side. He tried to rise. A grinding flash of pain streaked through him. He dropped back to the floor. His next breath was less painful, but any attempt to shift his weight sent lances of pain through his chest. *Great,* he thought, *probably broken ribs.* He coughed and spat on the floor beside him. He wiped his mouth with the back of his hand, then looked at it.

No blood. Good, he thought, probably don't have a punctured lung. He shifted to the side as he watched Jack stand above Ashe, shuffle on the slick floor, and face the elemental.

"Move you, idjit," Onyx yelled.

43

Jack stood and faced the approaching behemoth.

He scanned the room. There was nothing nearby he could defend himself with. He balled his empty fists. The idea of going bare-fisted against a giant made of ice was ridiculous, and he knew it. If only he had not put the shotgun down. He could see it across the room, leaning against the ice curtain.

The giant stalked toward him. It was an impressive creature. Eighteen feet tall, sculpted like Mister Universe, Jack marveled at the high detail etched into its features. The face sported wrinkles and laugh lines so minute that Jack could not believe he wasn't looking at a real person. The details were incredible, from the wrinkle-creased skin to the fringe of the knee-high boots that looked like white fur. Strands of individual hair seemed to splay away from the solid mound of ice on the creature's head as if it had just rolled out of bed. The detail was so consistent and vivid that if not for the sheen of ice, Jack would have sworn it was an actual person. Even the creature's kilt showed the individual patterns of thread strands in fabric.

Wonder if he's wearing that thing regimental, Jack's rebellious mind thought.

His thought was interrupted by a scream from Onyx. "Move you idjet."

Jack snapped out of his reverie as the giant swung its massive ice club down. Jack dove to one side, rolled, and came up running. His feet swung out from underneath him. He had forgotten about the ice-slick floor. He landed hard on his back and watched as a gigantic ice club swished past his nose. Jack rolled to one side. Above him, the giant's sandaled foot hurtled toward him. Jack rolled again. The giant nearly stepped on Jack as it recovered from its missed swing. Jack knew he could not stand on the slick ice fast enough to escape the giant. He needed a better plan. As the giant lifted its other foot to stomp down on him, Jack kicked both feet out; they struck the giant's foot and propelled him across the ice.

His slide slammed him into the ice curtain. He scrambled to his feet, picked up the shotgun, and thumbed the safety. He turned toward the approaching giant. His feet slid wildly on the ice, and he fell to his back once more.

The giant raised its club. Jack spun himself, kicked off the ice curtain, and slid on his back between the giant's legs. He pointed the shotgun up and pulled the trigger as he passed. The shotgun roar echoed through the cavern.

The giant let out a scream that shook several stalactites loose. They broke away from the ceiling and crashed to the ground. The giant collapsed to its knees, its hands cradled between its legs. Jack winced.

I guess that's my answer.

Jack got to his feet. He shuffled forward, raised the shotgun to the giant's head, and pulled the trigger.

The giant's head snapped to the side as the slug smashed into it. Pieces of ice were blown away, and a huge hole appeared in the giant's head. The giant head straightened; it turned to face him. Jack's blood ran cold as he watched the ice around the hole melt and slowly fill the gap until the head was once more whole.

Not again, he thought.

With no other option, Jack pointed at the giant and pulled the trigger.

"Click." The hammer fell on an empty chamber.

"Shit."

Jack backpedaled, skating backward on the slippery floor as he removed the shotgun magazine.

In one smooth motion, he dropped the empty magazine, pulled a new one from his jacket pocket, loaded it, and racked a round.

Setting one hand on the floor, the giant braced itself and stood.

Jack did not bother to aim. The creature was so close he could not miss.

Jack screamed and pulled the trigger. Flame erupted from the shotgun as the white phosphorus round ignited. A bright fountain of white-hot sparks flew toward the giant. Tiny, crackling embers shimmered and flickered toward the beast, creating a halo of light that hissed and fizzed out of the shotgun barrel.

The cone of flaming sparks struck the giant in the thigh. Ice shards were blown from the creature's leg. The flames quickly died as the superheated pellets melted their way into the ice. The giant stood and staggered back, its leg struggling to support its weight. It turned to face Jack. It raised its club.

Jack pulled the trigger. Five thousand degrees of flaming shot melted its way into the giant's kneecap. The giant dropped to the ground. Its club landed next to Jack as he pulled the trigger again. And again. And again.

Jack emptied the entire magazine of white phosphorus rounds into the giant of ice. Chunks of flying ice cut into Jack as massive, melted holes appeared in the creature's body.

The shotgun clicked on an empty chamber as echoes of the shotgun's roar died away.

The ice giant lay still.

Jack poked the barrel of the shotgun into the giant. The hot barrel sizzled as it made contact. The giant did not move. The creature began to shrink as it melted into the ice-covered floor.

"That was impressive," Ashe said as she stepped beside him.

"Modern solutions for mythical problems. That's my specialty."

"What was that?"

"Phosphorus shells. I use them at the ranch to start bonfires. Guess they work just as well to melt ice."

"Looks like," Onyx said as he joined them. He was soaking wet.

"What'd you do, take a bath," Jack asked.

"Shower is more like it. When that thing melted, so did the ice wall." He lifted his drenched arms and shook them. Droplets of water splashed around the trio. Onyx winced and grabbed his chest. "I think I broke a rib."

"The sword," Jack said as he looked toward the magma pool.

The way was open. The ice curtain was gone. Only a puddle of water now lay between them and the sword.

"Your prize awaits, Onyx."

Onyx winced again and nodded.

44

Onyx splashed forward to seize the blade of his grandsire. The crystalline hilt glowed red in the flames of the magma pool beside it. He reached out. His hand passed through the sword's hilt as if it were made of water. He felt a thin resistance, but when he closed his fist, he felt nothing, as if the sword had turned to smoke in his hand.

No, he thought, *this doesn't make sense. The guardian is dead; the sword is mine.*

"I am Onyx, son of Flinthar Eisenhart. Rightful bearer of Iismid," he said.

The crystal sword sparkled in the red glow of the cavern as if in response.

Onyx reached out for the sword once more. Again, his hand passed through it.

Onyx felt a hand on his shoulder; Ellis spoke behind him. "The sword does not seem to want to leave."

He chooses his words carefully, Onyx thought. *He doesn't want to admit the truth. I am not worthy.*

"What's going on?" Jack said.

Berry whispered, "The sword doesn't recognize Onyx as its bearer."

A quiet mumble of disbelief rustled through the group.

"This can't be; Onyx is the rightful leader of the Ienheid. He should lead our people by right of bloodline, and the sword should recognize this," Flint said.

"Aye," said Berry, "but Ellis is the Eldest."

Beside him, Bramble raised his hand to smack Berry but dropped it instead. "Yes, the sword may only recognize the eldest blood relative." Onyx watched as Ashe smiled and winked at Berry. He wondered what that was about, but his cousin's words sank in.

Onyx could not breathe. He blamed the broken ribs but knew deep in his heart it was the shattering of his dreams. He had fought hard to convince his cousins that the sword was real and attainable. He had traveled with them in a desperate race to find and claim the sword. Now they had found it, and it was still out of their reach, out of his reach. The group's disappointment was palpable, each struggling to come to terms with the sword's rejection.

Was he truly unworthy? Was his whole purpose only to get this far and fail, or worse? Would he watch someone else claim his father's sword and throne? Would that be worse, he wondered. *Was he doing this for himself or his people? Was he the best choice to lead the Ienheid,* he thought. Not if he was doing this out of some selfish pride. The Ienheid needs a true leader, not a vainglorious poser too buried in his own interests to help his people. He stood for a long moment, staring at the sparkling crystalline sword hilt. *Is my way the best way for my people,* he thought. After a moment of reflection, he had to admit to himself that his way was not the only one. Others were as dedicated, competent, and passionate about the tribe's success as he was.

With a shaky breath, Onyx stepped away from the sword.

"Ellis," he whispered, "claim the sword. It is your birthright, after all."

Ellis shook his head, "No, brother, this is your triumph. You claim the sword and the throne. You led us here; you shall lead the Ienheid. I do not want it."

Onyx smiled. "Which may be why the sword finds you worthier than I."

The shock and desperation on Ellis's face warmed Onyx's heart. His brother honestly did not want the sword or the responsibilities that came with it. Ellis looked at his brother, and Onyx smiled reassuringly. "Take the sword, brother. Regardless of what you face, know that I will always be by your side."

Ellis wrapped an arm around Onyx's shoulder and squeezed. "And I at yours,' brother."

Ellis walked up to the sword. He reached out, and his hand passed through the ethereal handle of the blade.

"Welp, there goes that idea," Berry said with a grin. "Who's next?" He looked around at his cousins and waggled his eyebrows.

Those around him laughed nervously. Each looked at the other, and then they all looked at Onyx.

Onyx could only imagine what went through their minds. *Which of them had ever considered ruling the Ienheid? A better question might be which of them had not.* They were all technically of Villnar's blood. Each of them had a blood claim on the throne, maybe not as strong as the direct descendants of Villnar, but a blood tie stronger than anyone now serving on the Ienheid.

Onyx resigned himself to the reality of the sword's choice. Some aspects of their character prevented the sword from acknowledging them. For him, it was surely his ambition. He had driven the others on this quest, hoping to get the sword and become king, but what of Ellis? His brother had no flaw, Onyx could see. If anyone was a bastion of honor and loyalty, it was Ellis. If he was not enough, which of them was?

Onyx sighed and looked toward his cousins. All of them had proven themselves on this adventure.

Onyx considered his cousins as they stared at him and waited for his word.

Beryl is fearless in the face of danger, always ready to act, and never backs down from a challenge. His determination always inspired others to push forward, no matter the odds. His bravery and resilience would make him a strong leader.

Flint's calm demeanor and analytical mind made him an excellent problem-solver. His plans always seemed to work out.

Berry's playful nature and sense of humor keep spirits high, even in challenging situations. His infectious optimism made him a joy to be around, even if Onyx would never tell him so.

Bramble, who, with his deep sense of justice, was so protective of family and friends. He was often the group's moral compass. He always led them down the most ethical path.

Opal, the peacekeeper, her empathy made her incredibly kind and supportive. She was always there to listen and offer quiet, thoughtful advice. Onyx could not recall any bad advice he had ever received from her.

Their loyalty and dedication to the tribe were unquestionable. If neither he nor his brother could wield the sword, he would be happy to serve any of these Eardfolc.

Onyx nodded. "Well, which of you is going to step up?"

45

When Bramble lowered his hand without smacking the back of Berry's head, Ashe grinned. She caught Berry's eye and winked at him. It might not have been the best time. They were all so wrapped up in claiming the sword that she did not think they noticed the deep red blush that blossomed on Berry's face and neck.

From what she could tell from the conversation, the sword not only could defeat the dragon, but like Excalibur, it granted kingship to its bearer. It seemed like a silly basis for a system of government to her, but bucking cultural norms outside her own seemed presumptuous, so she kept her thoughts to herself.

She watched as the five cousins approached the sword and attempted to claim it. Each one looked to Ellis, then Onyx, as if waiting for their approval like some pre-arraigned ritual. At a nod from Onyx, each of them, in turn, reached out to grasp the sword.

She had known these people for less than an hour, yet she felt like they had been her companions for years. Each of them showed a spark of amazing personality that made her want to be a part of their lives. There was a natural rhythm to their interactions as if they had fallen into step without ever having to find the beat. She had friends like that once, before Phil. Friends that she had slowly pulled away from, until it was just the two of them.   For a moment, Ashe wondered if that was by design, if Phil had isolated her from friends who might have seen what was happening and tried to stop it. She shook the thought off. There was no point in wallowing in past mistakes; you take their lessons and move forward. She knew that, but her vicious mind kept pulling her back, trying to make her relive the hardest times of her life.

Instead, she considered the cousins. Onyx's steady presence made her feel safe, while Berry's lighthearted jokes lifted a tension she had not realized she had been carrying. These were the kind of people who formed lasting bonds.

She looked around at the excited eardfolc. Even Onyx, rejected by the prize he had strove so hard for, had a thin smile on his face, hope for the success of one of his own. Ashe had a strong feeling that among these people she would always be welcomed and protected.

She looked at Jack standing to one side, alone in a group of bustling people. She felt for him. He seemed to be as broken as she was, unable or unwilling to trust enough to let people in, an outsider in any group he tried to attach himself to. She considered going over and thanking him for saving her life. After all, he had thrown himself across her when the Ice Elemental was charging her. She could still feel the strength and warmth of his arms around her as they lay on the ice, and the scent of him--pine, leather, and a hint of singed hair--had flooded her nostrils.

He looked so forlorn and lonely off to the side of the group; she wanted to comfort him. A part of her hesitated. After Phil, could she even trust her feelings?

Her judgment had been so wrong then; how could she trust it now? She barely knew any of them, yet it didn't matter. She wanted to contribute, belong, and do what she could to make their plans work out. Deep down, she yearned for a connection like the one they shared. She wanted to be a part of what they had, even if that meant facing a fire-breathing dragon. Their close bonds of undeniable friendship were something she knew she was missing in her life.

Onyx might be unable to take the sword, but the others were no less worthy. From what she could see, each of them would make a great leader, and any group would be better if they were in it.

Onyx's audacious dream of finding the sword and defeating the dragon had rallied his cousins, persuading them to seek the sword. Ellis's loyalty to his brother set him apart from most of the men Ashe had encountered. When everything seemed lost, he organized the cousins to attack and distract the dragon, allowing them to escape. Yet, despite their dedication, the sword somehow deemed them each unworthy. *Or had it,* she thought. *Was it that they were unfit to wield the sword, or that someone else was more worthy?*

Ashe considered the cousins: Beryl, who stabbed a fiery dragon to distract it so his cousins could escape; Opal, the peacekeeper; and the brothers Berry and Bramble, whose camaraderie was palpable, warming the air around them as they joked and made fun of each other.

The two stepped up to the sword. Bramble's hand rose in its habitual action but never landed. Instead, he nodded to Berry, "Idjets first," he said.

Berry bowed and swept one hand out toward the sword in invitation. "By all means, go first, then." Bramble harrumphed as the eardfolc around him laughed. He stomped toward the sword. Ashe wondered if he would trample his brother beneath his new authority if he were successful. Or was Berry right, and Bramble was as dedicated to his brother as Berry was to him? Bramble's hand passed through the sword.

Berry's smile wavered as his brother returned to his side. He swallowed as he looked at his expectant cousins. When he did not make a move to retrieve the sword, Bramble poked him in the back. "Get moving. We don't have all day, and it's getting warm here."

Ashe realized she was no longer shivering. It was warmer. The thick layer of ice that covered the floor was gone. She frowned. The slick, solid surface was now soft and mushy beneath her feet. It felt like she was standing on wet cement. Her eyes traced the path of steam flowing up around the crimson cracks in the floor, as the red light melted the ice and evaporated the water.

What would happen once the ice was gone?

The thought made her uneasy. A chill raced down Ashley's spine as inexplicable energy crackled around her like a premonition of troubles to come.

Anticipation hung in the air like early morning mist. Everyone held their breath as Berry approached the sword. Each step he took toward the Icenforge resonated with the weight of their shared hopes. Berry paused in front of the weapon; his expression was a mix of determination and trepidation. Ashe could feel the tension in the air; each of the eardfolc balanced on a razor-thin line of hope as Berry moved forward. The closer he got, the more Ashley felt the electric pull of terror tugging at her. She wanted to reach out, to stop him, yet something held her back, a desire to let him make this choice for himself. She clenched her fists, willing the outcome to be positive.

Berry's ever-present smile was gone. His face was a mask of seriousness as the weight of the moment pressed down on him. Sweat beaded his forehead, pooled on his brow, and ran down his temples--*nervousness, or was it just the heat?*

Berry moved to grab the sword. His hand passed through the handle. Rejected like the others. He sighed, and his smile returned as he moved back to stand beside his brother.

"Well, that sucked," he said.

46

Jack watched the dwarves as they tried to pull the sword from the stone. He stepped up beside Ashe. His feet splashed in water; small ripples spread across the cave. The ice that had once covered the entire room had melted, leaving a six-inch-deep pool of water on the floor. He hated wet feet, and cold, damp feet were the worst. He wiggled his toes, expecting a chill to run through him, but the water wasn't cold. It was warm. Jack bent and ran his fingers through the water. It wasn't warm like a summer lake; it was hot tub warm and felt like it was getting hotter. He looked across the cavern and saw steam curls rising off the surface. He straightened, ready to point it out, but something in the air had shifted. He realized the eardfolc had all turned toward him and Ashe.

"What," he said.

"We are the last two," Ashe said.

"The last two what?"

"The last two of the group that made it here," Onyx said, "you must try for the sword."

Jack laughed, "No thanks. I've no wish to be King under the mountain or whatever."

"The sword bearer is the Winter King, not just to those under the mountain. All the people of the Winter Court would bow to the will of the Winter King." Flint said.

"You said Villnar was eardfolc king."

"King of the Eardfolc, but also Winter King, Leader of the Winter Court."

"Winter Court," Jack said.

"The Sidhe are led by four royals, each responsible for certain tribes of Fae. The Eardfolc served the Winter Court. We followed the Winter King, but the last Winter King died, and the sword disappeared so that no one could replace him." Opal said.

"Shee," Jack asked.

"Have you ever read a book?" Ashe said, "The Sidhe, the Fae, Fairies. Come on. Didn't you read Shakespeare in high school? Midsummer's Dream and all that."

Jack just shook his head. "The only thing I remember reading was The Giver." He paused a few seconds, then exclaimed, "And Brave New World,"

Ashe sighed. "Where did you go to school?" she seemed exasperated. What was the big deal? It was not like he ever needed to know any of this stuff before today.

"So, fairies, elves, and such," Jack said.

Ellis shook his head as Onyx threw up his hands and turned away.

"No," Berry said, "and yes. Elves are people of the Fae. As are nyads and sprites. The Sidhe are all the people of the elements, Earth, Air, Water, Fire, and Spirit."

"Well," said Jack, "I don't want to be King of the Fairies either."

"Not all the fairies," Ellis clarified, "just the tribes of the Winter Court: the Eardfolc, the Selkie.

"Even the gremlins," Opal interjected, venom dripping from her voice. Beside her, Flint reached out and placed a hand on her shoulder.

"All the people of the Winter Court will bow to you." Berry continued, "All will look to you for guidance and protection as their Winter King," he explained, highlighting the Winter King's leadership over the various tribes of the Winter Court.

"No pressure then," Jack said with a shake of his head.

He thought Onyx was nuts when he met him, but now he was beginning to believe he was the one who was crazy. *I'm dead,* he thought. *Doesn't that make more sense? There was no dragon. I crashed the truck, and this is what my mind has made up to entertain me while I die. I'm lying on the side of the road somewhere, bleeding out as this crazy dream goes on. Yeah, that's got to be it.*

This can't be real. I must be dead. He said the last four words aloud.

Beside him, Ashe laughed. "Yeah, I thought the same when I saw that dragon. I must have died in that tree, or maybe my parachute didn't open, and I'm lying on the ground, broken and dying."

Jack started as she repeated the words that had just gone through his mind.

"But I figure," she continued, "I'm here, I'm in the middle of it, so let's see where it goes." She looked up at the sword and then back at Jack. She smiled. "When else will I get a chance to become queen?"

Ashe marched up to the sword, reached her hand out, and hesitated. She looked back at the group watching her. "Silly basis for a government," she said as she stepped up to the Icenforge.

"Long live the Queen," Berry shouted, his perpetual smile back in place. Ashe reached out to grasp the sword. Her hand passed through it.

All eyes turned to Jack. "Me, really," he asked.

"Makes sense," Bramble said, "You pretty much took that Ice Elemental down all on your lonesome; we weren't much help. You defeated the sword's champion, which makes you King by conquest."

"So, I...," Jack said, "I beat the bad guy, and I become King, like William at Hastings?"

"How do you know William the Conqueror but not Faerie?" Ashe said.

Before Jack could respond, Onyx interrupted. "Yeah, sure, just like that," said Onyx, "now pull the dang sword, and let's get out of here. I'm sweltering."

Onyx was right; it was getting hot. The once-frozen fortress now exhaled waves of heat. The water flowing from the melting ice covering the stalagmites now hissed and steamed on the floor. As he watched, it began to bubble and simmer, as if something deeper and more dangerous stirred beneath the surface.

Jack's heart pounded with each step as he walked up to the sword. The crystal handle pulsed with light; it glowed brighter as he got closer. By the time he was in arm's reach, the radiance was blinding. He had to squint as he extended his hand. His fingers hovered over the shining blade; they trembled with the weight of the moment. As his hand made contact, a brilliant flash exploded from the sword.

The room was flooded with light. Energy surged through him like a bolt of lightning. He felt the solid leather grip of the sword in his hand. He felt the weight of the blade as he spun it upright. He held the sword straight out in front of him. The balance was perfect. With a flourish, he stabbed the sword toward the ceiling as the room around him dissolved into blackness.

47

Jack stood on a tapestry of stars. Beneath him, behind him, above him, and before him, an endless universe of stars spread as far as he could see. His feet felt firmly planted on stone, yet there was nothing below but star-filled blackness. His head spun as he realized he was in space. He looked down. He felt like he should be falling, but there was no sensation of movement, just him standing in the dead of space. Panic rushed through him. *Space is a vacuum,* he thought; *I might not be falling, but...* Jack inhaled. His lungs filled. He exhaled. There was air. He was not in space, or space was not what he had been taught it was. The sudden terror of falling or suffocating passed.

Jack took a better look around. No star was close enough to call a sun. No planets were in view. No swirls of galaxies. No cloudy nebula of new solar systems. No recognizable constellations. Only stars, bright pinpricks of light in the black cloth of space, each holding its own enigmatic story.

Two of the stars shifted. They rolled around each other in a slow dance of light as they began to move toward him. With growing speed, they moved closer. They grew larger with each passing moment until they blazed before him. Orbs the size of small cars soon hung on each side of him. The one to his right blazed like the fires of the sun, while the one on the left, behind and lower than the other, flickered and pulsed like a strobe light synced to a heartbeat.

Suddenly, the star on the right blazed with a brilliant flash, and a deep and resonant voice boomed through the void.

"Welcome, Swordbearer," the voice said; the star flashed then dimmed with each word. "New Winter King of the Sidhe."

"The Tuatha De Danann bid you welcome," a second feminine voice said as the left star flashed in time to the words.

"Tuatha De Danann," Jack repeated as he looked down at the stars surrounding him. Another round of vertigo twirled through his head. He staggered even though the empty air beneath his feet felt like solid stone.

The ball of light on the left flashed, saying, "Husband, we should make our guest more comfortable."

The right star flared. It's light blinded Jack for several heartbeats. When he could see again, he found himself standing in a lush forest glade beside a gently flowing stream, a scene that had materialized out of nowhere. Two people stood before him.

"Again, we welcome you to Tir Na Nog," said the first voice. It belonged to a tall, imposing man and rumbled like distant thunder. He stood several inches taller than Jack and had an air of quiet authority. His eyes shone like polished emeralds, and he was resplendent in robes adorned with intricate vine and leaf patterns.

The woman beside him wore a flowing, delicate silk gown that seemed to have been spun from moonlight. It cascaded around her like a waterfall glistening in the early morning sunlight. Her crystal blue eyes floated above a gentle smile. She looked over at Jack, and her eyes seemed to strip apart his very being as he felt her examine his very essence.

"Why, Nuada," she said, turning to the man, "I believe this new Winter King is a Milesian." Her husband squinted as he looked closer at Jack. "What news have you of Queen Gloriana and her Arthur?" she said.

Her husband reached out and touched her arm. "Macha, Gloriana was laid to rest long ago. Flinthar is Winter King." He looked at Jack, and Jack felt like the look held condemnation.

"Of course," she replied. I forget. The mortal realms fly past us so fast. Have you killed Flinthar, then Milesian? "

A spear of blazing light appeared in Nuada's hands. "Is that why you hold his sword?" Nuada said.

Before he could think of moving, Jack's body reacted. His left foot shifted back, his arm moved away from his body, his knees bent, and the sword swept up until the tip was even with his left eye. He was ready to defend against a high attack or attack himself in a blink. The sword rested in his hand as if it had been there his whole life.

When Nuada did not attack, Jack said, "I pulled the sword from a stone in a frozen cave after destroying a giant made of ice."

Nuada blinked, and the spear of light disappeared. His expression shifted from aggression to curiosity in an instant.

"You must be hungry. Join us in our repast, and we will discuss recent events."

Jack turned. The stream was gone, replaced by a glistening pond surrounded by a floral garden. A long table sat beside the pond; three chairs nestled beside it. Behind him, he heard Macha giggle.

"Gloriana loved that sword in the stone idea," she whispered to Nuada, "I've always thought it was a silly basis for government."

Jack grinned. "You're not alone. So, how about I give the sword to you two and return to tending my ranch?"

"The Sidhe need a leader," Macha said.

"Sure, they do, but no one else could touch the sword. I don't want it. I'll give it to you, and you can give it to one of them."

"We cannot," Nuada said, "but you can."

He pulled a chair forward and held it as Macha sat. He lifted a decanter and filled a glass, which he handed to her. He poured a second glass and gave it to Jack. Jack went to grab it, but realized the sword was still in his hand. He grabbed the glass with his free hand and set the sword on the ground.

Nuada sat in the chair beside Macha and waved to the third chair in invitation. "Sit, be welcome. The sword is yours to keep or pass along. No one will force you to replace the Winter King, but your choice will have consequences."

Jack sat, stunned by Nuada's words.

That sounded like a threat, he thought. He sipped at the liquid. To his surprise, it was not the wine he had expected. It was thin on his tongue like water but sweet with a touch of tartness from some fruit he could not identify. He took another sip, and the flavor seemed different, like citrus. A third sip brought a third flavor, as if the liquid in the cup changed each time he drank, each flavor complementing the one before.

Jack set the glass down; now was no time to be distracted. He leaned forward in his chair and spoke to them: "Look, I don't want to be King. All I wanted to do was help Onyx get his brother. Then the dragon showed..."

The wine cup stopped halfway to Queen Macha's lips.

48

"The dragon," Queen Macha said. She looked at Nuada. "Didn't Gloriana say her Arthur trapped the dragon."

"No, my love," Nuada said, "that was Medb's northerner. He trapped him in ice with the others, if I remember."

Macha placed her wine goblet on the table and looked at Jack, her tone accusatory. "Just how was he freed then?"

"It seems the Milesians have melted away the glaciers that imprisoned The Children of The Morrigan," Nuada said.

"The fools." She said, her voice calm as if they were speaking of trivialities, not the world's destruction. She turned to Jack. "What of the Sidhe, Milesian? Have your people slain all of them?"

"My name is Jack," Jack said, irritated that they kept calling him Milesian. "And I was helping a group of dwarves recover the sword; I understand that they are Fae or Sidhe or whatever. So, no, I guess they aren't all dead."

"The Children of Earth have always been the first to respond to threats. It is good that they still hold to their pledge," said Nuada, "but we cannot take the sword. It is bound to the mortal realms and the one who claimed it. By right of conquest, you are now Winter King of the Talamh Sidhe, the Mortal Tuatha De Danann. The children of those who stayed behind when our people left the mortal realms."

Macha must have noticed Jack's lack of understanding. She explained: "Long ago, from your perspective, the Tuatha De Danann tended your realm. We were the stewards of the natural world. All that grew, all that breathed, and all that swam were under our care. For millennia, the lands and seas flourished. Then the Milesians came with their fire and iron, and" She paused with a long sigh, and her husband picked up the story.

"They drove us out of the lands they claimed as their own. Over millennia, we resisted their spread, but eventually, we held only a single garden. Ultimately, we chose to leave the mortal realms completely rather than make the land suffer more from our war."

Macha touched his hand, sympathy radiating from her as she spoke, "Our choice was to battle on and watch the world die or leave. So to protect what we loved the most, we left ."

"Not all left, though; some stayed," Nuada said. "They became the Talamh Sidhe, the Fae as you call them. Some stayed because they believed they could undo the damage the war caused and restore the land; others felt they could resist the Milesians from the shadows, and still others just refused to leave the lands they loved."

"They have failed, it seems; the world dies," Macha said.

"We cannot judge the Sidhe for this; I'm sure the selfishness and insatiability of the Milesians played a part. I'm surprised they lasted this long." Nuada said. He sighed and put down his wine cup.

"If the Dragon is loose, others of The Morrigan's Children may also be free," Nuada said as he stood. A spark of light appeared in his hand. It grew in brilliance until it was blinding. It dimmed, and Jack blinked until the dots in front of his eyes cleared. King Nuada held a crown in his hand. A circular band of silver with spikes of equidistant crystal rising from it. Each one split into prongs as they rose to circle the crown like antlers.

Macha moved beside her husband, taking the crown from his hand, "War comes to your world, Milesian. The elemental creatures created to eradicate your kind have been freed, and the Tuatha de Danann are no longer there to control them."

She stepped toward Jack as Nuada spoke, "The Sidhe need a leader. The sword has claimed you as Winter King, but all the Sidhe need direction, not just the Winter Court. The Talamh Sidhe are no longer unified, and they are unprepared. You have shown you have the skill to lead, and the sword has found you worthy, but you must lead more than the Winter Court." She raised the crown to eye level and nodded to Jack. "The Sidhe need a High King, one who can unify the Four Courts and fight The Morrigan's Children. We," she looked at Nuada, "We believe you should be that king."

Jack sprang to his feet, his hands held up in rejection. "Whoa, wait a minute, I don't want to rule the Winter Court, let alone four of them.

Nuada stepped forward and nodded, "You can refuse this call. You can return, and the sword will pass to another, less competent. They will try and fail, and you can watch your world suffer at the hands of The Morrigan's Children without the responsibility of stopping it. Or you can kneel and accept the crown of the High King as proof that the Tuatha De Danann stand behind you. This crown will be a beacon that no Sidhe dares refute. A rallying point for all the Fae that are still in your world. A symbol to mark you as the leader of the Talamh Sidhe and protector of your world. Accept it and rally the Sidhe to save your world, or refuse and watch your world crumble. The choice is yours."

Jack sat stunned. *How do you even respond to such a choice? He's basically asking me to fight or die.*

A vision of Onyx lying in his garden, four massive cuts across his back, came to him. He remembered blasting round after round of shotgun slugs into the Dragon. He remembered his frustration as he watched each wound flare up and then heal. *How can I even fight that kind of power?* The memory of the dwarves standing down the dragon with snowballs brought a smile to his lips. Others followed it: the burnt husk of the town of Arkona, a deer barbequed in a heartbeat, Otter facing the fiery dragon a hundred times his size, Bramble and Berry facing the ice elemental together. The beach at SoCal, the wooded ridge above the Flying J, and the farmers' market he and his wife visited the day of the accident.

There's so much to lose, he thought.

The wildfires that ravaged the continent had a cause; he was being offered the ability to stop it. If he chose not to, could he live with himself?

Jill's voice rang in his head. *Will you do nothing when you know there is a way to help? Can you stand by and watch as the world burns around you? Come on, Jack, you know what you must do; do it.*

Jack shook the voice from his mind, but he knew she was right.

Jack dropped to one knee in front of the King and Queen of the Tuatha De Danann. He felt Queen Macha place the crown on his head. "The Tuatha De Danann name you High King of the Talamh Sidhe, Champion of the Four Courts, with the right to name those who lead, Master of the Bloom, Warden of the Long Days, Herald of the Harvest, and Sovereign of the Snows. Rise and fulfill your destiny, Guardian of Life."

Jack rose, and King Nuada knelt to belt a leather sheath around his waist. "A sword of power deserves a home," he said as he lifted it from the ground at Jack's feet and slid it into the scabbard.

"May this blade aid you in your fight against The Morrigan's Children."

Jack was about to ask another question when his mind exploded with light.

49

Onyx stood numb as Ashe and Jack moved to the Icenforge. His heart had shattered as his hand passed through the sword hilt. All the dreams of his childhood smashed against the harsh reality that the sword of his grandfather had not found him worthy. As each of them tried to claim the sword, Onyx felt his hope rise, only to be slapped down again as they failed.

The Dragon must be defeated, he thought; *how would they do that without the sword?*

Despair filled him as the last Eardfolc stepped away from the sword. His mind was awhirl; he barely noticed as Ashley made and failed an attempt.

Of them all, only Jack was left. The words of encouragement flowed from his mouth without any forethought; his brain felt foggy, his mind numb as he urged Jack forward.

The sword seemed to light up as Jack approached it. Each step closer caused the sword light to shine brighter until none of them could bear to look at it. The light flashed as Jack pulled the sword from the Icenforge.

Onyx felt rage running through him as Jack grabbed the sword. That was the sword of his people. No Milesian should touch it, let alone be worthy to wield it. Rage swirled in him, then slowly settled as he remembered the care with which the man had tended his wounds and the courage he had shown against the Elemental and the Dragon.

Would even an Eardfolc have joined a perfect stranger on a mad rescue mission? Would I have? Would I have rushed forward to battle a creature from a nightmare to save a group of strangers?

Jack had; Onyx knew that if any of them had embodied the virtues of a King, it was undoubtedly Jack. When Jack listened to his worries about his brother and their struggle on the mountain, Onyx felt heard, valued, and respected. Jack hadn't jumped to the conclusion that Onyx was crazy, even though Onyx was saying crazy things, at least not immediately. Jack heard Onyx out, waiting for the full story before suggesting he get therapy. He felt like whatever he told Jack, no matter how crazy, would be considered and analyzed fairly.

Jack had demonstrated an unwavering commitment to the welfare of others. He set his own needs aside to help. Jack could be safe miles away right now, but instead, he was here, in the same danger as all of them, because he had chosen to help Onyx. In Jack, he saw the embodiment of what a king should represent: someone who helped others in their time of need without expecting rewards, and someone who was willing to wield his compassion like a sword to alleviate the suffering around him. Onyx recognized that authentic leadership is serving and supporting others, and Jack had that aspect down.

Onyx watched as Jack spun the sword, cut through the air, and held it out as if checking its balance; then, with a flourish, he thrust it at the ceiling. Jack stood there for a long moment, the sword held up, his expression blank. Then Jack blinked, and a blaze of light shone from his forehead. A crystal and silver crown of antlers gleamed upon his head.

The Crown of Hearn, Onyx thought as the others all gasped beside him. The very symbol of the unity and strength of all the Sidhe, an emblem that had not been worn for a millennium. Seeing it now on a Milesian's head shook Onyx to his core.

Onyx had only heard about it in legend—the crown of the High King. There had been no High King since Gawain. His fists clenched, and his legs trembled with anger. Not only had Jack taken his birthright, but he had also been given the rule of all Sidhe. Each of the Four Courts would have to bow to Jack, High King of the Sidhe and King of the Winter Court.

To be crowned with the Crown of Hearn was to embrace a legacy of honor and sacrifice. The crown bestowed upon its wearer not just authority but a profound connection to the land and its people. Legends claimed that the crown could summon the forces of nature and bend them to the will of the High King. Yet, with no king to bear its weight, no king to unify the Sidhe, the land had suffered. It had suffered because of beings like the one that now wore the crown. The thought sent shivers down his spine.

Would the Four Courts follow a Milesian?

Onyx recalled the way Jack had stood up to the Elemental and how he had faced the Dragon with courage. His resilience led Onyx to believe that the Four Courts might follow him and unite under his banner. Onyx relaxed his fists. He had accepted Jack as Winter King; he had no reason to refuse him as High King.

He glanced at the others. One by one, they dropped to a knee. Each one bowed their head in respect, loyalty, and acknowledgment. They all shared a purpose: to restore the Winter King, and as they knelt, each showed their acceptance of Jack as not only the Winter King but also the High King. Onyx could see it in their eyes--the same sense of certainty, of acceptance that he felt. In this moment, they were all united under Jack's leadership.

Onyx's gaze met Jack's. In that look, there was understanding. Jack had his loyalty, and Onyx had his back, not just as a follower but as a brother in arms--comrades who had faced the fires together and would gladly jump to each other's aid.

Ashe looked at him, her eyes filled with questions.

Onyx nodded to her and dropped to one knee.

"Long Live the King." Around him, the others echoed his cry.

50

"Long Live the King," Ashe said with a shrug as Jack stepped away from the Icenforge.

"What, you don't kneel for your king?" he asked with a twisted smile.

Ashe shook her head, "I'm an American, Jack; I bow for no one."

"Fair," Jack said. They stood silent for several breaths, not sure how to continue.

"Nice crown. Much cooler than that hat, she said, then took a double-take when she realized he was now wearing that silly hat. "Where'd it go?"

Jack raised a hand to his forehead and tipped his hat.

"It's right here," he said.

"No, the crown isn't." Ashe looked at Jack's beat-up hat; she searched the ground around them. Looking at Jack again, she realized he wasn't holding the sword. "Where's the sword?"

Jack laughed, "Not funny. It's right here." Jack reached to his waist and mimed, grabbing a sword. Iismid appeared in his hand. It was sheathed in a thick leather belt around his waist. Jack released the sword, and it slipped back into the sheath; both the sheath and sword disappeared.

Ashe's mouth dropped open. "How'd you do that?" she yelled.

"Do what?"

"Make it disappear."

Jack laughed. "Now, who's acting crazy?" he said. "It's right here." Jack placed his hand in the air where the sword hilt should have been, like he was resting his arm on it.

Behind Jack, Onyx shook his head, "She can't see it, Jack. The crown and sheath were made with spirit magic. Only the Sidhe can see it."

Ashe was finding all this hard to accept. A sword that made you king and a giant made of ice, but which was less believable, that a dragon was setting the Pacific Northwest on fire, or that a sword could be invisible.

Ellis nudged Onyx's shoulder; when he turned to look at him, Ellis waved to Jack as if he wanted Onyx to ask him something. Onyx looked at the others. They all nodded.

Onyx cleared his throat. "Your Majesty," he said, "may I ask where you got the crown?"

"What do you mean? It came with the sword; I'm Winter King now, right?"

Onyx looked nervous, as if he was about to say something that Jack might not like. Berry and Bramble wandered away. They looked at Ashe as if they knew an argument was about to ensue, one they wanted no part in. Ashe wondered how bad the news must be if the twins, who usually barged into every conversation, were avoiding it.

"Yes, you are Winter King. The sword chose you, but that crown isn't the crown of the Winter King; it is the Crown of Hearn." Onyx's words hung in the air.

"Okay, so a crown's a crown, right?" Jack said.

Onyx looked away, and Ashe realized the man really did not want to tell Jack whatever it was he was trying to say to him. Ellis stepped behind Onyx and placed a hand in support on his shoulder.

"Where did you get it?"

"When I grabbed the sword, I guess I must have blacked out because I found myself floating in space," Jack said. "I met these two people; they said they were Tuath De Dannan. The guy, Nuada, gave me the sheath, and the woman, Macha, put the crown on my head."

Ashe heard exclamations of surprise from the cousins. Opal turned and ran to the entrance to huddle up with the twins in whispered conversation.

How significant is this, she thought.

"Like the sword, the crown bestows a title, and uh," Onyx paused as if collecting his thoughts, "...responsibility as well." The weight of these words hung heavy in the air, underscoring the gravity of Jack's new role.

"Nuada mentioned that, but hey, in for a penny, in for a pound, I guess," Jack said with a smile, his acceptance of the situation reassuring the group.

"The Crown of Hearn is the symbol of the High King."

"Cool," Jack said, "So I am the King Under the Mountain and King Above the Mountain. Got it."

Onyx sighed and lowered his head, "No, Jack. The High King rules over the Four Courts; he is the ruler of all the Sidhe, not just one of the Courts."

Ashe shrugged as Jack looked at her. "I don't know anything about Kings and Courts. I just jump out of airplanes and fight fires."

"Master of the Bloom, Warden of the Long Days, Herald of the Harvest..." Jack said, listing the titles of the Kings and Queens of the Four Courts, Macha had told him.

"...and Sovereign of the Snows," Onyx and Ellis finished for him.

"Those are the titles of the Kings and Queens of the Four Courts," Ellis said.

"They are the titles Macha said I could grant as she placed the crown on my head."

Beryl gasped, then turned and ran to join the others at the exit. Their excited conversation echoed around the cavern, a stark contrast to the tense atmosphere inside the cave.

Onyx and Ellis exchanged a look before Onyx spoke.

"Jack, the King and Queen of the Tuath De Dannan, have declared you the leader of all the Sidhe. The Four Courts will be yours to command."

"Good, because they also told me to prepare for war."

"War," Onyx asked.

"The Dragon is not the only thing that came out of the ice; Morrigan's Children have been released. Nuada has apparently tasked me with saving the world."

It was Flint's turn to turn and run toward the exit.

Jack's words hit her like a brick to the head. Ashe's mind reeled as she tried to process what had just been said.

Saving the world? More monsters? And Nuada? It didn't make any sense.

If she had not already seen the dragon and a giant made of ice, she would have thought they were all playing her for a fool, that this was all just an elaborate joke. She felt a chill run down her spine. Her world had flipped upside down with the appearance of the dragon, but now they were talking about what? Gods and destiny?

Her reverie was interrupted by a series of loud barks. Otter was standing at the exit tunnel. He barked furiously for a moment, then ran up the steep tunnel before coming back and barking again.

"What's his issue?" Onyx grumped at being interrupted as he was about to speak.

Ashe looked at the cave entrance. The stone was now ice-free; even the giant puddles of water they had walked through only moments before were gone. The thin red ribbons shining through the ice were now bright red and glowing like hot brands.

"Uhm, guys..." Berry called from where the cousins stood by the cave entrance.

Ashe looked down where he pointed; the Icenforge was melting. Magma poured over the side of the small pool, engulfing the raised iron plinth. All over the room, the cracks that crisscrossed the floor were filling slowly with magma.

It was several moments before Ashe realized what was happening. The ice that held the Icenforge in stasis was gone, and the mountain's molten core was free to rise.

51

Onyx watched the iron plinth melt into magma. "The mountain has awoken," he warned urgently. "Flee if you value your lives!" He looked toward the exit to see Berry and Bramble already hauling all their gear up into the tunnel; beside them, Otter barked and pranced at the edge of the stone floor, the snow beneath its feet melting as Onyx watched.

Onyx, Ellis, and the two humans were suddenly aware of the imminent danger as the brothers reached the entrance. They were halfway across the cave when the magma began to seep onto the floor, blocking their path. The ice covering the stalagmites melted into fast rivers, creating a steamy barrier as the water met the molten floor.

"This way, Onyx shouted as he took two quick steps up the side of one of the stalagmites. The top spike had been shorn off as the Ice elemental stormed past it, leaving a flat platform at the top.

Onyx climbed to the flat surface and turned to help the others up. The four crowded up onto the impromptu platform.

Onyx gazed across the distance. The edge of molten flame crept slowly toward the ramp where his cousins now stood watching. *Look for solutions, not more problems,* Onyx told himself as terror tried to grip him. He scanned the ceiling, where most of the stalactites had been destroyed by the ice elemental. He could use one to swing over to the ramp. He reached for his backpack, but then remembered it was across the lava flow with the twins. That would not work. He had gotten them into this; he had to get them out. His brain kicked in, and he suddenly saw the answer. The stalagmites rose up in a zigzag pattern. They started just before the ramp and ran to the far side of the cave. None of their bases seemed more than four or six feet apart, and several of their vertical columns were broken like the one they were standing on now. He could jump to the next flat one, and then, when he reached the undamaged ones, he could trim the spike and form another platform for the others to use.

He looked across at the nearest stalagmite. It was so close that he didn't think even humans, with their ridiculously long legs, would have trouble. Even with his injuries, he was sure that he could make the jump across, but Ellis might not.

Without thinking any deeper about the problem, Onyx turned to the closest flattened stalagmite and jumped.

He began to tumble back but threw his balance forward as he landed. Pain flared through his chest and back, but he managed to stay upright on the flat surface. The calcite below his feet was slick. His boots slid on the surface. Compared to the slippery ice covering the floor earlier, the wet calcite was no problem. Onyx shifted his weight and stopped himself as he reached the edge of the broken spire. The others hollered behind him. He turned and, without a word, waved them forward. Across the distance, he saw Ellis shrug. He took two limping steps and vaulted across the gap using his crutch as a pole. Onyx braced his foot against the jagged edge of the plinth as he caught and helped his brother stabilize. Ashe was next. She did not take a run-up; she simply stepped across. Behind her, Jack did the same.

"Showoffs," Onyx said.

"The floor is lava was always my favorite game," Ashe said. Her smile was radiant, and all her teeth showed white in the red glow as her eyes twinkled above them. Onyx realized why this woman jumped out of planes and into flames for a living. "Ten jumps in a row, though, is going to be a strain," she said, looking toward the exit, "and the ones with spires are going to be a challenge standing on."

"I have a plan for that," Onyx said as he hurled himself across to the next platform.

They moved like this across three more stalagmites before Onyx called for a break. The next Stalagmite was undamaged; the spire protruded to the ceiling, its calcite covering gleaming in the red light from the magma below them.

Onyx checked the exit. The molten rock had moved slowly up the ramp and pushed the twins and Otter several feet back, but it seemed to have stopped there. The bases of the stalagmites were ringed by fire, but did not seem to be in danger of being covered in it.

The next stalagmite would be a challenge. Onyx was unsure if the sloped edges would give them a grip that was good enough to stand on. The best course of action would be to level the stone in some way. Onyx jumped.

His feet slid out from below him as he hit the edge of the stalagmite. He grabbed at the spire with his free hand, and it slipped off the wet calcite. He started to slide toward the magma. He wrapped one hand around the pillar and stopped his slide. He scrabbled his feet against the slanted spire, hoping to grab purchase. One foot hit a knobby protrusion below him, and he could push himself up until both feet were on slick but solid footing. He took a breath as he realized that the four of them could not hang from this thing, let alone jump from it to the next.

Onyx shifted his feet on the column. He found two stable footholds and a small crevasse to wedge his free hand in. He gripped his axe and slammed it into the stalagmite with a mighty swing. There was a shower of dust and sparks as the steel struck the calcite crystals and shaved the stalagmite flat. The space was about half the size of the previous stalagmite, but it would have to do. Onyx climbed up and turned toward the others.

"Come across one at a time. Wait until I get the next one cut before following."

Ellis jumped across, and Onyx helped him before jumping to the next. He landed on a shelf that looked like flowing water. It angled into the column, so he had solid balance as he swung his axe to trim the spire. He learned from the last one, so his axe hit lower on the pillar, cutting a bigger platform. He climbed up and helped Ellis as he jumped across. The next stalagmite was further away than any of the others had been. "That's a long way," Ellis said.

"Yep."

"Want to wait for the Milesians?"

"I am not letting no Reuzen throw me,"

"No, let them go first, then catch us."

"Oh," Onyx said as he looked at the space between the two stalagmites. "Nah, I can make it. Just send Jack first so he can catch you."

Ellis nodded. Onyx took two running steps and jumped. He landed easily and turned to grab Jack as he jumped.

Jack waved him forward. "Go ahead. I got this, no problem." Onyx nodded and jumped toward the next stalagmite.

He was still in the air when the screams started.

52

Jack landed solidly on his front foot as the calcite crumbled under his weight. He brought his back foot forward, but the slick surface of the stalagmite edge betrayed him. His foot slid sideways and off the plinth edge as his leading foot plummeted down the slanted edge. Pain erupted through Jack as his chest slammed into the top of the platform. The world tilted around him as he fell. His feet scrambled at the slick slant of the stalagmite but found no purchase.

Jack could feel the heat of the molten flow below him as he fell toward the burning floor. He screamed. Above him, Ellis and Ashe echoed his cry.

This is your reward for helping a stranger and thinking you could save the world, Jack thought. He closed his eyes as he twisted and plunged toward the lava.

Jack's shoulder slammed into something solid. His breath was knocked out of him, but he was not burning to death. The ground beneath him was not molten fire. *In fact,* he thought, *it's cold.* Jack opened his eyes. He lay on a broad circle of ice that floated atop the molten lava. A wave of relief washed over him as he realized he was safe for the moment.

He stood. His feet did not slip as they had when he first entered the cave. Steam rose from the edge of the circle where the ice met fire.

Jack yelled at the others, "Where'd this come from?" He stamped his foot on the ice.

"There was a flash from your sword as you fell," Ellis said, "and then it was there."

Jack reached across his body and grabbed the sword hilt. The grip seemed to throb with waves of cold as he held it.

Jack took a step toward the stalagmite where Ellis and Ashe stood. As he walked, the ice pushed forward with him. He stopped and looked behind him. The edge of ice farthest from him slowly hissed away as steam until he was again on a ten-foot circle of ice. Each time he took a step, the ice formed in front of him, covering the molten lava. Each time he stopped to look back, he saw the ice's edge melt in a spray of steam until only a ten-foot circle was floating around the sea of fire.

"Whatever's going on," Ashe said, "It's got you at its center."

"Yeah," Jack said, "Come on down, maybe we can just walk out of here."

Ashe paled. Jack raised his hands and flapped them in a come-on gesture. Ashe shook her head, "I don't know, Jack. What if it melts out from under us?"

Jack stomped on the ice. "Sounds pretty thick." Ashe did not look convinced.

"Look," he pointed back the way he had come, "when the ice melts, steam blasts up from where it meets the fire, right?"

Ashe nodded in agreement.

"Well, if it starts pouring out steam, we'll know it's melting and can jump up onto the stalagmites again."

Ashe still did not seem convinced. Before she could question Jack, Ellis spoke up.

"Sounds like a plan to me." Ellis slid down the slope of the stalagmite and hopped onto the ice flow.

"Welcome aboard," Jack said.

There was a huff from Ashe as she hollered, "Fine," and started down the column. When they were both on the ice, Jack began to walk toward the stalagmite from which Onyx hung.

"I thought you were dead from all the screaming," Onyx grumped as they approached him.

Jack grinned, "I'm glad you're okay too."

"It was the sword," Ellis cried, "it flashed and bang, there was," he paused and waved his hands toward the floor of ice, "just right where it needed to be. The stories were true, brother. I'll be damned, the stories were true."

As they approached the pillar Onyx clung to, the ice flow shifted to encircle the stalagmite. Onyx stepped easily off the plinth as they came. He tucked the axe handle into his belt as he stared up at Jack.

"Well, you could have said you could walk on fire and saved us all the jumping around."

"If I had known, I would have. Are you ready to get out of here?"

Onyx nodded, and they began moving toward the exit. They all huddled around Jack, their breath visible in the cold air. Each one tried to keep as far away from the melting edge of the ice as possible, often bumping shoulders with one another.

"Relax, guys, spread out. It's not like this has gotten any smaller. Have faith in the ice flow."

The ice moved with them as they walked, keeping its shape and size. The edges behind them melted and turned to steam as the lava ahead of them froze, creating a safe path. This soon became a problem. The air in the cavern became thick with steam. Soon, they were walking through sauna-thick clouds. The cavernous echoes of the cave became muted. They began to talk in whispers as if any loud noise would disturb something unseen out in the fog.

"This just got creepy," Ashe said.

"And a grand man made of ice wasn't scary to you," Onyx said.

"Scary, sure, but this is creepy. It's different."

Onyx looked at Jack in exasperation. Jack just shrugged and said, "Yeah, it's different."

Ashe must have caught the sarcasm in his voice as she threw a dirty look at him.

"Different," she said.

"Bah, you Reuzen, it's just a load a steam, isn't anything to be afraid of."

"Yeah," Jack said, his voice steady, "don't let your imagination get the better of you." His words were a reminder to everyone, including himself, to stay strong and not succumb to fear.

A fluttering of wings sounded from the fog. Everyone turned toward the sound.

An orange glow bobbed and weaved out in the steam with the rhythmic flap of wings. It flickered as it rose and fell. It was soon joined by a half dozen other bobbing balls of orange. They swirled around each other in the fog. The fog was so thick that Jack could not see past the edge of the ice flow. He turned to move toward the exit, but he was disoriented. He could hear shouts from the twins and the occasional bark, but the sounds were so muted he could not tell which direction they came from. He felt a hint of panic grip his chest. Whatever those orange balls were, they were getting closer. He had to move. Instead, he stood still. Uncertain. Close to panic, he took one step forward, second-guessed himself, and took two steps in the opposite direction.

"Calm down and pick a path, Jack," Onyx said; he squeezed the handle of his axe with both hands as he stared at the glowing balls of orange approaching. "If you bolt off, you'll drop the rest of us into the fire."

"Yeah, let's not lose the frying pan, Jack," Ashe said.

Jack took a breath. He looked around him. He was sure that the stalagmite on his left was on his right before the orange glow distracted him. He turned to put the stalagmite on his right and began walking. Ashe quickened her pace until she was walking two steps ahead of him. She watched the ice edge as she walked, but Jack could not help but look behind them. He would take two steps and then look back. Each time, the floating glow was closer. He studied the dense wall of steam in front of him, but could not make out the exit.

Ashe stopped and looked back. "We should run," she said, "We can match strides, sing some kind of cadence or something to sync up."

"What about them?" Jack waved to the brothers behind him. "They're going to need two steps for every one we take. It won't be long before one of them falls off the edge."

"We can hear you down here, you know," Ellis said.

"I am not running," Onyx said with a huff. "Stand right there and let these glowing galoots catch us up." He bounced his axe handle on one palm. Beside him, Ellis pulled a climbing axe from the loop at his belt. "We got this."

Onyx's confident declaration hit him hard. Jack's indecision earlier and his eagerness to get away had burned away any feelings of confidence he had after meeting with the Tuath De Dannan. His instinct was to follow Ashe's advice. Run. And run fast. He was unsure what the glowing orange light floating in the fog meant, but he knew it could not be good. Nothing new he had seen today had turned out to be good.

Who am I kidding? I am a failure. I couldn't save Jill; I couldn't run a bed and breakfast; how the hell am I supposed to save the planet? I am going to get everyone here killed. He was not cut out for this job; he now felt sure of that, but Onyx had his stuff together. His confidence and eagerness to jump into any conflict, no matter how badly outnumbered, outclassed, or outsized, was awe-inspiring.

Jack's earlier attack on the ice giant was not an act of bravery; it was an act of desperation, fueled by seeing Onyx struggle to rise and get back in the fight after being pummeled. He saw Onyx go down and got angry. That was it. He was not brave, he was not strategic, he was furious. That anger fueled his mad idea, and that idea paid off. That was no way to save a planet. Dashing toward the next fire or the next danger was never going to stop the planet's slow creep toward destruction. He needed a plan to remove the cause of the problem. He could not just run around handling disasters as they appeared. Defeating the Dragon would stop the fires, but what next? The ecological damage was done. The Morrigan's Children were free. Stopping its spread and returning to stability might not even be possible, but if he could protect others in the path of these creatures, it would be a life well spent.

Jack widened his stance and set his feet; the crunch of frost beneath his boots was swallowed by the oppressive silence of the foggy cavern. Steam billowed around the edges of the ice floe, his new sword, Iismid, sent up its own wisps of icy chill as Jack pulled it from its sheath. The faint blue glow of the blade barely cut through the shrouded gray. He scanned the murky cave, searching for movement, a shadow, anything--but the steam clung stubbornly to its secrets.

The fog shifted, curling and coiling like living tendrils. Jack's grip tightened on the hilt of the sword. His breath came slow and steady; every exhale formed a cloud that mingled with the haze. He could feel the weight of the unseen foe pressing in, a presence that made the hairs on the back of his neck stand on end.

You've faced worse, he told himself, but his pulse betrayed his unease. Beneath him, the ice pulsed faintly red as the lava below fought to melt it away.

Jack shifted his grip, readying Iismid. The sword hummed faintly as if sensing the storm about to break. Whatever lay ahead, it would not catch him unprepared.

53

Onyx stood his ground as the bobbing ball of orange grew bigger. He considered everything it could be and shuddered at the most obvious. He did not want this fight. He did not think they were up for it. He and Ellis would be fine; they had fought together in the Second Desert War before the last great peace agreement. He was confident they would overcome their enemy. They had faced tremendous odds on many occasions and always came out triumphant. No single foe could stand against them when they stood arm to arm. He was sure this time would be no different.

Onyx felt a soft shimmer of doubt as he thought of the fight with the Ice Elemental. Ellis had been knocked aside like a rag doll after rushing out alone. Onyx had been thrown across the room like a pair of dice. They were both injured.

Ellis was alone, Onyx thought. *I rushed in without him; isn't that proof that if we work together, we are unstoppable?*

The Milesians, on the other hand, were a liability. Jack might be some fancy fencer, but fencing had rules; real life did not. In this fight, there would be no referees, protective gear, or do-overs when things went wrong. While Jack waited for the right of way, his opponent would skewer him. Ashley, on the other hand, was an unknown; she was a firefighter and a parachutist, and maybe she could handle herself in a regular fight, but what he believed was coming was anything but a regular fight. They would be hard-pressed, and Onyx wasn't sure his friends could handle it.

Onyx looked out through the curtain of steam that masked the ice's edge. The orange ball was closer. Several more were now visible in the mist behind it. They all bobbed like corks in the ocean as they steadily approached. The rhythm of the spheres' motion looked familiar. He recognized it. His worst expectation was right, and this enemy might be beyond their ability to defeat.

The first orange sphere reached the edge of the ice flow. Onyx saw the blurred outline of a familiar winged creature through the wall of steam. Its rail-thin body and clawed hands made it look like an evil flying monkey. Like the dragon, it was wreathed in flames. They rolled along its skin and flared in the wind created by its wings. The creature barely slowed as it crossed through the steam wall.

I hate being right, he thought as the flaming creature rushed toward them.

"Ember-kins," Onyx and Ellis screamed together.

"Rank One, I have low," Ellis said as he stepped beside him and dropped into a low crouch. Onyx knew his axe had a longer reach than Ellis's; it only made sense for him to take the high position and his brother to take the low. He shifted his feet and readied his axe for an overhead defense.

The ember-kin was knocked sideways as it passed the steam updraft at the ice's edge. It recovered, wobbled in the air, and flapped its flaming wings. It flew at Onyx with a scream like the roar of a house fire. It extended its six-inch-long talons and swiped them toward Onyx's face. Onyx raised his axe and deflected the attack. The ember-kin's talons raked across the handle. Ellis ducked under the flying creature. He reached up and slammed his climbing axe into the ember-kin's calf. Gripping his axe handle with both hands, Ellis pulled. The Ember-kin slammed down into the ice. Onyx wasted no time. He stepped forward and split the creature's chest open with a practiced movement. The flames surrounding it flared then flickered out, and only ashes remained where the ember-kin had been.

Onyx stood. He stepped forward, elbow to elbow with his brother, ready for the next attack. More flame-wrapped ember-kin had passed through the wall of steam. Onyx glanced back and watched Ashley yanking a sheet of silver fabric from a pocket and throwing it over one of the ember-kin. The creature entangled itself in the cloth, unable to flap its wings, and it dropped to the ground. Ashley pulled a hatchet from her pack and pounced on the creature. A bit further away, Jack was a blur of moving steel as he feinted, beat aside an ember-kin's talons, and thrust his blade straight into its chest. Its flames died as it fell to the floor as ash.

Onyx did not see his next move. Two of the creatures were in front of him and Ellis. The beast to the right let out a screech like the pop of kindling and inhaled. "Fire!" Onyx and Ellis yelled together. They dropped to their knees and threw their arms over their heads, as a cone of fire spewed out of the ember-kin's mouth. When the flames died out, both brothers sprang forward, grabbed the Ember-kin in front of them, yanked it to the ground, and slammed their axes down on flaming skulls.

Onyx's hand stung as he gripped his axe. Pulling these creatures out of the air was the best way to defeat them quickly, but he wished he had been wearing gloves. The brothers turned in perfect unison to face the remaining Ember-kin.

It hovered in front of Jack. It bobbed and weaved in the air. Its talons slashed out only to be met by the edge of Jack's blade. The blade flashed left, right, then back to left as the Ember-kin tried to get at Jack. There was a loud pop like the sound of wood in a campfire. Experience and training had the brothers hollering "Fire" without realizing it as flames poured from the ember-kin's mouth. A cascade of flaming sputum poured toward Jack. A flash of blue surrounded him. Inches away from Jack, the flames stopped. Jack stood in the center of a blue orb of ice like a figure in a snow globe. Flames poured from the Ember-kin and cascaded off and around the globe of ice. Jack wasted no time. He jumped and lunged forward to catch the Ember-kin in the throat with the tip of his sword. The creature screamed as its flames died, fluttering to the ground as ash. As the ashes fell, Jack turned to help Ashley. The woman beat at flames that covered the arm of her jumpsuit, the ashes from another ember-kin at her feet.

54

Ashe beat out the fire, covering her arms. The Kevlar suit was built for jumping into hazardous terrain, not for fighting fires. When the flames were out, she checked over the burn and scorch marks left behind. The suit seemed solid enough until she looked down. Three long gashes cut across her abdomen. Ashe bent double as realization hit her.

If not for the Kevlar, her guts would be spilling onto the ash-covered ice. Her breath came in short gasps. She felt like she was underwater; the idea that she was a thin layer of cloth from disembowelment would not stop rolling around in her mind. She knew she was hyperventilating; she knew it was just a physical and emotional reaction to the fight, but she could not control it. She could not get enough air. She gasped in a shallow breath that failed to fill her lungs. She stood there, bent double, her breathing ragged and sporadic. Spots appeared before her eyes. She felt like she was going to faint.

A hand touched her on the shoulder.

"You're okay." Jack's voice came from beside her. "It's just the adrenaline crash. Breathe with me."

She heard Jack inhale next to her--a long, slow breath that lasted half a dozen seconds. It was followed by an exhale of the same length. "Breathe with me," Jack repeated as he drew another long, loud breath.

Her breath still came in ragged, short gasps. She closed her eyes and concentrated on the ridiculous sounds of Jack's breathing. In a few moments, her breathing slowed and began to match his.

"There you go, Inhale," Jack paused as she matched his inhale, "exhale," he said as he slowly blew out a breath.

Ashe's breathing normalized, and she stood. Jack stood next to her with a look of concern on his face.

"You okay?"

"I'm better." She looked down at her abdomen. "It was just so close."

"Yeah," Jack said, "That fire about got me." He took her hand and looked over the charred arm of her suit. "But it looks like you took the worst of it. I can't imagine how it missed me."

A gruff voice interrupted. Onyx approached them while Ellis scanned the steam wall, expecting more of the flaming monsters to come at them. "It's the sword, you idjit. It was made to fight creatures of fire. If this," he stamped a foot on the ice flow, "isn't enough to show you that, I'm not sure what it'll take. You are the Winter King."

"I'm still not totally sure what that means," Jack replied, "but let's get the hell out of here, then we can talk about it." He looked around. Only the wall of steam could be seen. "I can't tell through all this which way the exit is."

"Berry," Ashe yelled. "Where are you?" Jack and Onyx made faces at her, but she ignored them.

"Hello," echoed around the chamber, followed by a few barks.

"That way," Ashe said as she pointed to the right.

"Are you sure," Jack asked.

"I wander around in smoke-filled buildings for a living. It's that way."

Ashe hoped she was right. She was judging as much from instinct as any concrete knowledge. The echo seemed most vigorous from the right, so she was sure that was the way they should go.

Instead of arguing, Jack simply nodded and started off to the right.

That was too easy, Ashe thought, but the edge was moving toward her as Jack walked away, so she moved after him. The two brothers walked ahead of her. They gripped their weapons and eyed the steam wall as if expecting another wave of flying flaming monkeys. She did not blame them. Her eyes darted left to right, then behind them every few steps. If another group of those things, what had Onyx called them, ember-kin? If another group of ember-kin showed up, she wanted to be ready. The hatchet she carried had worked well on the things once they were down, but trying to smack them while they were bobbing in the air above your head was nearly impossible. In fact, if she had not thought to use the emergency tent as a net, that first critter would have killed her. Her breath caught in her throat at the thought, but she swallowed the panic and kept moving.

She thought about rushing back to claim the tent, but as she looked back, it rolled past the edge of the ice flow and dropped into the lava beyond. She hoped leaving it behind wouldn't be something she would regret, but she knew direct contact with the flames surrounding the ember-kin would have melted holes in it. The fabric was designed to reflect heat away from the occupant, rather than to contact the fire directly. Intense heat, such as when she had used it in the shelter, and brief seconds of fire contact were fine, but trying to smother flames with it would ruin it. That was why training always emphasized the importance of making sure the ground beneath your tent was free of flammable materials before you deployed it. A moment's negligence in such a situation could turn a life-saving shelter into a deadly trap. If even a single burning scrap of wood were to catch, it could burn through the fabric. On the fire line, far from safety, a simple mistake like that could be the difference between survival and disaster. The emergency tent, your only barrier against the elements, was built to withstand the heat, but once compromised, it offered no protection at all. This lesson was drilled into every recruit: check the ground thoroughly. A few extra seconds of preparation could save your life.

When she packed her gear back at the jump camp, she had envisioned using it in the predictable chaos of wildfire containment, not against creatures torn from nightmares. Yet here she was, her gear proving indispensable in ways she never could have imagined. The tent, meant to shield her from the blistering heat of a burn over, had saved them all from the dragon's fiery breath when they sought refuge in its makeshift shelter. The clearing hatchet, a practical tool for cutting through debris, had become a weapon in her hands, cleaving through two ember-kin that had surged toward them with fiery malice. She had packed it all, expecting the relentless rush of wildfire, not the surreal horrors she now faced. But the same instincts that prepared her for the inferno were keeping her alive in this new, terrifying fight. Still, she could not have even imagined using it to keep from being roasted by a dragon or to trap and eliminate a flying flaming monster.

As Jack walked, the ice flow moved in front of him, each step ahead advancing the ice as the ice behind submitted to the heat of the lava and poured superheated steam into the air around them. As they moved, the echoes became less pronounced, and the barking of Jack's dog became clearer. Soon, the direction was obvious. Rather than building up in front of them, the steam was now streaming up the exit tunnel where the twins and Jack's dog stood, urging them forward. Ashe took a deep breath. They were safe. At least, she thought they were until Onyx spoke.

"Uhm, Jack, you might want to hold up and let us go first."

Jack stopped in mid-stride. "Yeah, it'd suck if I stepped onto dry ground and the ice disappeared with y'all still over the lava."

Ashley watched as Ellis' eyes bugged out, and the little man sprinted off the ice to join his cousins.

She followed without hesitation.

55

The cousins crowded around them as they stepped onto solid ground. Questions swirled through the air, each one more urgent than the last. Jack's revelation about the Morrigan had stirred up a hornet's nest of worry in the dwarves. Usually polite in their conversations, the dwarves talked over and interrupted each other as they each tried to get answers to their questions.

"Had Jack really seen the Tuatha de Danann?"

"Was he sure the dragon was only the first of many?"

"How did they plan to stop The Morrigan's Children?"

The questions flew at them from all sides, swift and pressing, demanding answers Ashe could only guess at. She did not know what Jack saw. She did not know what Onyx planned. She did not even understand what this Morrigan they were talking about was. All she knew was that moments ago, she had fought for her life against fiery creatures she never imagined could exist.

Her hands shook as she considered how the fight could have ended. The panic she had felt on the ice, fueled by the rapid-fire questions of the dwarves, crept back up on her. She let Jack and Onyx answer the others. She was moving away before she fully realized it; the tumbling wall of questions receded behind her.

Ashley needed room and air, something to ease the tightness in her chest. She wandered to the side of the tunnel. She leaned her back against the wall and slid down to sit on the cold snow. She placed her head in her hands and closed her eyes. She concentrated on her breathing, fighting off the panic that threatened to squeeze the life from her. Her heart throbbed in her ears as the memory of claws and fire lingered in her mind. Each heartbeat felt like a reminder of how close she had come to dying. It was all too much.

Jack said it was the adrenaline that she would be fine when it wore off, but the panic grew. Her mind spiraled as she imagined all the ways it could have gone wrong.

What if she wasn't so lucky next time? Doubts chewed away at her usual confidence. This wasn't like firefighting. When she jumped into a fire, she knew the risks, the obstacles, and the complications. This was different; every challenge they faced was another impossible situation in a crazy fairy tale turned reality.

She hugged her knees to her chest and squeezed her eyes shut. The sounds of the group's eager questions and Jack's calm answers felt distant and muffled like voices in another room. All she could hear clearly was the roar of her own swirling thoughts and her pulse as it pounded in her ears. She felt utterly alone in her panic, a solitary figure amid a bustling crowd.

Footsteps approached. Ashe ignored them. She knew she had to pull herself together, but the more she tried to calm herself, the worse it got. If her panic took over, she would never get through this. She could not fall apart now. There was too much to do. She had to get off the mountain and return to the fire line. Even if she bolted and let these folks face the dragon without her, she still had to make it down the mountain.

Her panic was a living thing. It crawled through her chest and clawed at her thoughts. It was trying to consume her, reduce her to a blubbering bundle of tears and fear, trembling on the icy floor. She realized it wasn't just the fight or the danger they were in, but the feeling of helplessness. It was the sense that she had no control over what was happening, a feeling that was so memorable from her time with Phil. It gnawed at her. No matter how hard she tried to assert herself and shape her destiny, the forces against her seemed insurmountable. She hunched against the wall, struggling, not just with the physical danger but with her own emotional turmoil.

A hand touched her shoulder.

Why did people think they could touch you, she thought. *What made people even do that? Family and close friends, maybe, but near-total strangers seemed to think they could touch her. Sure, it was an attempt to comfort and show they cared, but jeez, a little space would help, too.* She was not used to such physical closeness, especially from someone she barely knew. She needed her personal space, especially in moments of distress.

The hand shifted and moved until she felt a small arm around her,

Ashley looked up to find Berry beside her. "Do you always wrap your arms around strange women," she asked.

Berry started. His smile slipped as he realized his concern may have been misinterpreted, but his grin quickly returned. "Strange women, no, friends, yes, whenever they seem to need to know I care," he said, his voice filled with genuine empathy.

Ashley put her head back in her hands and waited for Berry to say whatever meaningless platitude he had come over to say. She waited to be left alone so she could face her panic without having to explain anything to anyone. Berry stood quietly next to her, his arms around her shoulders. After a few minutes, Ashe realized her breathing had settled. The panic that threatened to overtake her was gone. A wave of relief washed over her as she relaxed and leaned into him.

"We heard the pop of flame and knew what you faced in the steam," Berry said.

He did not clarify what he meant, but Ashe knew he had been worried about her. He stood there without continuing. They barely knew each other, but he had been worried. Ashe wanted to look up at him and thank him, but she was unsure how to do it, so she kept her head down.

"My cousins and I fought in the desert wars," he said. "Redcaps were working with the ember-kin to push the desert outward. Our people were trying to stop them from destroying farmlands at its edge. My tribe and many of the Sidhe fought to stop them and push back the sands."

Ashley listened but did not look up.

"We didn't know the tactics we use now to fight them. We had never fought ember-kin before. We didn't know they could breathe fire. Many Eardfolc died before we learned how to fight them." He paused as if in remembrance of friends lost. For a while, he was quiet as he collected his thoughts, as if deciding how to go on. "My mate and I were the first to hear that crackle and pop on the battlefield."

Ashley raised her head. Berry unbuckled his jacket and pulled aside his shirt to reveal a chest covered in burn scars.

"She threw herself on me to put out the flames just as a second, Ember-kin released another stream of fire."

Berry took a shaky breath. "She did not survive it."

Ashley sat straighter and turned toward him. Berry held up his hand before she could speak.

Ashley saw the tears welling in Berry's eyes as he stepped away from the wall. He turned and placed his hands on her shoulders.

"I am glad that you made it back to us unharmed."

Berry turned and walked up the tunnel to rejoin his cousins.

56

Onyx exited the steep tunnel to find himself just below the peak of the mountain at the top of a deep crevasse that ran just below the peak and down into the glacier.

A spur of rock rose above them. It stood a good twenty feet above, rising on a curved swell of rock that made Onyx think of a wave of earth. He could see the flicker of flame from the fire they built against the rock. He nodded at their effort. The fire would warm the rock, reflecting the heat back at those camped in front of it, while the rock wall would break up and disperse any smoke an enemy could use to find them. He wondered about that enemy. He would have named it the dragon a day ago, but since the cave, he had to wonder if others were aligned against them. Was it only a coincidence that the ember-kin had risen from the magma? Or had they been sent to stop anyone from claiming the sword? The dragon's intentions remained a mystery, shrouded in the flickering flames of the fire.

Onyx sat at the fire as Ellis finished telling the others about the battle with the ember-kin.

"That's what I don't understand," Onyx said. "Why were the ember-kin here? Could they be in league with the dragon? Why would they be? What cause in common could ember-kin have with the dragon?"

The men around the fire shrugged or looked at Onyx in confusion. They weren't seeing the bigger picture.

Something was behind this, something bigger than the dragon, he thought.

"Well," Berry said, his smile widening, "It makes sense don't it, the dragon wants to set the world on fire, the ember-kin are pretty much made of fire."

Ashley had followed Onyx up the slope and finished Berry's thought, "so a burning world is probably ember-kin heaven or Valhalla or whatever ember-kin think of as paradise."

"But how would the ember-kin coordinate with the dragon? It's not like the beast speaks. It's a force of nature, an elemental force; it's not like it would use tactics to trap us below the mountains."

"The Morrigan would," Jack said.

Onyx and the others froze at the name. There was a long silence as everyone turned to look at Jack.

"The what," Ashe asked.

"The Morrigan," Onyx said, "A Tuatha de Danann General who led the war against humankind." The mention of her name sent a shiver down his spine, and he could see the same fear and awe reflected in the eyes of his companions.

"A criminal," Ellis said as he leaned to one side and spit as if clearing a foul taste from his mouth. "The Morrigan created the Dragon to eliminate humankind."

Jack stood, "I still find all of this hard to accept, but while I spoke to Macha and Nuada, they mentioned that the dragon was one of The Morrigan's Children. They said that others have broken loose." The disbelief in his voice was palpable, echoing the shock that reverberated through the group.

"What are The Morrigan's Children?" Ashley asked.

Onyx swallowed the lump that formed in his throat. He looked to the others, hoping one of them would respond. They all looked at him. Onyx swallowed.

"The Morrigan was once the greatest of the Tuatha de Danann generals. She led the Tuatha de Danann to victory time and time again during the millennia-long war with the Milesian."

Jack interrupted, "Milesian, what is that? They kept calling me that."

Onyx looked to Ellis, who nodded in encouragement. Thanks for the backup, brother. Onyx sighed and stood. He walked to where Jack sat and looked into his eyes.

"You," he pointed to Jack and then to Ashe, "are Milesians. Humans, Onhandige Reuzen, Homo Sapiens Sapiens. Milesian is the name you called yourselves when you first arrived. It was the name of the nation you built as you slaughtered your way to control the Earth. The Tuath De Danann fought for every inch of soil, but eventually, they were forced to surrender."

Ellis spoke up as Onyx returned to his seat, "Short lives and fast breeding outpaced the losses the Tuath De Danann suffered, and in the end, they were overwhelmed. The war lasted two millennia, but the Milesians just kept coming. Eventually, the Tuatha De Dannan held only a small island and prepared for a final stand."

"The Morrigan," Onyx continued, "had seen so many of the Tuatha de Danann lost that she swore to destroy every Milesian in existence. She created creatures out of Milesian nightmares to act as weapons, determined to destroy them. The dragon is one of them; the Jinn and the Kraken are others; the Morrigan created all of them to wipe humanity off the face of the planet."

He bowed his head and stared into the fire, "When the Tuatha de Dannan saw the devastation these creatures caused, they forbade their use and sued for peace rather than destroy the land. In the treaty that followed, the Tuatha de Dannan left the mortal realm, dragging the Morrigan kicking and screaming through the gate."

"They left behind her children," Berry said, "fearing they would cause havoc even in Tir Na Nog."

Onyx continued, "Many Tuatha de Dannan stayed; they gave up their immortality to stay and try to heal the land. They became the Aos Sidhe, the people of the mounds, the Fae of Milesian folklore. For years, they stayed hidden, but over the centuries, memories faded, and the Sidhe became stories out of legend. Elves, goblins, dwarves, and sylphs are all echoes of ancient history that your people only remember as myth. The descendants of those who stayed eventually learned to blend in, to look and act human, so they could continue to care for the world."

"And what became of The Morrigan's Children?" Jack asked.

"Some were destroyed, like the Abhartach by Cu Chulainn."

"The what by who?" Ashe whispered loud enough to break Onyx's train of thought.

"Ab-art-ache," Berry stage whispered, "Kinda like Vampires, Killed off by an Irish Hero."

Onyx shot a look his way, but Berry just grinned at him.

Onyx harumphed and continued, "Others were driven off, as Arthur did with the Fomorians." He stopped again as Berry whispered, "Giants."

"Still others were imprisoned like the Dragon."

"Well," whispered Berry, "you know that one".

"And now the Dragon is loose, and even if we defeat it, what other horrors will we face when it is gone?" Jack asked.

Onyx shrugged. He did not know. They only learned of the dragon's escape when Mount St Helens began to rumble. In the decades since, what else may have crawled from the melting ice prisons that once held them?

Ellis responded for him. "We can't be sure. Not all battles had stories told of them. Any number of the creatures Morrigan created could be gone from the world. Driven away or died off."

"Then we also can't know if any of them are gone," Ashe said.

"We know of the dragon's imprisonment, we know of the Fomorian exile, and the destruction of the Abhartach; those stories have been passed down through the ages. Of those that are left, there are many possibilities: the Kraken, the Albrac, and even the Sluagh may still be imprisoned, or they may be free. The Dragon might have been the first, but she also may have been the only one."

Jack shook his head and stood.

"No," Jack said. "Nuada said Morrigan's Children are loose. He said we need to prepare to face them. We must assume he meant all of them. We have to be prepared."

Onyx watched as Jack paced back and forth beside the group as he spoke.

"The King of the Tuatha de Danann charged me with preparing and leading the fight against The Morrigan's Children. He made me High King so I could rally the Sidhe. I didn't ask for this. I am not prepared for this." Jack stopped in his tracks. He turned and stared at Onyx's. "But damn it, I am going to be."

The big man spun on his heels and walked away from the fire.

57

Jack stood on the rock outcrop, watching a pair of vultures circle above the opposite hill. Below them lay the burnt carcass of a deer or a mountain cat; Jack could not be sure which. The corpse lay half on a fallen charred pine tree. It was not the first burnt corpse he had seen since crossing the fire line. He was sure it would not be the last. He thought for a moment about his new friends behind him and how close they had come to ending up like that carcass across the ravine. He had come close to failure several times. If not for Ashe's intervention in the stone shelter, the three of them would have died as the heat of the dragon's flame scorched through it. He was sure they would not have made it out of there if not for the cousins. He had made little contribution to their successes, yet he was given the responsibility to succeed — the responsibility to save the world.

Smoke roiled above him as the fires surrounding the mountain pumped clouds of black and gray into the sky. To the west, the setting sun dropped below the clouds of smoke. Jack held the Sword up to study it in the fading sunlight.

The pair of vultures that circled above dropped down to land beside the charred corpse.

Jack turned to face South. He held the sword behind his back, with his left hand, the blade pressed tightly against his arm. He breathed deeply several times. He moved slowly in the warmth of the setting sun; Jack raised his right hand even with his eyes. Two of his fingers pointed forward, and he dropped into a half squat. His right hand brushed his right ear, then flowed forward. He brought his left arm forward and stepped toward the sun. The sword was still held stiff against his forearm, and Jack spread his hands outward and circled them back toward the center of his chest. As he turned again to the south, he crossed his hands together. The sword flowed smoothly from the left hand to the right. He lifted his right foot. He stamped down and brought the sword around in a cross-block to the right. With a step forward, he reversed the sword to the opposite side. In a slow, deliberate motion, he thrust forward with the blade extended fully in front of him, both hands now supporting the sword hilt. Then, in a deliberate slow motion, he stepped back to a high block, the sword pointed down, dangling from his right hand, ready to sweep forward or shift to a cross block.

"Well, he can dance well enough," Onyx's voice broke through Ashe's admiration of Jack's flowing muscles, "but is he up to fighting a dragon?"

Jack continued turning and swung the sword in a flat arch toward the rising sun. His hands crossed as he stepped back to the south, standing straight, the sword now back in his left hand. He resumed the position he had started in, with a sword in his left hand behind his back, and his body relaxed.

Jack took a deep breath and sighed as he exhaled. The sword felt awkward after all these years, but he remembered the forms. His muscles complained at the no longer familiar movements, but he knew that when push came to shove, he could shove hardest.

The blade was well-balanced and light. It shimmered in the setting sun. Cold radiated from the blade. The grip was cold in his hand. He did not feel any chill from the wind that flowed across the spur or any of the frosty cold flowing off the glacier.

Jack stepped into the sword forms once more. As his hands came together, he slipped the sword from his left hand to his right and then burst into sudden action. Jack sped through the forms. He moved a little faster with each step until the sword became a blur. Once, twice, three times in rapid progression, the blade swung, spun, and sailed through the air.

Jack abandoned the traditional forms. His movements flowed into an impromptu battle with multiple unseen opponents as he spun, kicked, and slashed his way across the rock outcrop.

Jack turned South and stabbed out with the sword; all the frustration, pain, and worry of the last several days poured out of him in a savage, wordless scream.

A spear of bright white cold sprang from the sword tip and smashed into the opposite hillside. A plume of dirt, feathers, leaves, and ice splashed up from the point of impact. In a moment, the debris settled.

Two frozen vultures lay in an ice-rimmed crater where a charred corpse and a burnt pine had been a moment before.

"Well, maybe we do have a chance," Onyx said as he watched from his place beside the campfire.

The fire that raged across the mountains to the south flared. A spout of flame rose from the distant inferno like a tornado as it reached cloudward. It hurtled above the mountains like a swirling vortex of fire as it roared across the landscape. Wings of rolling flame seemed to envelop the entire sky. It came closer and spun toward the spur where Jack stood.

The dragon approached. Far larger than it had been outside the shelter, fire poured from between its scales, around its eyes, and out of its nostrils and mouth. Flaming wings beat and crackled as it let out a roar of challenge that echoed across the mountainside.

Jack stood on the spur and watched the beast approach. His mind was calm, and every doubt of his ability was quiet.

The sword grew colder in his hand and began to pulse with a bright blue light. In a few breaths, they matched his heartbeat.

The pulses were soft at first, a subtle tap against his grip. They grew stronger as the rolling meteor of flame barreled toward Jack. As they synchronized with his pulse, the cold touch of the sword hilt began to warm.

Iismid was ready to face the dragon, even if Jack wasn't.

58

A spear of ice flashed from Jack's sword, hurled across the ravine, and exploded on the far side; in response, a column of fire in the distance rose toward them.

Ashe sprang from her seat beside the fire and picked up Jack's shotgun.

"What the heck was that?" she cried.

"A challenge," Onyx said.

"I hope Jack's ready for this," said Bramble.

"I hope we are," said Berry.

The dragon hurtled toward them as its roar smashed through the air like a thunderclap. Ashe felt it shake her bones as the ground beneath her feet trembled. Her breath caught as the beast approached. It was far larger than it had been outside the cabin. A shiver of fear rolled through her. The battle with the ember-kin still swirled through her thoughts. Her pulse quickened as she remembered their chaotic bobbing dance in the air. She could still smell their sharp sulfuric tang as if her senses could not let go of the terror she felt.

Berry and Bramble stepped in front of her.

Her thoughts were disrupted by their move.

Chivalry isn't dead, she thought, *but I am not some helpless damsel.*

Their attempt to form a protective barrier was dismissive of her skill, and she would not allow that.

They're protecting me just because I'm a woman.

She let the resentment that thought created pass. She accepted their protectiveness as the gesture of concern it was meant to be, but she was not going to encourage it.

"I appreciate the gesture, guys," she said, "but I'm as much a part of this fight as you are." She racked the shotgun's bolt, and the "shrik tik" sound rang in a high-pitched contrast to the fading echo of the dragon's roar. The twins stepped aside and smiled at her as she entered the gap between them. All fear was set aside; her gaze did not waver; her new determination matched the ferocity of the approaching beast.

Ellis and Onyx stepped up to join them on the left.

"First rank, four," Onyx said. Ashe wondered at the words.

"Five," Berry corrected, "Right lead, flanking." he sounded less sure of his words than Onyx had, but the small man grunted his usual reply and nodded as Ellis said, "Left Lead, flanking."

"Center harassing," Bramble said on Ashe's left, then turned to Ashe. "Stay between us, keep pace. Strike when you get a chance. Berry and Ellis will attack it from the sides; we need to keep its attention on us." All four gripped their weapons and began to move toward the outcrop of rock where Jack stood.

Ashe nodded and followed as the dwarves began a steady but slow march toward the outcrop. Each of her steps equaled two of theirs, but within a half dozen strides, she matched their pace. She felt an effortless connection between them that made her sure she belonged here, with them, doing this. They moved together as a solid group, a ready and determined wall of weapons. As they moved toward the rock outcrop, she glanced back to see Beryl, Flint, and Opal holding back. Ashe stumbled on a stone beneath the snowpack and turned her attention back to their march toward the dragon.

The beast filled the sky like an approaching storm. Fear wiggled back into her thoughts as they marched. Each step over the frozen ground cast another doubt on her decision not to run blindly down the glacier while the dwarves handled the giant flaming beast in the sky.

Why didn't I run? What kept me here? I had the chance after the cave, I could have just started downhill.

She glanced around the spur of rock. They were surrounded by sky and glacial snow; no peak showed above them. They marched up the peak of the mountain.

I could have run in any direction. They are all downhill.

She looked at the dwarves around her. Their faces were grim, resolute, and determined. They had their reasons for facing the dragon, whether it was loyalty to each other or a duty to their clan; they were in this until the end.

Why am I here? she thought. She had no stake in this fight. Did she? The dragon's rampage had destroyed towns, ravaged wildlife, and left the land scorched in its wake. She could not let the destruction continue. If she could do something about it, then she must do something about it.

She heard a low growl behind her. She glanced back and watched as Jack's dog ran up and started to pace them. His hackles up, his teeth bared, the dog looked eager to wrap them around the monster's neck. Ashe began to feel the same. The beast moving toward them had destroyed millions of acres of land and an untold number of homes, towns, and businesses. It had killed or caused the death of hundreds. She would not allow it to continue its rampage. She knew fire, how it consumed, how it breathed, how it moved, how it latched on to any fuel to increase its size. This beast was no different, and it planned to consume the world. Like any wildfire, it was out of control and needed to be contained. Her training was in fighting fires, and what was this thing if not an embodiment of fire? As the thought rolled through her, the tingle of fear disappeared. She had done this before; she had battled house fires, starved forest fires, and beaten-out flames set in her path in dozens of fire calls. She handled those, and she could handle this one.

Her unease lifted as she adjusted her grip on the shotgun. She had seen what the flaming shot had done to the ice giant. She thought about the damage it would do to the dragon, and her feet felt lighter and her stride more confident as they moved together. The path grew steeper. Her fear and doubts fell away as her boots tramped across the snow-covered rocky ground beneath them. The dwarves beside her marched forward without question. They each had a clear reason, a purpose in this fight. Whatever her reasons for not running when she could, she knew one thing for certain: she would not turn back now.

59

The dragon filled the sky in front of Jack. Great fiery wings spread across his sight, beating in time as its fire-wreathed body rose and fell. Jack stood paralyzed, hardly able to believe what he was seeing. The creature was far larger than it had been in front of the cabin. He could imagine fighting that creature with a sword, but now its head looked big enough to swallow that cabin whole. A ball of fear formed in his chest as Jack considered the creature's size before him. The sword in his hand would be useless against such a foe. Fire poured from the creature's giant maw. Despair clutched at his heart as the torrent of fire rolled toward him, its heat radiating like the sun.

Jack screamed. The sword flashed blue, its magic responding to the peril he faced. A globe of ice appeared around him. Encased in its protection, Jack's terror turned to awe as he watched the flames swirl around the ice. The force of the conflagration was negated by the ice the sword projected around him. Jack's fear and doubt disappeared as the barrier redirected the flames away from him and toward the ground; in moments, Jack stood on rocks free of snow and ice.

A flash of resolve exploded inside him. Onyx had been right. The sword was the key to destroying the dragon. Jack tightened his grip on the hilt. The cold pulse he had felt earlier was now an electric thrum that surged through his arm.

I can do this, he thought. His determination grew as the dragon landed in front of him. The beast's control of fire was its greatest weapon. Its breath could unleash torrents of flame to reduce its enemies to a smoking husk, but Jack's blade, Iismid, protected him. The dragon's best weapon was now useless to it. Jack could defeat it. There was hope. The thought echoed in his mind, and his resolve strengthened. With every beat of his heart, his fear lessened, and his resolve to protect his friends, his home, and everything he held dear grew.

The dragon landed. Its great head reared back. The dragon had made the same gesture before snatching up the deer it had roasted on the road, and Jack recognized it.

Move, stupid, Jill's voice screamed in his head.

Jack stood still as he considered his options. A dive to the left would send him down the slope into the ravine. The right or back would get him out of the way, but to no advantage; the beast would strike again, and he would have nowhere to go.

How do you fight a larger opponent? Jill's voice asked.

Get in close, Jack thought in response, *eliminating any advantage they gain from their height and reach.*

The dragon's maw was inches from him when he rolled forward. He ducked under the dragon's head and rolled into the space between its front legs. He sprang to his feet under the monster. The air around him shimmered with heat from the fire that wrapped the beast, but Jack was as cool as an autumn day. His shoulder brushed against one of the dragon's flame-covered legs, but he did not feel it. He may as well have bumped into an unyielding, cold stone wall. The flames licked at him; they swirled madly in the air around him, but they did nothing. Enveloped in the protective magic of Iismid, the flames did Jack no harm.

Jack thrust the blade up into the dragon's chest, and a brilliant blue light flashed from Iismid. As Jack jabbed the blade up into the creature's chest a second time, the fire around the chest plates died. The red plates dimmed to green everywhere the sword struck. Jack expected the fires to flare up and heal the wounds, but they didn't. Bright blood began to rain down on Jack. The wounds from the sword seemed to block the creature from healing.

But the dragon did not fall. It twisted. Its tail whipped out over the ravine, and its head reared back once more to strike at Jack. He followed the beast as it moved.

The dragon struck down at Jack. Its jaw snapped inches away from his face. He had found the sweet spot. The dragon could not reach him. Jack spun the sword back and forth around him. He struck the back of the dragon's front legs, then turned and hit the back legs. Blood began to flow freely as the sword cut flesh and dampened flames. Jack swayed from leg to leg as the dragon spun around him. He stabbed and slashed at the legs, chest, and any part of the beast he could reach. It was like swatting a tree. The sword cut deep and dimmed the flames enshrouding the creature, but the size of it made the cuts seem meaningless.

The dragon spun in a circle, but Jack stayed between its legs. The dragon reversed direction and spun again to get a clear view of him, but he moved with it. Step after step, as the creature spun and shifted around the peak, Jack followed. The dragon's neck couldn't reach him where he stood, but Jack couldn't land a lethal blow in this position either.

Jack's head brushed the beast's scaled chest as blood continued to trickle down over him. He speared upward once again, tearing another gash in the beast's chest. The sword seemed no more than an annoyance to the creature. Too small to reach a critical organ, it seemed pointless. Maybe if he had the sword earlier, it might have made a difference, but now, with the creature grown so large, it seemed useless.

This is going to take a while, Jack thought—*the death of a thousand cuts.*

The massive legs rose above his head as the creature sprang into the sky.

How did I forget it flies, Jack thought. He dove to the side and rolled away as the dragon's head snapped in the air where he had been only moments before. Jack pushed to his feet, now the target of an enraged predator.

The dragon roared; the sound of its rage rattled across the mountaintops like a cannon blast.

Jack felt his frustration and screamed in response.

60

Onyx marched over the ice and snow of the glacier with his cousins.
Ahead of them, Jack stood battling the dragon on the promontory of
rock, the ice and snow around him melting from the dragon's fire.
The small group continued to march toward the battle. They walked
in step; each one truncated to pace Ellis' injured movement. Beside
him, the twins and Ashley adjusted their strides to match. Soon, they
were a workable shield wall, well, a wall at least, he thought.

When the dragon spewed fire on Jack, Onyx thought it would be all
over, but the sword interrupted the fire, and Jack, rather than
running in panic like Onyx wanted to do, charged forward. Even
now, watching the human bob and weave under the dragon made
Onyx want to scream in terror and run. He struggled to control that
instinct.

What was the line about fear killing the mind? He could not remember,
but he knew it was true. Fear could creep up on you. It could be far
off in the back of your mind, then suddenly, there it was, the only
thing you could think about. It would grow and nag at you until you

were so wound up that you had no choice but to give in to it. Once you gave in to panic, you were lost. No amount of effort would get someone back in the fight once they lost to panic.

Onyx felt the edge of fear creeping toward him.

Run, his rational mind screamed. His heart raced to match the urgency of his fear. The dragon was the size of an elephant when it chased him downhill; it was twice that size when it ate Jack's truck. It had grown again. They could take down an elephant or a T-rex, but this was the size of a jumbo jet. His fear tried to convince him it was hopeless, that there was no way they could hope to stand against something so big. Onyx refused to be a slave to his fear. He would stand firm against it. He knew he could not let it control him. He would not panic.

Onyx's fear gave way to amazement as he watched Jack battle the dragon. Every move the dragon made to swipe or bite at Jack was met with a countermove. The dragon moved right; Jack moved left. It tried to spin and catch Jack off guard, but Jack matched its spin and every movement step for step. Jack struck at the dragon with every move. His sword flashed in, out, and across the giant beast's chest and legs until blood flowed freely, and Jack stood covered in the beast's gore.

"Hold," Ellis said beside him, but it was unnecessary. Onyx realized they had not been advancing for some time. They had stopped the march without even noticing as they watched the fight. They all stood in awe as Jack danced with the dragon. What else could he call it? The man and his opponent were synchronized as each tried to take down the other.

The dragon took flight. It hovered above Jack and roared. Jack roared back. The dragon struck down with one claw; Jack stepped out of the way. The second claw swiped forward, and again, Jack moved just in time to avoid the swing, only to step back in and slash the sword across the dragon's flesh. Flames died, and blood flowed.

Onyx had seen great fighters in his time, Champions of his people, of the elves, and other Sidhe tribes, but Jack was beyond the best of those. A grudging respect replaced Onyx's fear and shock as he realized he was watching a master work his craft. Half a dozen times, the dragon came within a hair's breadth of catching Jack, only to have Jack dance behind the swing and slam his sword home.

The hovering dragon sprang into the air, ignoring Jack as it began to circle above. It banked and plummeted down. Its neck curled back, and it shot a line of burning liquid toward Jack.

Again, the globe of ice appeared as the fiery stream reached Jack. Onyx flinched from the heat as the flames licked around the world. Gobs of burning spittle splattered toward the group. As the fire dissipated, a strip of rock between Jack and Onyx's group was laid bare. The dragon dropped onto the bare rock and struck at Jack again; its back now to Onyx.

"Charge," Ellis hollered, and the four dwarves ran forward. Behind him, Onyx heard Beryl yell, and a flurry of snowballs sailed over his head to smash against the dragon's flanks.

The fire sputtered out, and red scales turned green. Onyx's axe rose and fell. The dragon roared in pain. It spun away from Jack. As it did, its tail swung around. Onyx and the twins were ready for it. They jumped onto and then over the tail as it swung past. Ellis, hobbled by his leg splint, did not make the jump. He was slammed sideways and, with a thin cry, tumbled down the slope toward the ravine.

Onyx's heart clenched in horror as he watched Ellis go over the side, but he had no time to worry about his brother. The dragon's teeth snapped together inches in front of his face. As his axe rose and fell, cuts appeared on the dragon's face, only to flame up and heal while he watched. What good could they do if they could not injure the thing? Onyx felt the shadow of fear creep back.

It whispered to him. *Break away. Run. It is hopeless.* He steeled himself and pushed the feeling of dread down. He was Onyx, son of Flinthar; he had led the group that found the Frost-Forged Blade. He would not break before the dragon.

Another volley of snowballs flew past Onyx. They smashed into the dragon's shoulder. The twins moved forward and buried their weapons in the now green scales. The dragon's head spun away from Onyx and smashed the twins with the side of its head. The two eardfolc hurtled over the cliff edge and down into the ravine. Onyx realized the wounds they had made remained. The cuts made where the snow hit did not heal over; they bled a deep, dark crimson.

As the next flight of snowballs smashed into the dragon's face, Onyx knew what he needed to do, but now he faced the dragon alone.

61

Ashe watched as Berry and his brother tumbled over the cliffside, leaving Onyx to face the dragon alone. She screamed and pulled the trigger on the shotgun. A cone of sparks blew from the barrel, and flaming shot struck the dragon in the face--phosphorus pellets lodged in the soft tissue of the dragon's snout and eyes. The beast's head reared back as the phosphorus joined the burning flames that wreathed the dragon. In the blink of an eye, the wounds were healed as, seconds too late, a hail of snowballs smashed into the dragon's face.

"Run," Ashe shouted.

The stubborn eardfolc stood still. His feet planted firmly, his axe ready, his knees bent as if about to launch himself into the air to strike at the beast. The monster turned its head sideways, opened its jaws, and moved forward to snap up the morsel in front of it.

Instead of running, Onyx lifted his axe and brought it down on the now green scales of the fire-beast's muzzle. The beast let out a muffled squeal as the axe bit deep and lodged in the bone of its jaw.

He tried to yank the axe out, but it didn't budge, and he didn't have enough leverage. Onyx rose into the air as the dragon lifted its head. It spun its head to one side and slammed its snout into the ground. Onyx still held the axe. He was smashed between the dragon and the rock as the beast dragged its face across the ground.

Behind her, Otter let out a long series of barks. The dragon's head lifted toward the dog, and the creature lunged forward. As the dragon moved, she realized she was directly in its path. She raised the shotgun. Onyx still clung to his axe. He was in her line of fire.

"Let go," Ashe yelled. Onyx wiggled as he shifted his weight back and forth as if he hoped to get the axe loose that way.

Ashe turned to run. A flight of snowballs flew past her.

The three eardfolc ran past her, camping tools and fistfuls of snow held as improvised weapons. As they passed Otter, the dog charged, too. Ashe turned, ready to offer support with the shotgun. The dragon's head pulled back. It inhaled.

"It's going to blow," Onyx yelled. Ashe raised the shotgun, determined to face her end fighting.

Jack appeared above them, surrounded by an intense aura of blue light. He ran along the dragon's scaled back; the sword in his hand glowed a fierce, brilliant blue. He reached the base of the dragon's neck and slammed the blade down with a scream. The sword plunged to the hilt, and with a flash of lightning, the crystalline hilt illuminated the mountaintop.

The wyrm reared and let out a roar that shook the mountain. Jack was thrown off its back and crashed to the ground, the sword still embedded in the creature's spine. With three wing beats, the winged titan sprang into the air and soared high above the mountain peak. Tongues of flame coiled around it as if the fire in its heart was trying to break free. Vibrant pulses of orange, red, and yellow flames flickered and twirled around it as if alive. From the mountain below, columns of fire burst upward to join the dragon fire, swirling like a tornado of flame above the mountain. The dragon became a roiling inferno above the mountain, challenging the waning light of the setting sun.

At the heart of the fireball, a spark of blue light ignited, a tiny twinkle in the vast inferno. Flashing within the conflagration, it pulsed like a heartbeat and grew as if it fed off the flames roaring around it. As the light intensified, it began to whirl and spin through the fiery mass. Where the blue light shone, fire died. Soon, the blaze of the blue light was greater than the glare of the fireball the dragon had become. With a blinding flash, the light of Iismid pulsed one last time, and the fireball exploded outward, scattering embers and cinders across the mountainside. The thunder of the shockwave echoed across the valley for miles.

Knocked flat by the explosion, Ashe stared at a sky devoid of fire. As embers of ash floated down around her, she scanned the heavens.

There was no sign of the dragon, the sword, or the blue light, only the blanket of smoke that had hung over the mountains for the last few days.

She stood and looked toward the cliffside, hoping to see the twins. She realized that all the fires were out. The flaming hellscape, once a lush and radiant living ecosystem, was now a curling veil of ash and burnt timber. The distant mountains, which had been forests of flame moments ago, were now only charred earth, covered in the skeletal remains of a devastated forest.

Jack lay unmoving among the ashen rock of the peak. Ashe's heart raced. They had been through so much in such a brief time that they had all become friends, forged together by circumstance into a coherent group, an alliance that stood against the forces of destruction and prevailed. They all may have been strangers hours ago, but now they were bound by the challenges they had faced. Ashe felt a surge of gratitude for the bond they had built, a connection that surpassed the madness that enveloped them. They had shared experiences that most people would never understand, and that shared experience would hold them together as they moved off the mountain and into the next challenge, this new, unbelievable world of dragons and fairies threw at them. As she looked at Jack, immobile on the ground, she realized each one of her new friends held a place in her heart, and she could not bear to lose any of them. *How unfair would that be,* she thought, if Onyx were to be believed, and she no longer had any reason to doubt, *they had just saved the planet.*

She ran toward Jack. She stopped several feet away, unwilling to reach out to him and find that her worst fears had come true.

Her voice trembling, she called his name, willing him to respond.

62

Jack lay on the cold, wet ground. His neck chilled as it made contact with the ice-cold stone below him. He stared at a blue-grey sky. The orange glow that had permeated the sky for the past week or more was gone. A grey pall of smoke rose from the hilltops below and drifted around the mountain peaks. A solid mist of smoke hid the scree and sand-covered slope into the valley below. From his position, the part of the distant mountains he could see were now bare, burnt-out slopes into the far distance. Only small patches of the majestic forest they once held remained. Jack sighed.

He heard someone call his name as far above him, something glinted in the sky. Jack tensed. A ball of glowing blue hurtled toward him. Iismid, The Frost Forged Blade, was falling straight at him.

Jack rolled to one side as the sword slammed point-first into the stone protrusion where his head had been only a moment ago.

Jack stood. Once again, he stood before a sword in a stone, a relic of ancient times, a symbol of power and destiny.

"Here we go again," Ashe said. She stood behind him, her hands trembling, her face a pale mask as if she had seen a ghost.

"Looks like we did it," Jack said.

Ashe's gaze wandered over the distant mountains. "The trees will return, the forest will recover, but..." Jack heard the melancholy tone of loss in her voice.

"Yeah," Jack agreed.

"We did it," a voice behind them said. The two turned to find the twins grinning at them. Soot-stained and singed. They both bowed as Jack turned. "Your majesty."

Jack looked toward their small camp. Opal was rebandaging Onyx. Otter lay beside Onyx, his head across the eardfolc's legs.   Beryl and Flint moved beside the fire pit, packing their gear as they broke camp. Jack did a quick count in his head and realized someone was missing. "Who is missing?" he asked.

Looks of concern passed across both twins' faces. Together, they yelled, "Ellis," and moved to the cliffside. A small figure hobbled up the pebble-strewn slope at the bottom of the steep slope, only to slide back down.

When his slide stopped, Ellis stood again and began half-crawling up the slope.

The twins looked at each other and grinned. "Looks like he needs a hand," Berry said. "Maybe even two," Bramble said.

The twins turned to Jack, their expressions confused. "Uhm, may we, Your Majesty," Berry said, gesturing down at Ellis.

"Of course," Jack said.

The twins grinned at each other. As one, they dropped to the ground and slid down the rocky slope toward their cousin, like kids on a playground slide. Giggling the entire way.

"Can you get this cow off my legs?" Onyx yelled to Jack. Jack turned to see Opal pull the bandages tight with a jerk. Onyx hissed. He spat and said, "Uhm, Your Majesty." He flashed a hateful look in Opal's direction as he did.

Jack whistled. Otter's head lifted from Onyx's legs as the dog rushed over to Jack.

Jack bent slightly as the dog arrived and began petting him.

Onyx stood with a bit of help from Opal. The two moved toward Jack. Beryl and Bramble joined them. As they reached Jack, they all dropped to one knee, their heads bowed. Their unity a testament to their family bond, a bond that would carry them through all of the challenges ahead.

Beryl spoke, "All Hail Jack Season, High King of the Sidhe, Winter King and Wielder of Iismid, the Frost Forged Blade." The formality of the ceremony added a sense of gravity to the moment, marking the beginning of a new era.

The others responded with "Hail, Jack Season."

Jack stared as Ashe poked an elbow in his ribs. "Long live the King, Cowboy," she said with a chuckle.

Jack looked around, panicked. Even the dog had dropped his head and let out a short bark.

"Not you too, Otter," Jack said. The eardfolc in front of him were solemn. They obviously took this idea of the High King far more seriously than Jack had. He sighed and touched Onyx on the shoulder.

"Rise, Gentlemen. There is no need for such a ceremony. We have a long hike off the mountain," he said, looking at the sword once again, stuck in the mountain's stone. But first, we must resolve this."

Jack walked up to the sword. He reached out to grab it, but stopped.

"Onyx Eisenhart," Jack called.

"Yes, Your Majesty," Onyx said.

"Come forward and claim the sword of your forefathers."

Onyx blinked. "Jack," he said, looking around at his cousins for support. "I am not worthy. The sword has already rejected me."

"The sword may have rejected you, but I know no one more worthy to stand at my side and lead the Winter Court through the crisis we face."

Jack remembered the words of Nuada. "The Morrigan's Children ravish the world your people have sworn to protect. Your axe is broken. A weaponless Eardfolc has no place in the battles to come. Take Iismid. Rally your people as King of the Eardfolc, then rally the Winter Court and prepare them for what is coming. The dragon is slain, but more evil creatures roam the land. Accept this obligation and join me in hunting them down."

Onyx rose and moved nervously toward the sword. He reached his hand out. Jack could see his hesitation; *how bad it must have been,* he thought, *to travel so far and fight so hard only to lose the prize you had expected.*

Onyx looked up at him. "Jack," he said. Behind him, Opal and Beryl cleared their throats loudly. Onyx corrected himself, "Your Majesty."

"No," Jack interrupted. "I am High King of the Sidhe. I accept that and the charge that the Tuatha De Dannan have given me. The Tuatha De Dannan said I could name my own Court. I will not face this crisis alone. I will need allies. Fae, who know how all this works, and among those Fae, I need ones that I can trust. I need someone who will rally to my cause when I need them. That is you, Onyx. You and your cousins have my trust. You earned it when you blindly trusted me, a perfect stranger, to help get to your brother and complete your quest for the sword."

Jack straightened his back and stood tall. "Onyx Eisenhart, as High King of the Talamh Sidhe, I command you to claim that sword and take leadership of your people."

Onyx walked up to the sword buried in the rock outcrop.

"Jack," he said, "I..."

"Onyx Eisenhart, I name you Sovereign of the Snows," Jack said. "Take the sword, Winter King."

With a sigh, Onyx reached his hand forward to place it on the hilt of Iismid. A flash of blue light burst from the sword hilt, and blue sparks roiled along the exposed blade.

Onyx gripped the hilt and pulled the sword from the stone.

Snow began to fall.

Jack removed the sword belt and handed it to Onyx as the sound of wing beats echoed across the mountain.

63

Ashe's heart skipped a beat as the tremendous beating of wings echoed across the mountaintop. All eyes turned to the sky. Onyx drew his sword, the crystalline blade flashing blue-white in the dim light of the setting sun. A blue aura spun around Onyx as the snow fell harder around them.

The eardfolc spread out in front of Jack and Ashe. They held their weapons ready against the coming threat.

"Guys," Ashe said as she racked a round into the shotgun. "You need to quit this; I stand with you, not behind."

A gap opened between the twins, and Ashe stepped up to fill it.

The thrum of wings beating the air resonated across the mountain, amplifying their sense of dread. It sounded like dozens of winged creatures flapped frantically across the sky as they rushed to reinforce the dragon. The sound sent a fresh wave of anxiety through Ashe, mixed with the remnants of adrenaline from their earlier battle; it made her heart race frantically in her chest. She knew their reprieve was fleeting, and whatever came next could change everything. Ashe scanned the sky; her heart raced as she prepared herself for the coming fight. There was movement above a distant ridgeline, and the entire group spun to face the incoming threat.

Ashe could just make out the silhouette of a Blackhawk helicopter as it rose into view and began circling the small stone shelter they had sought refuge in just hours before. The group released a collective breath; their spirits lifted as they realized they had succeeded.

Has it only been a day since I jumped over Lawrence Lake? she thought.

It felt like a lifetime ago; so much had happened, and so much had changed. Yet, with unwavering determination, the group was ready to face whatever was coming next.

The Blackhawk circled the cabin several times, its rotors slicing through the air with a sharp whirring sound before pivoting sharply toward the glacier, its path now aimed directly at them.

"Looks like our ride is here," Jack said.

"What will we tell them?" Onyx asked.

"The truth," Ashe said with a grin, "I got blown off course, and you guys helped me out of a tree." She looked at the blood seeping through Onyx's bandages. "That mountain lion came out of nowhere, but we managed to fight it off." She patted Berry on the shoulder, "One of us even lost a finger."

"Sounds like a plan," Berry said.

"Any plan is better than no plan," Jack said, "Keep it as close to the truth as you can, and we should all be fine."

Ashe turned to Jack. "Well, it was not the adventure I expected when I hopped on an airplane this morning."

"Me either," Jack said. "You up for another," he asked. "There might be more of Morrigan's Children out there; this may have only been the beginning."

"Wouldn't miss it for the world. Besides, what girl wouldn't want to hang out with the King of the Fairies?"

Onyx grunted beside them, "The Morrigan's Children are still out there. But I don't think they're working alone. Someone sent those Ember-kin to the cave."

"Who could it be?" Ashe asked.

"Many of the Sidhe still hate the Milesians; they still want the world cleansed. It would not be a stretch to imagine one of them sending the ember-kin to stop us, hoping to aid the dragon. It may even have been a Sidhe who orchestrated the attack."

"What's that mean to us?" Opal asked.

"It means we won't just be fighting Morrigan's Children. We may also have to tangle with Sidhe," responded Ellis.

The group crowded together and started moving down the slope as the helicopter circled above, trying to find a place to put down.

As the Blackhawk approached, it spun to expose the open sliding door on its side. Ashe could see three people inside, two were dressed in the orange and white of Search and Rescue. The third wore street clothes, a standard MFS helmet with the shield up, and held a camera to one shoulder. Below the helmet's raised shield, the bill of an outlandish yellow ball cap poked out.

The Blackhawk landed halfway between the peak and the old stone hut. Its blades created a storm of white powder around it. A storm that smashed into Ashley and her friends with the force of a hurricane. Sharp stinging flurries of snow were thrown in their faces. Ashe couldn't see a thing as the cyclone kicked up by the spinning blades slammed into them.

She squinted through the chaos, her eyes tearing in the icy downdraft. Sharp, stinging flurries of snow and ice crystals slammed into her face. Behind her, Jack and the eardfolc raised arms to protect their faces. Shadows blurred in the whiteout. The crew was hopping off and moving toward them. They seemed to have as much difficulty in the cyclone of snow as Ashe and her friends were having. The sound was deafening. She felt the huf, huf, huf of the spinning blades echo in her toes.

Behind her, Ashe heard Onyx mutter something.

There was a flash of blue light. The snow swirling around the helicopter fell like a white curtain severed from its fixtures.

The rotors still whipped the air around them, but no snow or ice flew up. They had a clear path to the helicopter.

Ashe led the way, trudging through the snow now settled around them. The search and rescue team reached them first, their faces reassuring as they guided them towards the helicopter.

In his distinctive yellow cap, the cameraman approached with a wave and a stunningly broad grin.

"Ashe!" he said, his voice drowned out by the noise of the rotor blades.

Ashe recognized him immediately.

"Charlie," she yelled, brushing past the SAR team. "What are you doing up here?"

He raised the camera. "Here to get footage. I convinced Blake that reporting on the lost wildland firefighter's rescue would be a feather in his cap." His eyes went wide as he looked at the group following behind Ashe. "So how was your day?" he asked.

Ashe laughed as she climbed into the helicopter. A sense of relief washed over her. Despite the chaos of the past day and the threat the Morrigan's Children posed, they had made it.

With a final glance, Ashe stepped into the helicopter, followed by her friends. The door slid shut, and the roar of the blades became a distant hum that reverberated through the cabin.

Safety was within reach. As they soared above the peaceful land, Ashe felt a sense of pride. They had beaten the dragon. Hope filled her heart. No matter what lay ahead, she knew they would overcome the darkness together.

64

The rescue of seven dwarves and a lost firefighter barely made a blip among all the stories that emerged about that day. The destruction caused by the fire dominated all news coverage. The pictures of the dragon exploding above the mountain, on the other hand, filled the Internet for weeks. The fiery wings enveloping the mountain peak had everyone asking if it had erupted. The obvious dragon shape rising within the fires was dismissed as a coincidence or wishful thinking by a select few, like the images of Jesus on toast. The authorities attributed the images to a backdraft from the surrounding fires caused by natural weather patterns. The concussive blast that smothered the fires burning across half of three states was referred to as a weather anomaly by some and a miracle by others.

Jack shook his head at people's willingness to obscure what was plain before them. The world does not believe in dragons, so the last thing it could have been was a dragon, despite the obvious proof. After a week of debate and discussion, a celebrity was caught in a scandal, and the world's focus shifted away from images of the dragon rising from the fires on the mountain. The dragon's return, indicating the planet's turmoil, was overshadowed by celebrity gossip and soon forgotten.

Like its owner, the Fallen J Ranch emerged from the wildfires with only minor scorch marks around its edges. The old hay barn bore the brunt of the damage, with its back half reduced to ash. The main barn and the house showed signs of smoke damage, with blackened windows and bubbled paint in places, but overall, the ranch had weathered the storm. Jack knew he would need to repaint the house and bunkhouse and tear down the rest of the hay barn, but these were things he had planned to do before the fires.

Jack walked around the ranch. Signs of the fire were everywhere. Charred patches of grass and ash-covered ground were reminders of the blaze and the destruction he had avoided. The paddock, where he planned to have horses one day, was now marked by scorched fence posts. Jack's heart ached at the sight.

Beside him, Otter walked sniffing the air. As they walked, the dog would stop, his nose held low to the ground, and he would move away from Jack, chasing down unfamiliar scents. His fur was still singed in places, but he seemed unfazed by his injuries. He darted ahead, investigating the remnants of the fire. Every now and then, he would stop and bark at charred tree stumps like he was warning them to stay away. The dog's unhampered spirit offered Jack hope amid the wreckage.

The garden lay in ruin, with brittle stems and shriveled leaves reaching from the dry soil. The heat had wilted the plants. He knew that it would take time and effort to restore the place to its former glory, but he was determined to bring life back to the ranch.

Most of the damage was cosmetic, but Jack's spirit soared. The repairs would not bankrupt him. He would rebuild his ranch the same way he had started it, going step by step until it was done.

Jack jumped as his phone rang. He picked it up and saw that cell service had been restored. He clicked on the incoming call.

The National Forest Service was sending a group of surveyors to the area to review the damage on the mountain. They wanted to book the Bunkhouse for the season.

Jack spent a few minutes explaining the cosmetic damage to them.

"No problem," said the voice on the phone. "How soon can you be ready for guests?"

Jack momentarily considered, "My last booking left when the evacuation orders started coming in; I don't believe they will return. So, it's ready to book now; you can come in anytime if you don't mind the smell of smoke."

"Wonderful, would tomorrow at ten pm be too late?" the voice asked.

"No, I'm up well past then and would be happy for the company,"

"Great, see you then."

Jack puttered about the ranch the following day. He double-checked that the bunkhouse was ready to rent and walked out to the hay barn. His foot twisted out from under him as he circled the collapsed and burnt timbers around the back. On the ground was a scorched piece of leather, a sleeve from a jacket. Jack picked up the leather. He smiled and tucked it in his back pocket. He already had a plan in mind for redecorating. The scrap would go on the mantle beside his trophies as a reminder of his day on the mountain and the friends he made there.

The sound of revving engines filled the air. Jack stepped onto his porch to find a shiny new truck and two motorcycles approaching his driveway. The motorcycles were custom-made choppers with elongated front forks and ape-hanger handlebars. Berry and Bramble rode the bikes. Their smiling faces brought a smile to Jack's lips. His joy at his friends' arrival was a testament to the bonds they had formed on the glacier.

The truck door opened as he reached the driveway, and Ashley Ember slid out to greet him. She held a set of keys in her hand and jangled them in front of Jack's face.

"From Onyx Eisenhart, Winter King and King of the Eardfolc, greetings and a gift for Jack Season, High King of the Talamh Sidhe." Ashe turned to Berry and whispered, "Did I get that right?" The small man raised a thumb and nodded.

"What is this?" Jack said.

"A truck, Your Majesty," the twins said; both of them bowed as Berry continued. "Oni," he paused and cleared his throat, "The Winter King said you lost yours to the dragon, so the Eardfolc have chipped in to replace it in thanks for your assistance and as a token of our loyalty to the Talamh Sidhe."

Ashley grabbed Jack's hand and plopped the keys into it. "Registration and insurance card are in the glove box. They are all in your name. We would love to stay and chit-chat, but we're off to Vegas. It's a long ride, and I am burning up my sick time."

Ashley leaned in and hugged Jack. "Thanks for getting me out of that tree, Jack."

Before Jack could respond, the two bike engines roared to life. Ashley hopped behind Berry, and the trio rolled down the drive.

Beside Jack Otter woofed.

"Well, boy," Jack said, "at least someone's riding off into the sunset."

Jack felt a surge of excitement as the motorcycles vanished into the distance. He knew more of the Morrigan's Children were out there. He didn't know what dangers they would bring.

The future, after all, is uncertain. Isn't that what made it exciting, he thought.

No matter what came at him, Jack was ready to face it head-on. His ranch, the land he cherished, and the world he fought to protect were safe, and he was prepared to keep it that way, no matter what challenges lay ahead.

Epilogue

The chill air cut into Lieutenant Collin James as he stood watch on the Coast Guard Cutter Dauntless's observation deck. The choppy waters of the Weddell Sea had the cutter pitching and rolling as it moved away from the Ronne Ice Shelf. The Dauntless carried supplies and scientists bound for the polar research stations around the South Shetland Islands.

This is as south as any ship can sail, Collin thought as he adjusted his binoculars. In the distance, faint wisps of cloud swirled like ghostly ribbons in a lazy haze above the distant peaks. They formed a strange column that peeled away from the white mists and descended in thick, swirling clouds. The spinning column solidified and stretched downward toward the ocean.

The sea erupted into chaos as the two forces met. Waves crashed and spiraled outward, crashing high into the air as the ocean awakened to greet the swirling clouds. A deafening roar filled the air as a solid column of spinning water burst into existence. It rose like a creature forged from water and fury. It pulsed with a strange, rhythmic energy. Its surface shimmered with reflections of the churning sky and frothy waves.

Collin watched enthralled as a waterspout began to take shape. It solidified with otherworldly grace and spun toward the ship as if guided by an indomitable will. It grew taller and more defined. It twisted and turned with raw, untamed power. Its movement looked deliberate, as if it were aiming for the ship. Captivated by the storm's sheer power, it took every ounce of Collin's will to look away and call in a distance report.

The power of nature that unfolded before him was both beautiful and terrifying. It was a stark reminder of the power the elements hold. The spinning column stood defiant, bridging the heavens and the sea in a spectacle that left him breathless.

"Waterspout, off the port bow!" he shouted; his voice rolled over the low hum of the engines, and the bridge crew snapped to attention.

Collin, heart pounding, lowered his binoculars. The sight was like nothing he had seen before. A twisting column of mist and water that churned with unimaginable force and rose hundreds of feet into the air. The base of the spout tore at the ocean, lifting spray and debris high into the air. Dark clouds filled the sky above in seconds, and driving rain pelted the observation deck.

Captain Rivera's calm and authoritative voice cut through Collin's turbulent thoughts. "Distance, Lieutenant?" she asked, her tone firm but collected, a steady anchor amidst the chaos.

Collin tore his gaze away. His pulse raced, but his training kicked in, forcing clarity into his voice. "Two nautical miles and closing fast, Captain," he replied, his eyes darting between the spinning tower of water and the roughening seas around it.

Rivera responded almost immediately, her voice a steady counterpoint to the raging elements outside. "Understood. Prepare for evasive action and keep me updated every thirty seconds," she commanded, her tone leaving no room for doubt.

Collin nodded, though she couldn't see him.

"Aye, Captain," he said. His hands tightened on the console as he relayed orders to the rest of the bridge.

Collin took a deep breath, letting her composure steel his resolve. The storm was closing in, but with Rivera at the helm, there was still a chance they could outmaneuver nature's fury.

Collin leaned over and tripped on the microphone for the intercom. As the storm approached, he called out the distance to the bridge.

Between updates, the Executive Officer's voice came through the intercom with orders. "All stations prepare for severe weather. Secure the deck. All non-essential personnel below."

The deck crew lashed down loose equipment and cleared the deck for severe weather. Steel doors clanged as hatches were sealed. Collin's eyes locked on the spout as it veered, and the wind shifted toward the cutter.

The wind howled like a rabid beast as the spout approached the ship. Collin shifted his feet as the ship spun windward to point its bow at the oncoming storm. Rain fell like a sheet in front of him, driven horizontally by the wind. His visibility dropped to mere yards.

"Lieutenant James, to the bridge," Rivera ordered.

Collin spun and descended the ladder to the bridge. A thrill of concern flowed over Collin. It didn't last long; he was confident every man knew his job. The atmosphere inside was tense, but the crew's professionalism was reassuring. The Dauntless had carried them through worse storms over the last three years. Collin turned to the Communication station, "Prep damage control, full inspection once this storm passes."

The ship was designed for this kind of punishment, but nature was unpredictable. The Dauntless pitched violently as the wind-driven water screamed across its deck. Collin grabbed a railing to steady himself, the steel cold and unyielding beneath his grip. Outside, the world was a blur of spinning water. The storm's fury drowned out all sound, but the crew held their ground.

All of Collin's attention was on the swirling wall of water that assaulted the ship. The windows blurred with spray. The lights flickered. The hull groaned.   The ship's steel protested under the battering wind and waves.

"Damage," Collin called as the lights dimmed and returned.

"Engine room reports failure of starboard battery array. They've switched to backup, voltage holding steady." Collin smiled; despite the chaos, everyone was working with precision.

An eerie silence suddenly replaced the chaos. The rain stopped. They had passed through the waterspout's twisting wall of wind and water. They were inside the funnel. Collin could see the impossibly tall cylinder of spinning water now encircling the ship. For a hundred yards around the Dauntless, the sea was calm.

Collin blinked and rubbed at his eyes. He lifted his binoculars. He couldn't believe what he was seeing. In the center of the swirling whirlwind was a man.

He walked across the water like a man on land, indifferent to the storm. The wind howled around him, and lightning flashed, but the man walked on. He moved with a calm and purposeful grace, as if he were the storm's center. Stunned by the sight, Collin watched silently, his disbelief slowly mingling with a growing sense of awe and terror.

Across the waves, Collin saw the man's glowing eyes as he raised a hand and brought it forward, pointing at Collin. Lightning began to strike down at the ship, each bolt a blinding arc of pure energy that split the sky. Blinded by the flash of light, Collin's vision seared white. His ears rang with the blasts of thunder that overwhelmed the constant electric hum of the ship's systems. Sparks began to fly from the equipment as they faltered in the wake of the lightning strikes. As his sight returned, he staggered, trying to make sense of the chaos around him. The ship rocked violently beneath his feet as the storm wall crashed into it. The bridge became a maelstrom of flickering lights. Sailors stood fast at their posts, panicked faces lit by the glow of the bridge's panels.

The lights went out, and alarm bells rang. The thick, acrid scent of burnt wiring filled the air. The crackle and pop of failing systems mixed with the roar of the waterspout as the vessel struggled to stay on course amid the growing disarray.

FIN (for now)

Book 1   1/24 - 6/25

Storm Season- The Morrigan's Children Book 2 available in 2026

Find the further adventures of Jack Season at

https://www.pervasive-art.com/shop/books/2

Instagram: @pervasivemedia

Facebook: Pervasive Press

Email for catalogue or questions: strambooks@gmail.com

Dear Reader,

Thank you for spending your precious time with my book.

You have read this far, and I hope you have enjoyed my story, but before you go, I have a favor to ask.

Independent Authors succeed or fail because of their fans and their reviews. In the vast ocean that online publishing has become, an Independent Author is easily lost among the crowd.

Reviews help to push forward sales by encouraging shoppers that the book they might buy is worth both the money and the time they will spend on it. Fans push sales by sharing the stories they love with their friends and their family.

All I ask is that if you enjoyed this story, share it, tell your friends, tell your family, tell the WORLD how much. Your honest review or recommendation on any platform means the world to me.

Please drop a short review on Amazon, Goodreads, or this book's page on any bookseller's site. The success of this series will guarantee that I write future ones.

I am looking forward to telling the rest of Jack, Onyx, and Ashe's story. I hope you'll join me as we follow their further adventures together.

T E Marts - June 2025